KEY WEST INTERLUDE

Paulette Marshall Mystery Series

Lois Richman

authorHOUSE®

AuthorHouse™
1663 Liberty Drive
Bloomington, IN 47403
www.authorhouse.com
Phone: 1 (800) 839-8640

Published by AuthorHouse 11/29/2016

ISBN: 978-1-5246-5188-6 (sc)
ISBN: 978-1-5246-5189-3 (hc)
ISBN: 978-1-5246-5187-9 (e)

Library of Congress Control Number: 2016919642

Print information available on the last page.

Any people depicted in stock imagery provided by Thinkstock are models, and such images are being used for illustrative purposes only. Certain stock imagery © Thinkstock.

This book is printed on acid-free paper.

For KARL A. LOZIER, CAROLANN Brockman, and Joyce Geib, who were my biggest supporters through this process, and always for my daughter, June Diane Richman Chastain, who sent cards, notes, and calls to say "Believe." I love you all. On a professional level, thank you to Detective Mark McCall, a retired police officer from Cincinnati, Ohio, currently living in Key West, Florida; Sandra Inman, a private detective from Los Angeles; and Howard Kolwalsky, an old time friend and advisor. From the past, Sonia Wolfson from the publicity department of Twentieth Century Fox, and Fredda Dudley Balling, writer, columnist, advisor, and second mother.

A respectful mention for the principal of Key West High School at the time, Mr. Menendez, for his story. And while embellished by me with an artist's imagination—admiration for his honor, concern for others, and his courage, continues to this day. Check out his letter on loisrichman.com.

CHAPTER 1

~∞∞∞~

CLUMSILY RACING ACROSS CAMPUS IN her new seven-inch heels with two-inch platforms, Paulette Marshall cut through hundreds of students to reach the center of the school's courtyard. The bell for first period had rung, the second bell quickly behind it, and no one was on the way to class.

Screams came from everywhere. Paulette scanned the courtyard. She did not recognize any teachers, administrators, or any of her students. Meanwhile, her records, final reports for the semester, and various papers necessary for the day's lessons were spread out all over the courtyard.

Carlos Ornez came over to Paulette and looked around before he spoke. He turned full-faced toward his counselor. Sweat and dark stains covered his San Fernando Junior High School football shirt. His arms were all bloody. "Mrs. Marshall! Mrs. Marshall!" he screamed.

"Someone stabbed Oscar! I came to tell you that you won't see me for a few days. We're on the way downtown."

"Oscar? Where is he?" she asked in disbelief.

"They killed Oscar just now. This minute! They stabbed him with a long knife. One time. It took only one time. In the back! Over there. Paramedics are on the sidewalk. Right there!" Carlos pointed into the middle of the crowd.

By now, many of the male students were breathing heavily and beating their chests, preparing for action. The girls were screaming and hugging each other and hiding their faces while pulling out their hair full of hair spray and long curls.

"The medics say no use," Carlos said in a daze.

"You have to stay. Aren't you a witness?" she asked.

It seemed as if Carlos wanted to do what his counselor was asking of him—he was always polite to certain staff members—but he was swaying between paying attention to Paulette and sprinting to what she felt was a prearranged meeting.

Oscar was a well-known member of the Bloods gang—except in San Fernando where he was an exceptional student. He was a wavering one even though he had been told by Paulette and his teachers how smart he was and how he could educate himself out of the ghetto. He seemed to almost believe them, but the rumor, according to Mr. Haber, was one more negative neighborhood incident, and Oscar would be lost to the school system forever.

"The Crips and their vans. Selling drugs and coming over here to recruit. They stole my younger brother. Stole my girl. Now this. They are history in San Fernando. To the death!" Carlos shouted.

Paulette shouted after her star student and biggest protector on campus. No doubt he heard her call after him, but Carlos had disappeared into the crowd.

The school police held back the crowd of young students refusing to go to class. They had watched the whole process—seen the same results over and over so many times before.

Heartsick, Paulette stared at the paramedics as they put Oscar's body inside a plastic black bag and zipped up the two sides.

There was nothing further Paulette could do. She returned to center court to recover whatever she could of her files and crumpled papers strewn all over the courtyard.

Meanwhile, two Los Angeles County Police helicopters were circling the front entrance of the school, searching for any students attempting to leave campus without permission. They also covered the entryway next to the main office where school police had vacated their posts to rush to the scene.

"Sorry, missy," the school custodian said as he came over to help Paulette pick up her papers covered with footprints, sand, and dirt.

"Do you know what happened? How Oscar died?"

"Stabbed in the back. Right through his backpack. No books inside," the custodian said, a sad look covering his usually jovial face. "Woulda' saved his life, for sure."

Paulette stood tall. "Thanks, Henry. We'll talk later, okay?"

"Sure thing, missy," Henry said as he stared straight ahead in an effort to ignore Paulette's tears.

Mr. Haber, the teacher in the classroom next to Paulette's small counseling office, sat at his desk, very still, his hands clasped tightly in the prayer position, his eyes staring straight ahead.

"No shining words, please," he said. "I'm one and a half years away from retirement. My wife says leave this coming summer, but I have some boys I'd like to see cross that stage. Go on to high school. Oscar was the best of them."

Paulette was shaking, thinking, and then she said, "I am so sorry. I loved Oscar like my own. There are so many other things I could be doing with my life right now. Working here, especially at this time, is, well …"

"You're here for the same reason I am. Maybe there's one student we can save. Pull out of this godforsaken hole and have him or her find a better future."

"You're right. For me it was Oscar."

"He wasn't your last hope, nor mine. And there's always next year." Mr. Haber's words were slow and lumbering as he spoke. "Or neither one of us would stay."

The day was long. No lessons were taught, no personal or individual counseling was going on. The whirr of the helicopters continued on campus and throughout the neighborhood, a constant reminder of the early morning tragedy. The news media swarmed the entire area during the hours of class, seeking facts and reactions. Girls continued to cry in the bathrooms and outside their classrooms.

Most students were absent by third period. They had either run away or were waiting, still in shock, for their parents to sign them out and take them home to apartments where eight or more slept to a room. A place where no doors separated the units, no bathroom privileges existed, and there was hardly any food.

Paulette phoned her husband, Dr. Christopher Marshall, MD, FASC, but each time she hung up before leaving a message.

What could she say? Furthermore, he was in surgery all day. Chris had been afraid an event like this would erupt—convinced that her dedication and love of her students should not outweigh his concern for her safety.

She said so many things, so many good things to her students, no matter whether they were listening or not. Words that must be spoken. She felt their pain while holding her own inside. By the final bell of the day, everyone was drained. The few students who remained walked out quietly, single file through the front gate where check-in had occurred only hours before.

"Tomorrow," Paulette said with a wave as she watched her students cross the street. Three more days of classes and school would be closed for the Christmas holidays, which were going to be a very long and sad two weeks.

CHAPTER 2

PAULETTE LOOKED AT THE FEW students who came into her small office on the day Oscar, her prize student, was stabbed in the back. She wanted to cry like they did, except her job was not to feel sorry for their circumstances or conditions or the fact that so many of their brothers and close friends had been killed before this or for the current tragedy. Her duty was to assist them through the trials of the teenage years and instill in them the sense of a better future.

At their middle school in San Fernando, no buses arrived every morning from other communities, thus ridding the school system of cries of unequal opportunities. Everyone walked to school or was dropped off. Every student was on lunch tickets. The continuing problem was the vans that arrived every day five to ten minutes before the final bell. The vans were the kind with no windows. Their panel doors opened from the rear.

So long as the vehicles caused no serious disruptions and kept on moving, the police were unable to stop the drivers who sought out innocent, eager girls and young men looking for "treats" in small plastic bags. Payment was collected on alternate days and in different ways, so it was always hit or miss for law enforcement.

Oscar was lucky enough to live in a small house a few blocks away from the middle school. He walked to school with his twin brother because his father went to work for the county before the school was unlocked. On Friday nights his father's right to the truck ended, so Oscar and his family never left the neighborhood either—except when certain high school students swept past and picked Oscar up for a special meeting.

Finally, Paulette left a message on Chris's phone, asking him to cancel dinner plans for the evening. They were to meet another couple at The Marina restaurant. She would be late. Surely the incident would have been all over the news by now. Paulette knew better than to pretend glibness over the phone. She also knew what her husband and their son Billie would have to say when she arrived home.

First, she expected Billie to ask her why she worked at the worst school site in all of LA County except for Watts. The label "education with electronic gates and guards with guns means an education under extreme stress, which is exactly how the students felt.

Billie would look at his mother with disdain the way he did each morning as she drove down the Santa Monica Mountains from Mulholland Drive, leaving their home in Bel-Air for the town of San Fernando to counsel students with police records who had been arrested for drug abuse or robbery and charged with mischievous intent before they reached high school age.

Her husband Chris would say nothing, having spoken his peace and given up long ago on trying to direct any part of his wife's career.

Chris might still ask why, but once he had whatever answer she gave him, he would be satisfied, sigh, and move on. All she wanted when he arrived home tonight was a big hug. She longed to have him brush her hair away from her face with his slim, tender fingers, then gently kiss her forehead, and tell her he understood—even though she knew he didn't.

Paulette drove home slowly, which she had been doing often lately. The message on the answering machine was from Chris. "I cancelled dinner with the Albertsons. However, I still need to see you tonight."

Paulette finally reached Chris at the hospital. "Oh, honey. Those are the best words I've heard all day. I'll fix a nice dinner with a glass of wine. I have no message from Billie. Have you heard from him?"

"He's down the hill for the night."

"Did you hear the news about our school today?"

"I'm sorry for your bad day. Mine had less drama and fewer people, but was just as impactful."

"You sound like a news reporter," Paulette chuckled. "I'm looking for a nice, long hug when you walk in. I'm too tired for much else except to sit with you. Maybe you'd rub my feet. We could take a shower together …"

"I … um … You'll stay awake, won't you?" Chris asked crisply.

"It's barely five o'clock," Paulette reminded him.

"So it is. I've kept outrageous hours, but I have to get back. I have a meeting later tonight."

"That's what's outrageous about your practice, but okay. See you later."

Chris did not pull into the garage. He parked in the driveway.

The chimes at the front door woke her from a dead man's sleep. "What's this?" she asked as Chris entered, surprised that he rang the doorbell as if he were a guest.

She was caught completely off guard when she saw Chris, waiting to be invited in—he was still the handsomest man she had ever seen: tall and thin but with a perfect body shape. He also had wavy black hair, dimples on each side of his cheeks, and perfectly straight teeth. His sensuous lips could be envied by the Kardashians. And his hands—they were as long and as delicate as a concert pianist's.

CHAPTER 3

PAULETTE CLOSED THE FRONT DOOR after she let Chris in. Shocked by the whole setup, she had nothing to say as Chris headed for the living room and the sofas facing the huge picture windows looking westward. The night lights were upon the horizon. The summer sunset over Catalina Island had stopped time as usual. Its slow-moving beauty of brown and yellow swirling around the sun was coming to a close, as it did every day around this time—the evening's artificial lights leaving a glow over the San Fernando Valley.

"Your dress is pretty," Chris said lightly. "But then you always look great."

"Nude or dressed," Paulette joked as she swung around to make her skirt twirl. "Like you used to say when ..." Paulette did not finish her sentence. She stopped dead in her tracks. At the exact moment when she looked into her husband's eyes, she felt further away from him than she had ever been. "You want a drink or something?"

"No. I want you to sit down and listen."

She did as he asked, kicking her shoes under the table. His tone reminded her of Chris's dictatorial manner whenever he tried to control her. She was about to say so when he said, "You and I? We loved each other once, but living with you no longer excites me as man."

The wind was blown out of her lungs. She could not breathe. The love of her life could not even look at her. Instead, he stared at the high ceilings and over at the paintings he hated. She liked modern: scenery rather than close-up portraits of people. He liked canvases painted dark colors like the one done in black with a white dot in the center—and nudes, yes, nudes—all over the house.

Chris moved his collection of beautifully painted naked women from their home office and workout room to his apartment near his office in Beverly Hills. When they were at home in his study and workout room, he showed them off, bragging about the fame of the artist and the fortune he spent.

Before Chris continued, he stared at the custom drapes that were the wrong color. To match all the custom dark wood he'd spent a fortune on, he wanted a muted color. A broker said it would be easier to sell the house if it was decorated in monochrome. Paulette chose desert rust and had the drapes installed without consulting him. To her, it didn't seem necessary. To him, it was the last straw.

And the imported stones he brought back from Italy for the fireplace? The treasured collection of rocks in a variety of earth tones Paulette actually painted over them with a solid color that matched a rock she brought back from a trip to Arizona.

He continued: "I ... I ... in fact, I want to move on with my life. Separately," Chris informed Paulette on his last night of pretense. "I am filing for a divorce, and I want to buy your half of the house for cash. Can we do that without all the legal mumbo jumbo? You'd have a cashier's check for over a million dollars in exchange for your signature on the new deed, and ..." He dropped the rest of the sentence.

It was the Chris of today speaking, but the one from the past Paulette remembered. After all they had been through over twenty-two years together and now this? "This can't be," she whispered. "When did you figure all this out? In Tahiti last month? On our first vacation in two years? Just the two of us?" She was stunned, her words changed to accusatory but gently spoken.

On that night, as Paulette faced her adversary on the couch where lovemaking began in the past, her husband, who was always relaxed in this setting—a drink in his left hand, his right arm outstretched so she could fold into it and lean against him, smell him, kiss him—sat at the very edge of the seat, so far off the pillow it was as if he had no butt.

That's when Paulette noticed Chris had come into the house with his briefcase. It was sitting at his side and he was playing with the handle. This he did with the lack of his usual grace, his fingers as white as his knuckles.

This was not about Chris's comings and goings this past year, nor was it about his so-called midlife crisis. This was about their life together and how it had gone awry.

Paulette was embarrassed at how she could pretend their life as husband and wife was as casual as she had acted when he first rang the bell tonight for permission to enter his own home.

In the past when they discussed problems in their marriage, Paulette was the type who specifically avoided arguments at all costs. Her excuse? She would do anything to keep the peace. The only thing that she always stood up for was her career, despite the response from her husband and son.

"There is someone else," Chris said after he cleared his throat.

"How could there be?" Paulette demanded to know. "When was there time? We're both so busy." Anything, she thought, to keep the dialogue going. Anything to ignore what she already felt in her bones was coming. Something she could not stop nor avoid.

"It's Christy in my office. I want to marry her, take care of her two little girls by men who abandoned her. And we want to begin our life together in this house."

Paulette felt pretty stupid. Her breath disappeared long ago, and the blood was draining out of her body. Yet somehow she was still able to quip: "And now she's pregnant with your child."

With that off-the-cuff comment, Paulette felt a chill rise up through her back, forcing her to sit up straight, cross her legs, and grasp her knees with intertwined fingers.

"How?" Chris replied, his face going blank. "Even Christy's mother does not know about this pregnancy."

To Paulette, Chris seemed taken aback. Paulette had met Christy once at her husband's office about a year ago. She was one of those too-beautiful California blonde beauties, only, from what Paulette could tell, Christy's was all natural. Running down the middle of her back were curls that covered her shoulders and went almost to her waist. She had pretty eyes and a little too much makeup for a girl so young. Although Paulette thought she was a bippy, Paulette never imagined this entry clerk was after her husband.

He seemed to recover from Paulette's guess about Christy's pregnancy when he said, "Yes, as a matter of fact she is. We want to start a family of our own right away," making Paulette feel as if she had been taken into his confidences. "Bring them here ... to this house."

"How old is she?" Paulette asked. "All of twenty?"

"Twenty-four," Chris replied.

"Someone from your office?" Paulette sighed. "How ordinary. In your position, I would expect you to find someone your equal. Another doctor perhaps."

Chris defended his choice. "She's pretty and she's got great skin, an asset to show off to those women in Beverly Hills who want to look as young and pretty as she is. Remember I do plastic surgery all day long. That's what pays the bills."

One last chance to place guilt, Paulette started to say, "What about me?" but she did not dare. Pride alone would not allow it.

"You know our son Billie and I are close. That will never change," Chris spoke into the air space between them.

Paulette had so many more questions like: Has Billie ever met this woman? Does our son know you want to take our home away from us? She did not create my home, my status, my very life!

Instead Paulette was screaming until the sound of her words shut off her hearing. "Are you *crazy?* This was our ... my house, and I am keeping it, period! I have rights and I will go to any length to maintain them!"

Chris slid further back onto the couch, saying nothing, a surprised look on his face. And damn it all, he sat there and said nothing more!

Paulette was set for battle, her decision final. What did he think? she wondered. That I wouldn't yell and holler? Didn't he get it that any woman put in her position would react exactly the same way? How could he? Answering her own question, she replied, He's a man, isn't he?

Love and confidences gone, the only topic that seemed appropriate concerned departures.

Finally Paulette said, "I see. Now you have someone at work and at home to say, "Yes, doctor. No, doctor. Of course, you are always right, doctor." If I sign this house over you can continue with the same lavish lifestyle we had. Continue … without me. Of course. How perfect for you." Her voice was barely audible and filled with unaccustomed sarcasm.

"Thank you," Chris said.

"Love to help you out here, Chris," Paulette said. She took in a long, deep breath. "But these rights must be sorted out by the proper authorities. Let's just see what the court thinks."

CHAPTER 4

As PAULETTE WALKED CHRIS TO the front door, she mentally patted herself on the back and thought: *Well, not bad for the first time out of the gate.*

She was actually standing up for herself, Paulette Marshall, soon to be a divorced woman!

After she slammed the door shut and bolted the double lock, she began to sob. How was she going to remain the bright and cheery person she always was, full of sunshine and looking forward to the future, under these conditions?

The next morning Paulette returned to campus.

A riot late the night before had destroyed the entire campus. There was gang writing on every building. Books and computers from the second floor were tossed out onto the sidewalk. All the windows were broken, wood pieces slivered and hanging onto the broken glass.

Inside the classrooms, monitors were smashed, the overheads crashed on the floors, made useless. Extra supplies in the closets were thrown into the center of the room, the desks spray painted.

"Outside subversives" was how the police labeled the intruders. They had climbed the electronically operated fences at about midnight. The library, filled with newly purchased books donated by various businesses for the school's use, had their pages torn out while others were glued together.

Six months later, the ninth graders were ready to graduate—minus Oscar. The two-week break for the Christmas holidays calmed down the environment. No audience, no gang violence. It was as simple as that. During that time students were huddled in their apartment, surrounded by family and friends. The school was open for breakfast and lunch, but it was a quiet procession in and out—and no dramas.

A new principal who had connections came from the district office. The gangs wrote on the walls; the writing was painted over by first period. Paulette patrolled the halls, pulling inattentive students out to do yard duty, the rules be damned. She was the queen, and this was her territory. Should anyone complain, her standard remark was: "You want a good education for your child or not?"

On a personal level, those six months whizzed by like it was a week. She and Billie went to visit her parents over the break. What Chris did Paulette had no idea, and in order to keep Billie out of the middle, she never asked him about his father's comings and goings.

Meanwhile, Chris was serving her with all kinds of papers she turned over to her best friend and attorney, Kathleen Moore, whose only concern was to know how Paulette was doing emotionally.

When asked how the divorce was going, Kathleen was basically non-specific, which is the opposite of behavior expected of attorneys. "Oh, they're flapping in the wind, but all they get are postponements." Whenever Paulette asked to be brought up to date, Kathleen would say, "You just keep your son happy, and we'll make it through this."

She hardly saw Billie. It was his last semester, and he was, as always, Mr. Popularity. There were games and parties and other get-togethers that included his mother. They sat separately, which did not seem to bother Billie. Like so many millennials, he avoided speaking on the phone. But he would communicate all day long text messaging on his iPhone. And that's how they stayed in touch.

However, signs of her son Billie were everywhere: his dirty clothes stacked high; the refrigerator empty the day after she went shopping; and of course, notes for gas, lunch, and weekend entertainment money.

Before Paulette left for San Fernando Middle School at the beginning of the final week of school, she stood in the middle of the cavernous living room of the Casa del Marcella, staring at the traffic creeping up Laurel Canyon, a coffee cup in her hand, her mind on how it used to be. Actually, she had been through enough of that. She was thinking of consequences.

If Chris had his way, her presence in the home would be wiped clean. Her mementos would be packed up and taken down the hill into a two-story, anonymous Beverly Hills home in the center of the daily traffic she abhorred.

She wondered what good any amount of money is when a person's very lifestyle has been ripped away. All that plotting and planning and saving—was it worth it, only to end up in a divorce between two best friends, lovers, and the parents of one son?

There was nothing in the dissolution papers about the displacement of a wife and mother. That was Chris's way. Nothing was left to protect her from the uncharted waters ahead. All of this seemed so new, so strange.

The final hearing was set for the first few days after school closed for the year. She was, in fact, a thousand percent better than a year ago when he had slammed her with the petition for dissolution of the Marshall marriage.

The proposed final agreement between the parties regarding the family residence was up for the judge's approval. The court might go along with California's unwritten "best use" law and grant Chris full ownership after payment of one half of its value. Or the judge could follow the written letter of the law for community property and allow the mother to stay in the family residence until her children left the premises on a permanent basis—or in Paulette's case, until their son, Bill, graduated from Brown University.

In the meantime, Paulette was going to do something outrageous of her own once this hearing was over. On the spur of the moment, she booked a one-way ticket to Key West where she would visit her cousin Doug and his wife Flower. She had even had her eye on a rental for the entire summer.

CHAPTER 5

~∞∞∞~

PAULETTE AND HER ATTORNEY, KATHLEEN Moore, were due in courtroom two of the LA County Courthouse, Civil Division, in downtown Los Angeles, California, at 9 a.m. Late as usual, Kathleen picked Paulette up, and they headed over Coldwater Canyon.

"Not the 101?" Paulette asked.

"I worked all night on your file," Kathleen explained. "You know how Jack is when he doesn't have his dinner—and his sex on time."

Paulette said nothing, but the longer ride and the extra amount of time only added to her frayed nerves.

"All rise. Judge Adam McDuffy presiding," the bailiff said in a ho-hum monotone twenty years on the job could extract from someone. As His Honor whisked through the doors of his private chambers and settled into his oversized black leather chair, the bailiff said, "You may be seated."

The judge was a man of seventy-five, silver-haired, and a little too thin beneath his robe. Kathleen had hoped for McDuffy, she had told Paulette months ago. One reason was he viewed the law the "old way" which gave them the edge. And she was glad he was still there because it had been politely suggested several years ago that he retire and, for starters, take his wife on a vacation to Hawaii. Not him. Word was he planned to die in his chair in his courtroom.

"I see there has been an exceptionally long postponement. Counselor, can you explain?" Judge McDuffy asked.

Chris's counsel answered: "The first time, Your Honor, was to reassess the value of the family residence. Prices in the area have fallen considerably. Lower than at the time of the initial filing."

The judge flipped through the papers. "On Mulholland Drive, huh? Isn't that where Marlon Brando and Jack Nicholson live?"

"I don't know, sir. I only know the original assessment did not come in at an amount satisfactory to my client. With the size of the monthly mortgage and the property vacant most of time, we urge the court to award the petitioner the right to purchase respondent's half of the premises for all cash. In addition to the financial agreement between the parties, my client has volunteered to purchase a home in the same zip code at his own expense. The purpose is to enable their son, Billie, who has graduated from high school and will turn eighteen next month, to live close to his childhood friends."

Kathleen responded by presenting exhibit C to the court, arguing, "Is petitioner kidding? Exhibit C proves the value at today's market is not only unfair but inequitable. Statistics show that the value has almost doubled in the last five years as LA draws in new industry, residents, and jobs. The sections of Beverly Hills, Bel-Air, and Brentwood have been prime locations for over seventy-five years.

"Even actor Tom Cruise had to carve his mega-mansion out of a mountainside with less view—while admittedly more house—than my client's home.

"Further, your honor, my client, as the custodial parent, still has the major responsibility of nurturing a young man who will soon embark on a life filled with new challenges. The confidence and security he will feel, knowing he can return to a home he has lived in since he was twelve years old, is immeasurable."

"I object!" Chris's counsel said. "A price was settled at today's market value of two point five million dollars. I have the papers here to prove it. Your honor, there is a substantial loan on the property that must be paid off, along with the amount of the down payment to be reimbursed to my client. Such funds were taken from his sole and separate property."

The clerk took the sheet and stamped it for the file, marking it exhibit C.

"The terms and financial arrangement between the parties are still at issue and will require another hearing in a separate department," the judge informed counsel. "As you know, we are here today to determine the rights of residency. And on that matter, I have made my decision."

"Judge ..." Kathleen interrupted.

The judge glanced over at respondent's counsel before continuing. "The court has taken care of due process. I will read my decision if that is all right with you, Ms. Moore. Although I agree a price for the property is in question, I will leave that issue in the hands of arbitration. All this over a house," he mused, apparently distracted by which celebrities surrounded the property in question. "Looking from one side of the table to the other, he said, "You both could have picked up your papers with a property settlement to follow. Gone into Arbitration. Not wasted the court's time."

"The docket … Then the parties could not agree …"

"That's crap," the judge snapped as he looked over at the bailiff.

"Neither was a separate trust established by respondent to protect monthly payments on the property should she win," Chris's lawyer pointed out.

"Now, how would she know to do that when neither party knows what the outcome is?" the judge interceded.

"Suppose the price goes down even lower while the parties wait for another hearing?" Chris's attorney argued.

Kathleen remained standing at her table. She momentarily leaned down to hear Paulette whisper, "I had no idea …" Kathleen gave Paulette a signal of silence as she watched the heated, low-hum conversation happening at the other table.

"This is a good sign, right?"

"So far as the judge? Yes." Kathleen squeezed Paulette's hand under the table.

Checking the file and handing it to the clerk, the clerk began to read the decision. "According to the laws of the State of California, respondent will maintain …"

Paulette did not hear the rest of the boilerplate. All she knew at that moment was that she had custody of their son, and the Casa was hers until some date in the future.

After the hearing, when Kathleen dropped Paulette off at the Casa, she had a few errands to run, but she'd be back before three thirty and the rush of traffic on the 405 freeway that begins at four.

Checking her watch for the umpteenth time, Kathleen was already thirty-seven minutes late! Kathleen was LA stylish, beautiful, smart, and basically a responsible person, but her lateness, even for court appearances, was a real issue.

Stopping at the front door for the hundredth time to check that she had the proper amount of luggage for her trip, Paulette was ready to blow this city called Los Angeles, the nurturer of her dreams and ambitions, her failures and successes, and visit her cousin Doug and his wife Flower in ultimate Paradise—Key West, where lost souls find their true nesting spots.

"Oh, Chris, what have you done?" she said to the walls, her emotions running all the way from high and free, only to take a nose dive into self-pity. She never wrote a check without his approval. In fact, she had no idea where any of their money was.

Still waiting, Paulette went out the back side of the house and onto a wide, open porch. She looked for the doe that had appeared in what little was left of the green portion of the Santa Monica Mountains below. It was nowhere in sight, nowhere hidden in the trees.

She went back inside just as the phone rang. "Oh good!" she said aloud. "Kathleen is on the way!"

CHAPTER 6

"PAULETTE? PAULETTE MARSHALL?"

"Yes."

"It's Ellie Johnson. I mean, Ellie Livingston. I was married to Brent Livingston. I'm really a Darby, but ..."

"Heavens, yes! Ellie? My God, I thought you were ..." Paulette gasped. "I expected this call to be from Kathleen, my friend who's taking me to LAX. How are you?"

"I was wondering if you know how my mother is. I came in through Miami. Actually, I'm across the street from Willow Estate, my mother's place."

"Your mother may have sold it by now. I read the Darby Trust was thinking seriously about giving the property to the city of Miami. Upkeep and all. She is up there in years. It was in the real estate section of the *Miami Herald*."

"When?"

"Maybe two months ago or so," Paulette replied. "Time has been slipping away. They thought ... we thought you were dead. Years ago, when your husband's boat went down in that hurricane," Paulette said as gently and kindly as she could. "Maybe your rights have expired."

"Well guess what? Think again! I'll sue for my rights if I must," Ellie said.

"You can't blame your poor, brokenhearted mother. Why didn't you call her long before this? She hasn't heard a word directly from you, only through the grapevine, since you ran away at—what?—eleven years old?"

Paulette did not wait for an answer before continuing. "Let me give you Iris's cell phone number. She's probably the last person Claire talked to." After giving her the number, Paulette added, "It's so good to hear from you, but I am in a rush. I'm catching a plane to Key West within the hour."

"Key West? Why Key West?"

"And that's my story," Paulette replied anxiously. She was ready to hang up, but the little voice from inside said: Stop and tell her the truth. "Christopher and I are officially divorced as of today," she added.

"I'm so sorry."

"So am I, believe me. So am I." Paulette sucked in as much air as possible as layer after layer of darkness began to take over her vision.

Ellie had dropped the call. Finally having the courage to dial Paulette's number, but then hearing the news about her mother, Ellie felt like a stranger, completely out of step with the world she had left behind so long ago.

She cried: "Where is my Mama Mae?"

Ellie did not have to leave Cove Island where the only true closeness she had ever felt to other people who had such close-knit families—since she had no idea what that meant—she learned after she arrived on their island, battered and beaten by Brent and then nearly drowned by the hurricane.

What did her husband, Brent L. Livingston III, care? He had to save his boat. Had to make it to a boat hold where they were supposed to go a few days before the storm that was headed straight for them.

"We never thought you would be whole again," Mama Mae had said as Ellie began to gain consciousness on a regular basis. Mama Mae was the island queen of Cove Island. She was surrounded by eight young girls, four birthed by her. They all loved her, obeyed her, and looked out for her. She rescued many others before Ellie came along, but Ellie was in the worst shape. Her hair was chopped off. It looked like a self-cut job with chunks of hair sticking out. Her bruises darkened her skin, and her gashes were deep.

Born on the island, Mama Mae was young and beautiful like the ladies she cared for now, but time had taken its toll, and now she weighed almost three hundred pounds. Roughest was the fight against the heat of summer. Her family took turns splashing her with water from the sea. She was also fed filtered water to keep the rest of her system working.

She cleaned Ellie up and made homegrown broth. There was a broken ankle and two black and blue and swollen eyes. Her clothes were in shreds, and she was incoherent. Somehow she had pulled herself across the rocky shore far enough to yell for help.

Eight months later, the two women stood at the dock where deliveries were made to their small village before the ship traveled oceanside to the large hotel where most of the young people and all of their men except for the infirm were employed.

"Here," Mama Mae said, lovingly brushing Ellie's wisp of hair away from her forehead. She handed Ellie a colorful scarf the girls had made and then a purse made from straw that was sold in the hotel's shop. "We don't have much," Mama Mae said, "but what we have is in the sack."

Ellie shook her head no. "I can't take this," she said.

"Now you go on back home and find your people. They ain't around no more. You come back, you hear?" There were tears of love in Mama Mae's eyes, tears that Ellie had accepted contained pain and hope. Thanks to this woman and this island, Ellie finally understood what was meant by accepting and giving love.

CHAPTER 7

PAULETTE AND KATHLEEN WERE ON the 405 freeway heading for LAX. The carbon monoxide was settling into the continual layer of smog that hung heavily all the way from the Pacific Ocean to the Santa Monica Mountains. Carved out of those mountains over seventy-five years ago was the 405, which runs north and today is a sixteen-lane nightmare. Could it be true that 380,000 moving vehicles drive the 405 each day? According to the *Los Angeles Times* it is.

While Paulette's purse contained a folded copy of the judge's order, making her the temporary victor in this ongoing battle with her ex-husband, she felt as stiff and hollow as a balsa wood door.

Paulette had known for some time that the ground no longer pulsed below her feet like it once did when she and Chris first arrived. Needlessly, she was taking her frustrations out on the traffic and overpopulation. "These people drive hours to get to work," she observed. "Charging gas on credit cards they cannot afford, their mortgages going well beyond the reach of any ordinary man's income. There are other Utopias better than this one. Did I thank you for all of ... this?" Paulette asked.

"Not yet. But it's nice to hear."

"You're the dearest and best friend I've ever had. To think about what you gambled to be on my side—I can't thank you enough."

"You're welcome. Now stop. Just return in one piece. I want to see your smile again. See you light up. All that energy put back in the right places. Don't tumble too far down when you get to Key West, or you might fall into a trap that mires you in a place you can't leave. I've heard stories."

"I promise. Just get me out of here, will you?"

"Doing my best, girlfriend, doing my best," Kathleen replied, changing the subject. "You going with something more Florida before you board?"

"On the plane," Paulette groaned. "I'm too exhausted to move right now."

"I didn't mean in the middle of the 405," Kathleen teased her.

"I cannot believe how unceremoniously I was dumped."

"You? You want unceremonious? Someday let's reminisce about my first divorce and how I lived off food stamps once he left. I'm a native to LA. My struggles are right in this space. It's you who has to go through self-discovery only to realize LA is home after all."

"Thomas Wolfe," Paulette replied. What she wanted to confess and have Kathleen understand was how living off food stamps would be far easier than the pain she was enduring now; how releasing Chris made her feel as though she had lost both her legs and arms and was left out on some dark, wet street to die alone.

"Here you have friends, family. Go to Key West and let him go," Kathleen urged. "But come back here. Ahh, here we are! You have twenty minutes to be at your gate, or I'll have to return for you. I'm going back to my office to work on another divorce hearing for tomorrow."

"Yeah, 50/50, and she gets her payback by keeping the house," Paulette chuckled.

"That does not sound at all like you," Kathleen said, almost slamming on the brakes.

"Maybe not, but you expect me to be rational at a time like this?" Paulette was out of the car and leaned over the top and screamed, "*I am not rational! Beware! Do not listen to me!*"

Kathleen shook her head. Paulette came around to the driver's side where she said, "Love ya. Call ya." She raced back to the curb and blew Kathleen a kiss as she pulled out her tickets.

"Oh, I almost forgot!' Paulette gasped, holding onto the open window. "You'll never guess who called earlier. Ellie Livingston, risen from the dead. At first I thought I was speaking to an imposter. Strange coincidence. She's in Miami."

"What did she want?" Kathleen asked while glancing in the rear view mirror. There were horns blowing from behind with drivers raising their arms with all kinds of embarrassing signals, reminding her she was blocking the way.

"Did I know anything about her mother. If her next stop was LA, I invited her to stay in my house. She hung up before I could finish."

"Definitely an imposter. Good thing you're going out of town."

"You would have to know the whole story. Poor girl. I wonder if her mother realizes Ellie is still alive. Here's a legal question for you: If Ellie wants to claim her share of her parents' estate, even though she ran away at age eleven, would she still have any rights?"

"That takes a lawsuit," Kathleen replied. "Now go! Let loose and have a great time, meet a new guy and stay out of trouble. But don't forget where your real home is. Call me?"

"I will, I will!" Paulette replied, excited. She turned to the porter who returned her license and her ticket and tagged her bag. "I'm going to Key West!" she giggled.

"Yes, ma'am. You sure are. Next door to your left."

CHAPTER 8

ON THE FLIGHT TO MIAMI International Airport, Paulette was shoved, jostled, and stuffed into her seat next to lovers, their arms and legs wrapped around each other as they balanced champagne glasses.

Passengers were dressed in typical Florida attire of flowery shirts, white shorts, sandals, and straw hats. Most were set to deplane in Miami and head for the Caribbean on the new Oasis out of Fort Lauderdale. Add crying babies, teenagers hollering at each other over music plugged into their ears, and older couples who ducked the luggage toss, and the picture of today's airline travel was complete.

Cute, she thought with a smirk.

Climbing across three seats to the window seat, Paulette wished she had booked her ticket earlier, at least soon enough for a first class seat. Never mind. If this is what it took to get to her destination ASAP, then so be it.

Strapped in, Paulette shook off her shoes and wrapped the small blanket supplied by the airlines around her shoulders. Five hours of engines whirring below her feet; five whole hours before landing; five hours to ask the important question of what to do with the rest of her life. So how could she sleep?

Paulette blotted her forehead with a Kleenex as the crowd disembarked into the sweltering heat in Miami. Her ankles were swollen, and her inner thighs were damp from the moisture stuck inside her panty hose. Sweat was pouring from her armpits, and crawling around her waist was a reddened ribbon from the too-tight waistband of her skirt. (When did that happen?)

Too excited to change clothes before the sign-in for her bright yellow Ford Mustang convertible, she was whisked to a warehouse several miles from the terminal for her rental. The plan was to drive south past Miami and onto the Stretch, the famous thirty-mile highway from Homestead to Key Largo, where she would pick up a sandwich and a cold soda, change clothes, and continue on US 1 to the Overseas Highway until she was literally at the end of the road.

Freedom, here I come!

After texting Kathleen that she was safe and her flight uneventful, Paulette called her cousin Doug Sanders. The last time she saw Doug was on a trip four summers ago with her son, Billie, and Howard, one of his school friends.

Doug and his wife, Flower, were living in a small apartment at the time. They apologized for not having room. However, Paulette had already rented a cottage on the beach at the Sundance House: one room for the boys and one for her, which included a massage and special concoctions at the tiki bar. The boys scoped downtown, while she luxuriated at the hotel for the long, three-day weekend.

"Hey, girlfriend, you're right on time." Flower's voice was upbeat as she handed the phone to Doug.

"I'm glad you're on schedule," he said. "Flower has your room all set up. We're very excited to show you around. We love doing that."

"You've done it before, but thank you."

"Hey, cous'. This time is special. Both Flower and I have been where you are—through difficult, painful divorces. But look at us now! There definitely is life after divorce. She makes me very happy!"

"We can't wait to take you on the sunset cruise in front of Mallory Square. Tomorrow we'll do a walking tour along Duval Street. Stop at Sloppy Joe's. Breathe in some Ernest Hemingway. You win?" he asked.

"If you call watching your heart walk into the arms of someone else winning, I suppose the answer is yes. I was granted use of the house until Chris finishes college and half the funds to maintain it. Then Chris and I have to settle ..."

"How's Billie about all this?" Doug interrupted.

"I flew to Brown with him a couple of weeks ago following graduation. He has more adjustments to make than his parents' divorce," Paulette admitted. "College and all. Otherwise he knows we both support him on most things he does."

"That house thing is not your life," Doug said. "Any man of Chris's financial reputation would want to win that mansion and its view just for show."

"I suppose so," Paulette replied, knowing she could not listen to much more without starting to cry.

"The divorce? It was inevitable."

"What does that mean?" she asked, shocked by his comment.

"Let's talk later. Just get yourself down here in one piece. Once we begin to party, and we do party, you won't give a damn about LA."

Determined not to release her tears, Paulette quickly said, "I'll be there by five! Thanks for the accommodations until my apartment is ready."

As she opened the trunk and rummaged through her luggage, a thought snagged her. Was Doug talking to Chris? Otherwise how did Doug know their divorce was inevitable? They hardly knew each other, Chris and Doug. And she never talked over her personal problems with him or Flower.

CHAPTER 9

So FAR PAULETTE'S PLANS WERE moving along. After a stop-off at mile marker eighty-eight in Key Largo, she would definitely have three full hours of blissful solitude all the way to mile marker zero, at Key West's southernmost spot, marked by the famous buoy where millions have pictures in front of the landmark. Her timing was perfect for travel from Miami to Key Largo. The sun would set within the next two hours. Slow, seemingly motionless shadings of nightfall were moseying along the open sky at their own summertime pace.

Now she was ready to shed her LA court suit and put on a bright, flowery Lilly Pulitzer dress and matching sandals. "What's more Florida than that?" she wondered out loud.

As she put the top down on her yellow Ford Mustang, its five-speed transmission and V8 engine purring and stereo system blasting, Paulette drove the Stretch speeding over the limit and singing eighties songs.

At mile marker eighty-eight she pulled over to buy some finger foods: chips, peanuts, and a sandwich. She left her purchases on the seat, put the top up, and locked her purse inside the trunk. With her Florida clothes wrapped around her arm, she crossed over US Route 1 to a fifties two-story pink motel called the Flamingo Terrace Motel.

Paulette casually glanced upward, only to see a huge, athletically built man dressed in black pants and wearing a white Cuban shirt tapping on the jalousies next to the entryway door of a room halfway down the open walkway on the second floor of the motel.

She turned around in a circle, looking for signs of life. *Didn't anyone else hear the yelling and banging? See anything?* she wondered as the man shouted, "Hello! Hello!"

Various couples wandered around, but they seemed to be involved in their own moments, ignoring the world around them.

"I cannot be the only one!" she mumbled as she walked toward the entrance of the motel to look for a staff member.

Coming from the south and traveling at the speed of sound was a black Chevy with darkened windows, its wheels blowing up so much dust that Paulette was unable to read the license plate number. The hot car circled around back and came to a dead stop at the entrance to the stairs next to the main office. The driver faced forward, his engine revved up.

Seconds later a man raced down the stairs like Superman, his heels sliding to a stop on the driver's side. The car window opened part way and a hand brought out what Paulette thought was a hammer. The man then quickly raced back up the stairs.

Paulette looked around again. Again, no one paid attention to the banging on the window, which, to her, was loud, almost thunderous. The man who ran back upstairs was beating his fists on the same door. When there was no response, he used his elbow to smash in the side window. Climbing through the broken glass, he pulled out not a hammer, but a gun—a small automatic handgun!

Two shots were fired, and the shooter exited through the bright and shiny pink door, blue plastic gloves covering his hands. He sprinted to the passenger side of the parked car and jumped in. The dust flew everywhere as the car made a quarter turn and headed north on US 1.

Paulette was too stunned to move. Recovering, she crossed the street, grabbed her cell phone, and dialed 911. "We have an emergency here."

"Your name and location," the operator said.

"It's a pink motel. The last sign I remember was mile marker eighty-eight."

"Is the motel opposite a gas station and a little sandwich shop? The Flamingo Terrace Motel on the east side of US 1?"

"That's the one!"

"We're on it," the operator's voice was muffled. "But we do appreciate your call." She took Paulette's cell phone number, and said, "When the police are ready, they will call you. How long will you be at this location?"

"About five more minutes if I have anything to say about it."

"Can you wait at least thirty minutes? By then an officer will be available to take your statement."

"I guess so," Paulette said.

When she hung up, she entered the lobby, her clothes still tucked under her arm.

Moments later two police cars arrived and blocked the driveway entrance to the motel, their blue and red lights flashing, their siren blasting.

Two young officers jumped out of the second vehicle, removed their weapons from their holsters, and bounded up the far set of stairs two at a time. Next, a team of paramedics arrived.

Paulette went back outside as the two officers came down the stairs empty-handed. They ran to their car, got in, and sped off, heading north. Meanwhile, a white paramedic truck arrived and dropped off two medics and a stretcher.

The truck backed up to the stairway and waited.

Several minutes later they came down the narrow stairs carrying the gurney and a blue body bag, zipped and closed. A strap held the bag to the gurney.

At the truck, the paramedics released the wheels and jammed the gurney inside the vehicle. The truck headed south again, its siren blasting through the late night air.

Paulette crossed US 1 to her rented Mustang and unlocked the trunk. Her suitcase was open and nearly empty. Her purse was gone along with all her money and her IDs. Shaking in disbelief, she reviewed her steps. She had definitely locked the car. She even clicked the lock and waited for the sound of a wounded animal before she crossed US 1 again.

"Oh, great. Just frickin' great!" she collapsed on the side of her dream vacation car. "I came here for some R & R. Now look what has happened!"

She went across the street and found one of the officers.

"I've been robbed!"

The officer stared at her. "You're in a vacation city. Never let anything personal out of your sight, and certainly hold onto your cash and your credit cards," he said.

Paulette was on her own.

She looked in the glove compartment for the rental agreement. Grabbing it, she weaved back through the traffic and showed the only ID she had to the officer, who was writing on a small pad.

She told him, "My stuff has been stolen."

"Stolen how?"

"I have no idea. I only went into that little store across the street to buy some food and witnessed this incident. It's now three hours later. I returned to my locked car and nothing. I've been robbed!"

The young police officer was hesitant. His attitude to Paulette was as if he was holding back a "No shit!" remark.

"We're here for hours yet, ma'am," he said finally. Pointing to the other side of the driveway, he added, "Why don't you follow that officer and give him your statement? You say your car was locked? Wait." He nodded to his left and pointed a finger. "That's our captain over there. He'll take care of you."

"What about my stuff? My license? Credit cards? Money?"

"You have a cell phone? ... Good. Use it. You are not a suspect," he reassured her. "You're free to go."

"What happens about my things? Can't you do anything?"

The officer did not respond. He only moved closer to the murder scene, his back to her.

CHAPTER 10

AFTER STANDING IN THE VERY same spot for quite some time, Paulette finally got the message that all the cops were going to do was ignore her. She was a side issue they would get to later.

She phoned her cousin Doug.

"Don't waste your time up there," Doug told her. "That sort of thing happens in the Keys all the time. Between the natives, shopkeepers, and tourists, the cops can't keep up. A couple thousand isn't worth the hassle. No sunset ride down here for you tonight, dearie. You gassed up?"

"I'm full."

"Good. We'll settle everything in the morning. I know people up there. I'll fix it so you can report your losses from here."

"You can do that?"

"Cous', this is the Keys. We can do anything we want. In the meantime, Flower and I will grab a bite at Margaritaville and be home on the shy side of midnight. We'll leave the front door unlocked. Why don't you settle in? Shower, relax. Out back, there's plenty of wine in the cooler," he said. "If you're a coffee drinker, a grinder and a coffee pot are in the small pantry to the side of the back kitchen counter just around the corner from your room."

"I could check into one of those glamorous motels," Paulette said. "See you guys in the morning."

"No way," Doug said. "We have a nice big house now, and who better to stay with us than you? We can't wait to see you. And I don't want to greet you from some lobby of a hotel. I got a call from your future landlord about your new apartment. They started painting. Should be ready in a coupla days. Maybe Monday."

"Okay, all right," Paulette said, grinning. For her first night in town, she felt much more comfortable being with people she knew, and she was grateful. Doug reminded her, "We have some time before set up and then there's the welcoming party. That Sunday, we also have another big day: a noontime brunch at the Pier House. Afterward, a small group is coming over to see my new boat. You into boats?"

"Not really."

"You can't live in Key West and not be into boating," he said proudly. "Otherwise you might as well live in Kansas where it's a whole lot cheaper."

CHAPTER 11

~∞∞∞~

NEAR KEY WEST NOW AND way past the time of a spectacular sunset, Paulette called Chris's home number. Ms. Bippy answered.

"Is he there?" Paulette asked, disappointed. She only wanted to remind him of a very romantic time when they were virtually penniless and their future was filled with so many dreams and great potential. Before leaving for California and his internship at UCLA, they went to the Keys for a few days and stumbled onto the spot where the sun is exactly opposite the moon. Back then, she stood unsteadily on the rocks in front of the Marina Restaurant. She spread her arms out as far as possible and released a long "The hills are alive; oh, there are no hills, but there will be when we arrive in LA, doctor."

And the phenomenon disappeared.

"In surgery," Leslie said pastily.

Ms. Bippy must have been sleeping. How could that be? Why be a working stiff when you don't have to be? Paulette's thoughts were bitter.

Just for kicks, she called Sherman Oaks General Hospital, the burn unit.

"Dr. Marshall, please," she said in her most official voice.

"He's in surgery. Who is calling?

"Mrs. Marshall."

"Oh! Hold on!"

"Hey, honey, is it time?" Chris asked.

Chris's voice was lighthearted, even friendly, as if he were sitting at the kitchen counter on a Saturday morning, having breakfast.

"Hey, Chris. It's me," Paulette said, cheerful herself.

"Yes?" his voice was abrupt. His change in tone pitched a solid rock into her heart.

"I'm at the spot where the moon and sun can be seen at the same time. Remember?"

"Paulette," Chris said sharply, "that was a long time ago. Only a memory. The only call I want from you is when you're ready to sell the house. But then you already know that."

The line disconnected, and Paulette's face flushed. She knew her behavior was one of those unexplainable moments. I mean, how do you act when you're first divorced and you run into trouble and he's the only one you've been close to? Her question was rhetorical, said as a method to hide her embarrassment for such a ridiculous action, an action that set her up for rejection of the worst kind.

Paulette arrived at the Mitchell residence across the street from Higgs Beach at 11 p.m. As promised, the front door was unlocked.

She went back to her car and took out the nearly empty suitcase and threw it angrily on the bed and headed for the bathroom. The only way to soothe her nerves would be a hot shower, so hot her skin would be red before she turned the faucet back to a normal warm. *Must be my Swedish blood*, she thought as she checked for a clean towel.

Bless Flower. There were not only clean towels, but she had hung a bathrobe and a night shirt on the back of the door! It took about ten seconds to fall asleep.

CHAPTER 12

WHEN PAULETTE WOKE, IT WAS daybreak and the house was quiet. She went to the alcove at the staircase to make coffee but decided against it. She could do all of that at home or with Flower and Doug another time. She was going to walk the famous Duval Street. There was so much to explore!

Eighty, eighty, and eighty: air, water, and humidity. This was the weather report—all of it essential medicine for healing and renewing. No more allowing the usual continuing on ad infinitum. No more silly, embarrassing, and intrusive calls to her past. Take chances, meet new people, make contacts, make calls—step up to the plate instead of always stepping aside like a good fifth grade teacher.

Even without knowing the territory, Paulette was raring to discover a wondrous place in the early a.m. What was stopping her? She had only ventured out tethered to a partner who was himself tethered to his cell phone, thus making the trek challenging.

Earlier Paulette had been sitting out on the Mitchells' front porch to watch the sun rise as a few runners whizzed by, iPhones on, earphones plugged in, and dogs at their sides. Maybe this was her future destiny, to always be sitting alone, waiting for the paint to dry. No! It was time to step up to the plate.

First step: stop waiting on others!

Paulette walked across the failed grass, unable to grow as a result of the coral rock beneath it. She was at the beginning of Duval Street, but she did not know if she was facing east or west, north or south.

A block away, the setting was so Key West. Across the empty street was a small bookstore with two big front windows, filled with the latest best sellers. Behind the building were identical and intriguing guest houses. One was painted white and trimmed in turquoise, the other sanded down to its natural wood.

She bought a copy of the *Key West Citizen*. Before opening the paper she drew in her surroundings. No one was out and about this early, so she could peer into the windows, the alleys, and hidden corners without other people around.

Across the street was a coffee shop. The smell of pastries and fresh coffee floated over to where she stood, looking at the finished redo on an old Victorian. She picked out a key lime croissant and ordered a latte. (Oh! The calories in that!)

"We also have seating on the restaurant side," the woman behind the counter suggested.

"The open air porch looks much more appealing. I'm on vacation from LA. Your air is so fresh. I'm looking forward to being here for a few months."

When was the last time she had actually sat alone in such an intimate setting, reading the paper and drinking coffee that someone else had made? Maybe never! Things were definitely looking up.

"At the end of the street, I saw lots of boats for hire. If I took a day trip, would I be back by early afternoon?" Paulette asked the server.

"I don't know about that, but if you really want to hear about our history from a fisherman's point of view—and save some money—you got a car?"

"It's parked at my new apartment."

"Drive to the Garrison Bight Marina on Roosevelt. Turn left just before the US 1 sign." The woman checked her watch. "You should be on time for the first run. There's an old sea captain named Hernandez. The locals call him Captain Maxy. Great guy. He'll give you an interesting morning, that much I know. Plenty of customers come back and tell me what a fun day they had going to Fort Jefferson and snorkeling."

"I don't have a full day, but …"

The hostess leaned over the counter. "Why not give it a shot? You won't be sorry, I promise."

CHAPTER 13

AT THE GARRISON BIGHT MARINA at the end of Roosevelt, near the drive out of Key West on US 1, Paulette went into the small office and asked, "Can you guide me to Captain Hernandez's boat? Do I pay you for a ticket?"

The sunburned, sun-bleached blonde-headed kid, about seventeen or eighteen, pointed down the main docking area.

"Captain Hernandez?"

"That's me!" He was dressed in khaki pants with multiple pockets and wearing a white T-shirt with Key West written across it. He wore a wide-brimmed straw hat. His skin was of lizard quality, deeply lined and darkened by years in the sun. But his eyes sparkled as he replied. "You comin' with us or just askin' a question? 'Cause we're leaving in about two minutes."

"Oh no! I want to go with you! How much is it?"

"You have gear?" he asked as he looked around to see what she was carrying.

Paulette glanced at his hands. On closer inspection, the captain was about sixty-five. He had rough hands and several scars on his fingers and the fronts of his hands, which at one time must have been serious, mean gashes.

"Nope. Come on aboard. I have plenty. You ever dive before?" he asked.

"No, sir. How much?"

"We're going to Fort Jefferson, stay an hour or so. The gentlemen aboard want to dive first, then drink and play some cards below. That bother you?"

"No, sir. It won't."

"Cash?"

She nodded.

"One hundred twenty-five dollars. Where you from?"

"LA. Los Angeles, California."

"Folks that formal out there? Yes, sir and all?"

"Only when I'm teaching," she laughed as she took the captain's hand and carefully came aboard, cautiously landing each foot one at a time on steps not quite big enough for her feet.

The captain's assistant untied the ropes while the captain started the engines and gave out the safety instructions over the loud speaker.

"There are life jackets under your seats. Yes, I see you boys know the drill—and Miss? You as well."

The helper began lining up the tanks and rechecking the pressure gauges as the captain steered clear of the marina. Almost immediately they were out on the inlet where numerous boats headed for the Atlantic while others were going in the same direction as the captain.

The water was as calm as the day; the sky the bluest she had seen it in a long while, with only a few white clouds high above. The ocean side under the highway and in the channel was calm and clear, the water from dark amber to light turquoise.

Paulette thought of her vacation with Chris in Tahiti two years ago. The only difference was here there were no mountains, and for East Coasters, Paulette thought, coming to the Keys would surely save time and money and be just as exciting.

Before they reached the fort, which was straight ahead by a mile or so, the captain turned off the two engines and the young helper jumped to his feet.

"If you noticed, we cut the engines. We'll glide from here. There's white sand ahead. I'll bring her up to an embankment, and you will enter the water wherever you feel comfortable. The depth is only five, six feet." He turned and said to his helper, "Get the gear."

What kind of adventure did she get herself into? The water was not shallow. It was up past her neck and also dark.

She was wet now, her gear rinsed in salt water, her mask spit into. She waded for about a minute. Soon after that, her foot reached the embankment the captain had pointed out. It was time to put on her mask, fit her breathing mechanism into her mouth, dunk her face in the water, and study the terrain below.

Below the surface was a sight to behold. She had been on glass-bottom boats before, but having her body in the water—and being told not to step on the coral below—made her feel like part of the scenery.

There was white coral and young pink coral—coral that was fan-like, which was created by nature herself. Also purple stems that sprouted into waving fans in the lower areas and swam around the swaying green sargasso reeds was very exciting. Fish of all different colors of the rainbow spread out in every color, size, and shape imaginable. They swam in and out of the rocks, the shells, and the sand below, nibbling as they went along.

Who would want to catch and kill these precious creatures? she wondered.

After an hour or so, she was exhausted. Thrilled by what she had seen, but still not on target when it came to her energy level, she surfaced as she swam to the boat and climbed aboard.

Sure enough, from below deck, Paulette could hear laughing, smell liquor, and see the gambling table set up in the center of the sleeping quarters. And as she was cautioned, they were smoking big, fat stogies, their glasses filled with whiskey that smelled all the way up to the deck. Enjoying their time together and truly away from it all, they were laughing, talking loudly, and telling dirty jokes.

"So you're from LA. Not many Cubans out there," the captain commented.

"No. Mostly Mexicans. Lots of people from other countries and just as many moving in from all over the US."

"What do you do in LA?"

"I'm a counselor, sometimes a teacher, at a gang school in the San Fernando Valley."

"Nice. My wife—we've been married forty-five years—she has always stayed home. We have five kids. All of 'em live in Key West."

"How great for you."

"Great for her, a little confusing at times for me. We never stayed home with our kids. That was the wife's job. Never went into the delivery room like my sons did—and proud of it!" The captain shook his head, a small grin on his face.

"You like fishing? I mean being a captain and going out like this?" Paulette asked.

"Actually, I do. For years I had a fleet. Kept the boats up myself, so I didn't get out here as much as I would have liked to. When I was younger, I brought my kids out here. Broke them in early. None of them are fishermen, though," he added.

"For years, I wished for a family like yours. I was too ambitious. When I reached my late thirties, I had troubles having more children."

"You close?"

"I have a son. We try. It's my fault if we're not. I gave too much energy to my own education. Focused on that instead of my son."

"There's no sense second guessing about your kids. It's too crazy-making. Besides, you are far too beautiful and probably a good therapist who helps many people. The books should have taught you that."

"It might have gone better if there had been more than one. Everything is magnified. He had no one else to blame and we gave him all the blame."

The captain laughed. "The problem with five is only one can be the favorite."

"And it would be your last."

"How did you know?"

"You look like a caring father," Paulette said, smiling.

"I loved them all, but my youngest—Susanna—she's had a rough time. Got in with the wrong crowd from the beginning."

"That's what my job is all about. I wish we, as counselors, had caring families like yours to work with."

"Thank you. Most of the credit goes to my wife. And the church. We are Catholics, strong ones. All our kids went to Catholic school until they reached high school. My son Michael is a chef. Went to school for it. Owns his own restaurant."

The captain was twirling the small rope he had been holding onto in between his fat, crooked fingers. To Paulette, he seemed like a contented man—not the restless soul she had become in such a short time.

"You in town alone?" he asked.

"I'm staying with my cousin Doug Mitchell. You know him? Next week I'll have my own place for the summer."

"Sure. Doug and Flower Mitchell. Been here for ten or so years. Straight up people. You shouldn't be here by yourself. How about joining our family one of those Friday nights when we all go to my son's restaurant? Mix with some real natives?" He smiled.

She noticed how bright and alive his brown eyes were. They sparkled and seemed to dance as he talked and retreated when he was listening.

"That sounds just wonderful. Is your house number the one on your payment receipt?" Paulette asked.

"I have a separate cell phone like the kids of today. For my friends and my business. I'll write it on the back of the receipt, and we can go from there."

Chapter 14

Captain Maxwell Hernandez was ready for a good, long, uninterrupted nap. There was something he had chewed on the whole damned day, and he needed to get rid of it.

What a nice surprise to meet a new lady friend. She was not only beautiful in an approachable way, but she was warm and feminine, even funny. She had the long hair with curls, like the style he saw on television with more curls coming to the front. Susanna told him those were mostly hairpieces. He couldn't wait to tell her one of his customers was from LA where the long hair and curls were the real deal.

Max did not ask his customer why she was in the Keys. Since he would figure a way to see her again, he would ask more about her the next time. Right now, he was too exhausted to think straight. He needed food and rest, and then he'd be ready to go again.

His irritation this time was about the four wannabe divers in from New Jersey whose good time left a stench in his cabins.

Like so many of his clients exposed to the phenomenal fishing or those who went to dive at the restored reefs—almost as beautiful as those at the Great Barrier Reef—the response was always the same: a big, friendly pat on the back and words to the effect: "Man, are you lucky! What a life! Wish I could break away from my job. Make a living like you do."

Little did they know!

Maybe he was on his last nerve because there was a true lady aboard, and below was a low-class group of overtipping rowdies.

This bunch of guys was okay, and they were overly generous with their tips, but when was someone going to really explore Fort Jefferson and appreciate it like it should be?

Max's night trip coming up felt bad for a number of reasons—Two.

Cubans—no doubt in the Keys illegally—were to be taken to Islamorada and returned to Garrison the following day.

Max and the inexperienced boy he hired for the day washed down the boat in preparation for the evening run. He paid his helper, saying, "Monday morning first thing? See you then."

He patted the boy on the back and sent him on his way, even knowing it was the wrong move. He needed an assistant on the night run more than during the day, but he let the boy go after overpaying him. Max was definitely losing his touch.

Where was Allyson Jackson these days? She always spent time giving the history of the fort while customers were suiting up. Allyson was his secretary and bookkeeper, who took care of bookings when he had a full fleet. For a time after that, she was the buffer between wound-up clients and the crew's demands. Somehow she knew when they were properly booked, leaving enough hours for cleanup and sending everyone home at reasonable hours. Running the business by himself he was no good at it. He certainly missed her.

All day Max felt out of sorts. His problem was with his circumstances. Restless by nature, what he yearned for most of all was some variety—something exciting and unusual instead of his uneventful, mindless daily routine.

Why Max felt this restless on this particular day he blamed on the need for a change of scenery, not his health.

If the young lady had not been aboard to have a friendly chat and to flirt with, Max would have gone into his fantasy world, imagining a woman who would wrap her warmth around his body like a call girl rides her pole.

This kind of thinking led to some mighty negative formulas for getting rid of Rosetta, his perfect and dedicated wife of forty-five years. *Forty-five years with one woman is way too long*, he thought. Same house. Same wife. Same job. Same routine. Just like his father before him and his grandfather before that.

In his imagination, Max carried pages and pages of unfulfilled dreams. They were always about escape. His nightmares, when he was able to sleep, had him reviewing all the opportunities he had passed up. Sometimes the loss of these opportunities, whether he was awake or dreaming, had him running so fast he could hardly breathe.

So many thoughts were about how Rosetta should conveniently die before him. These he quickly discarded. She had not been aboard one of his fishing vessels in years. Furthermore, she did not swim, so how could she end up "accidentally" in the water?

Further thoughts went to stabbing her in their bed while he was out at sea. But who would assist him? Then how much money would it take to permanently keep the guy's trap shut? Finally, how long would it be before the truth was uncovered?

How about a slow poisoning? "Dummy me," he said aloud. "I never cook, and she doesn't swim." Too much drama, too much planning, and way too risky, he finally decided. However, it never stopped his elaborate dreaming.

None of his thoughts were new. He only hoped that some "ah ha!" moment would arrive that would set him free. Over the years he was bored by narrow Catholic thinking about duty to one's family. He wanted to become a born-again Christian and sing emotional, heart-wrenching songs.

Max's advice about kids since he had five of them? They don't grow up and move away as a parent might expect. They grow up to hang around, rent free, complete with their car—which he paid for—and their electronics. They stay in the bedroom of their childhood until well into their thirties, many times bringing a kid or two with them.

Max's generation may be made fun of for being behind the times when it comes to expensive electronic and computer gadgets, but his generation was wise enough to know these new toys, bought by his kids and others like them, were out of date the moment the salesman rang up the sale. If he bought all of the gadgets that had come down the pike in his younger days, where would his family be now?

The simplest way to rid himself of the problem, of course, was to go against his Catholic belief system, divorce his sweet, kind, and loving wife, and let the neighbors talk all they want. Let his family think he was no good. So what? He couldn't care less. All they ever did was suck off him anyway, and after they got what they wanted, they paid him no mind.

Watching the years fly by without change, Max had his share of serious lovers. For one reason or another, he always dragged himself back home, either out of guilt or because of a heightened sense of responsibility for what he had caused to come into this crazy world. That he chose to marry a child as young and inexperienced as he was, one who never changed and wanted nothing more than to stay home and take care of her family on his dime—his choice was his own bad luck.

Max went to the Key West library to research information about the city's historical cemetery between the early 1900s until the death of his grandson Tomas a year ago. The family buried the Hernandez family child in their plot after he drowned in the family's above-ground swimming pool while Rosetta was caring for him. After that, Max's notes became somewhat sketchy. The library, however, had plenty of data from authentic sources whenever he was prepared to begin again.

As far as his family plot was concerned, while there were many gaps in the data, his secret desire was not to straighten out his genealogy (as he had said), but to find some shred of evidence that would keep him plugging along in the belief that one of his relatives owned certain unclaimed rights to land grants stolen from the early Cuban settlers. Like many Mexican families in Texas whose property had been illegally confiscated by the federal government, Max felt such a right existed for him right here in Key West.

Whenever he told anyone about investigating the land grants, hoping to receive remuneration in cash from the federal government, the response was that his odds of such an event happening was lower than winning the lottery.

Finding a rare and pure passion Max never felt before, especially in a library, was the most unexpected move he had ever made.

"I am Miss Browne with an 'e' at the end." Those were the exact first words she spoke to him.

CHAPTER 15

MAX WAS STRUCK BY MISS Browne with an "e" at the end of her last name the first time he spotted her behind the information counter at the local library. Her curly red hair was loosely tied to the back of her neck. She was tall and thin and had a fine figure underneath her colorful dress. She was in her early fifties but still a knockout—a woman who worked in a profession perfectly suited for her. She was charming but standoffish, a whole lot stuck up, and too educated for her own good. Those were all assumptions, of course. Once he got to know her, he discovered they were true.

So far as Maxwell Alexander Hernandez, US naturalized citizen, boat captain, reader, journal writer, and music lover was concerned, no one else took the time to know Miss Mabel Browne the way he did.

True, Mabel was a bookworm, but she was also a foodie, an excellent chef who taught him the art of eating, going well beyond his rice and beans existence at home. And she was sure hot in bed, hungry for sex like no woman he'd ever been with. She also had a redhead's temper.

Max's crazy thoughts ran at full speed whenever he was around her, so crazy they went well beyond what a man his age should be imagining let alone attempting to carry out.

A few months ago, Max was over at Mabel's having one of her gourmet meals when he threw out, "If I divorce my wife, will you marry me?"

"A good Catholic like you? Never happen!" She laughed at him.

She always followed his persistence with her explanation for remaining single. "I've been on my own too long," she would tell him. "Single and having a married lover and sleeping alone works for me. Let's keep things as they are. Otherwise I might take a walk. I've done it before. If I ever saw any of your five kids around town, I would freak. That just would not do."

The remark felt as if she had scraped his balls against rusty nails as his heart cracked into a thousand pieces. Maxwell might divorce his wife but would never abandon his kids.

"We could start all over somewhere else," he told Mabel in an insincere, shallow tone, grabbing at straws, knowing that life without his children would be a torture he could not endure.

And then there was Susanna, light of her father's eye and envied by the rest of the family.

Or what about Max's neighbors' reaction to his "taking up with a white woman?" Max already knew what they would think. They could all rot in hell. That's how much he cared.

"What we have here, Maxwell Hernandez, is a Mexican standoff. What if you walked away?" Mabel asked.

They were standing in her 1930s kitchen with its open fire pit at waist level—the only signs of age in the entire mansion that she had modernized. He was cooking steaks and she was turning over the noodles with cheese and broccoli.

"Me? I have it all. Why wouldn't I want more? I want you," he said, grinning and looking away. "Come away with me on a cruise."

She only laughed at him. "On a fisherman's holiday? No thank you. A trip to Manhattan to the downtown library or the Metropolitan Museum of Art to view the masters—now you're talking my language."

From Max's point of view, what would he do in a big city like that? It was no vacation for him to see treasured books or to analyze art he knew nothing about.

Despite their passion for each other, the price was ultimately too high. For that reason alone she was by far the wiser. "Oh, and what about my three cats?" she would tease him, attempting to force him to face facts.

"I'm with Rosetta because we knew each other's families," he explained. "They're all dead now, but when they were alive, we brought pride to them like our children will do for us."

"Then go home and be prideful," she would say, shrugging.

Their affair went on for five years. Max ended it when he finally came to terms with how being an unattached wealthy white woman, thousands of miles away from any of her own family, she could not possibly comprehend what the importance of close ties to his family meant to two poor, young arrivals from Cuba who started saving their money a few dollars at a time.

Being a fisherman, like his father and his grandfather before him, fishing was all Max knew. He lacked a college education, but he loved books, especially reading about the history of his own culture, going all the way back to the Conquistadors and their lost gold.

His father shared a few stories about Max's grandfather. The rest of his family history was pure conjecture. How did they make it through World War II and the Great Depression? Questions they had never thought about until it was too late.

All he knew was earlier generations died relatively young as a result of the poor conditions in Cuba, followed by years of surviving inside hot, damp, open camps at what was then the outskirts of Key West.

That Max was a leader among his own kind did not mean much to him. In fact his visibility and so-called importance in recent years had become an entrapment, causing him to do what he hated most—lie and sneak around.

Max was inside his old red truck, on the way to his home on Petronia. He finished cleaning the boat and putting supplies in place for the next run to Islamorada at 6 p.m. with the two Cubans.

He drove by rote through the side streets, avoiding the main highway, namely Roosevelt Boulevard, which was always filled with anxious tourists heading for downtown Key West. Arriving at White Street, he turned right then right again at Petronia, which was a dead end street. However there were no signs to warn tourists of this fact, thus drivers had to turn around in order to exit the area.

Today was another hot, steamy day, with a groundswell of 104 degrees, when Key West's traffic was on the upturn with the summer visitors, mostly from around the state of Florida.

When these sightseers, eager to break the law, ignored the No Parking signs on both sides of his street, Max's blood pressure rose to the breaking point. Today he was prepared. He would park front and center at his garage door, which sat at the rear of the property. Backing in to face the street, he was more than ready for the attack.

"Come on, you assholes. I feel the urge to call parking enforcement today," he yelled out the window. He relished the thought of a nasty challenge, which he always won. "Move or face getting ticketed!" He smirked as he turned the corner.

Damn. Not one tourist was blocking his right of way.

Free of cars, he was disappointed—not somewhat disappointed but very disappointed. It was essential he face some kind of confrontation today to keep the adrenaline going, which reflected exactly how empty his life had actually become.

Five o'clock. Dinner time. Slowly, deliberately, and then with resignation, Max unsnapped his seat belt and climbed out. He clicked the locks on his truck and headed in the back door where he could count on the smell of pulled pork, rice, and refried beans wafting throughout the house.

Rosetta Hernandez, Maxwell's wife of forty-five years, rushed around the hot, steamy kitchen, fussing over first one pot and then another. She was stirring and complaining about the meat. It was not cooked quite as perfectly as she had hoped. She heard the heavy footsteps of her husband come in the back door. He dropped his keys into the glass ash tray and walked into the kitchen. She took off her apron and lifted the lid to scoop out a taste of tonight's dinner in a large wooden spoon, poised for him to sample.

"I'm around five feet tall," she would tell people whenever they asked—knowing Susanna was the only offspring who took after her. The boys were near six feet like their father—and handsome. Susanna, afraid she would become overweight, even fat like her mother, weighed and measured her food every day while Rebecca, who ate nothing but lettuce, was taller and "paper thin" as her mother would say with a worried look.

On the other hand, Rosetta never discussed her weight, which had slowly increased over the years. Rather than exercise and diet, she would buy bigger clothes that hid the larger arms and thicker waistline. Then she hit sixty-five when what she wore no longer mattered.

Max tasted the food and kissed his fingers to his lips.

Finally, Rosetta could smile. Her day had been worth all of its difficulties.

She had much to be proud of. She and Max were married at eighteen, right after crossing the stage at Key West High School, the first members of their families to do so. The result of a good Catholic upbringing, they grew to a family of five children, all educated and on their own except for Susanna Rose.

Susanna returned home with their precious grandson, Xavier Tomas, after filing for a dissolution of her marriage in Dade County from Mario Ruiz, son of millionaire drug runner mobster, A. Ruiz.

Determined to prove she was an abused wife, Susanna produced pictures showing bruise marks on her face and upper body, the result of her husband's fancy work. What forced her to file was the incident that ended on their front lawn. The fight began in the early hours of daybreak, and by late evening Mario was so drunk and high on OxyContin that he began slapping her around.

Near the end of the struggle, he pulled out a small pistol from a drawer in the dining room breakfront. "I'm gonna kill you! Both you and your father!" he threatened.

Mario cocked the gun and pressed it to her left temple. Unable to pull the trigger, he hit her across the face, leaving a large black and blue welt on the side of her cheek.

Hearing a sound in the backyard, Mario was distracted. He yelled, "Who's there?"

His grip loosened on Susanna's arm, and she yanked free. She scrambled across the front lawn to the next door neighbor's house where she phoned her father, who arrived wild and packing. Then she called 911.

Mario's only witness was an unreliable neighbor who lied on the stand. Reading the police report and Mario's standing record of violence, the judge hit the hammer fairly quickly. He would give full custody of their young child to Susanna, with monthly visits under court supervision. Susanna's only restriction was she could not leave the county or the state without the court's approval.

The police tied Mario's wrists together, his bulging muscles and tattoos aglow. "I am not leaving!" he informed the officer. "This was my parents' house. It's mine now. You understand? My ex-wife is the one who must vacate the premises. Isn't that how you guys say it? 'Vacate the premises?' And I say get your asses off my property!"

By the time her father gathered together the portable crib, high chair, toys, and some loose clothes lying around, the police report was filled out and signed, and Susanna was released from the scene.

Meanwhile, Mario wrestled with the inexperienced officer, who wasn't very good at containment. "See him over there? Anything for his spoiled brat daughter. He's the reason for the divorce. She's nothing but a nasty woman who does not deserve to raise my child! Hurt my son, and you will be dead before I get there!" he yelled over at Max.

Max's face turned red from the neck to his hairline as he fingered the small pistol nestled deep inside his fisherman's pants. This was the gun he kept aboard his boat for hire. He happened to bring the weapon home for a cleaning, with plans to return it to the boat before his next hire.

"Dad! We have to go!" Susanna urged.

Max ignored his daughter. On the lookout for one small opening, one lunge, one breakaway attempt, and Max would have shot this lowlife in a place from which there was no recovery.

CHAPTER 16

PAULETTE WAS HOPING TO REACH her son Billie. It was only three o'clock in New Hampshire, and his last class today was over at two.

"Oh, I'm so glad I caught you!" she said.

"Yep," Billie replied.

"You okay and all? I've tried you several times. Left messages. It's an adjustment here. I rented my own place for the summer. But you knew that." She laughed nervously. "How's your room? Your roommate?"

"Mom. I can't talk right now. I have someone here."

"You're not okay. Why can't we talk? Texting I get no response. Just tell me. No matter what it is, I love you, you know that."

"Yep."

"Do you want me to call another time? Be specific and I will, I promise."

"Nope. You and Dad and the divorce—it's about that. Why didn't you discuss it with me? Include me? So we didn't have to ... *I* didn't have to go away like this."

"Like what? You chose Brown. We went there together before you graduated."

"I meant you."

"I ... I wanted to take a break from almost a whole year of harassment over how your father wanted the house so he could move his new pregnant wife in."

"So? It's not a big deal. I mean the house. Another family."

"Oh, Billie. But it is. To me it's everything: the past, now, the future."

"Mom, there's no future there. You'll become like those rich old ladies who die alone in their mansions."

"Well, thanks a lot."

Between the nerves of having to discuss what was wrongly walked around for her son's sake and having him think she was ready for the grave, Paulette was thrown off.

"I'm sorry. Can we talk another time? Gotta go."

"Give me a time," Paulette urged.

"Tomorrow. Tomorrow around this time, okay?"

No one knows what a wrenching to the heart and the digestive system such a conversation can bring to a mother except another parent. And she was so upset, she was wrenched, her intestines tied into such a tight knot she was ready to throw up.

All she could do when she talked to Billie tomorrow was be calm and ask him if his father ever discussed the divorce when Billie was over at his father's apartment—and then apologize for how it was.

She thought and cried and desperately prayed for a solution that could bring peace to an untenable situation. Then she realized all she could do was move forward, go to the high school tomorrow, and continue from there.

Her mother used to say, "Nothing is forever." Paulette could only hope that Billie's resentment would not last that long.

A ticket to LA already in her hand, Ellie Darby Livingston left three messages on Paulette's phone.

Last night there was some creep sneaking around at the back of her friend's condo in South Beach. He wasn't a vagrant or a druggie. He was too well dressed in a dark shirt and pants for that. Also, he seemed familiar with where he was walking back there. He even had a good flashlight. He stopped at the telephone and cable box, looked around, shut the box, and then slowly walked away.

Ellie picked up the one-time cell phone she had purchased in the morning but put it down. She couldn't call the police. How could she leave a real name and address and not get into trouble? Her maybe ex-husband knew that. This had to be Brent's work. No doubt about it. He must know where she was and was checking up on her.

She ran around the condo, closing all the windows and pulling the drapes. Soon the music began up the street at Fourteenth and Collins. Ellie would go out for a while, and if he was still there when she returned, she would rethink the trouble she might be in should she be the one to call about the disturbance.

She asked herself if she was being paranoid. Or if this could be culture shock.

Last night she arrived from Cove Island. As she walked from the boat docking area to Biscayne Bay Boulevard, wherever she looked there was a sense of urgency. Noise was everywhere she turned, and there was a disjointed feeling of not being able to catch onto what the flow was as if she was in the center of an unstoppable merry-go-round.

Where could they all be going in such a hurry? No one waited patiently at traffic lights, not pedestrians nor drivers. Required stops were slow glides regulated by a nervous foot as drivers in back of the lead car impatiently inched forward, a hand on the horn.

Ellie walked past the Fontainebleau, up Collins Avenue, and sat on a bench for what she thought was but a few minutes. Rousted in the middle of the night, she must have fallen asleep and was shaken lightly by a cop who looked at her condition. He must have decided she was down and out, but certainly not a hooker or a druggie. He said, "Ma'am, you need to move along. The hotel's customers walk here."

But he left before she got up from her lying down position.

He turned around and took out a five-dollar bill from his pocket. "Here, lady. Get yourself a cup of coffee, some dinner," he said.

"Thanks," Ellie replied, taking the money as if she had lived on the streets all her life and counted on the generosity of strangers for her survival.

Right across the bay was Whipper Will, there as it had been when she left so long ago. Whipper Will was the largest private residence that faced the Fontainebleau Hotel, on the Miami Beach side, the Intracoastal separating their very different lifestyles from the disenfranchised.

In his will, because her father told her so before she ran away, she was to inherit the premises and be allotted the funds to maintain it.

Paulette had said in their first conversation that the property would soon belong to the city. No doubt Ellie had been declared dead so her mother could take full control over her father's estate, which was just fine with Ellie because she connected far too many bad memories inside those walls to ever want to return. Miss Claire, as all her friends called

Ellie's mother, would be seventy years old by now. Was she even still alive?

If, in fact, Ellie had remained at home and not made the stupid move to run away, she could be a millionaire herself, enjoying the fruits of her ancestor's labor and living the life offered to her through blood line. She even went so far as to imagine how she could be mingling among the Miami moneyed crowd as the belle of the ball her mother had always been.

If so, Ellie would never have met a rich man like Brent, who was vengeful when he drank and a fairly nice guy when he was sober. She would have met a nicer millionaire.

Staring across the way at such luxury that Ellie had experienced first-hand, it was not about the money or any share she might have the rights to. It was more emotional than that. After all these years, it was about finally facing her mother and knowing her mother would dismiss the passage of time and the angst her daughter had caused by abandoning her real family. Her mother always rose above it all, no matter what the problem.

The real question was: Would she do the same when it came to her daughter?

CHAPTER 17

"MORE BOXES, I SEE," MAX sighed. He had arrived home an hour ago, tired and out of sorts, his day not over as he had a trip to Islamorada still to go. All he wanted now was to sit down and have a full dinner that smelled and tasted familiar.

The trip this morning to Fort Jefferson with the wanna-be divers from New Jersey had been more tiring than usual. The only up was the solo lady on the trip he gave his private phone number to. His true hope was that she would call and they could get together before she went home. He liked that idea.

Take a deep breath and continue the drill that works at home, he told himself.

"You're the best cook on the block—in the whole city!" Max said as he scooped up his dinner from the pots and piled his plate high.

Watching Max gobble down his dinner, Rosetta gasped, "No, Max! Wait for the rest of the family!"

"More boxes in the hall, I see," Max said again, washing his first serving of pulled pork and brown rice down with a Corona despite his wife's pleas.

"Where will we put all those boxes Susanna's ex-husband shipped to her?" Rosetta whined as she fixed a plate for herself and sat next to him.

"Don't you worry," he said, reaching over and patting her thigh. "Let me take care of it. We have the garage in the back."

"Not the boxes! I mean taking care of my grandson," she said with a sigh.

"What about Xavier?"

"I love him with all my heart. But I am not looking forward to raising another grandchild while my daughter does a bank job."

"She takes a job working at a bank," Max corrected her. "Bankers' hours are good," he said, mainly to assuage his wife. "I'm just a put-your-money-in-the-shoebox kind of guy myself—thanks to my parents. Working at a bank is only a beginning."

"Look how long she's lived here. Six months before she got a job, and now you're complaining?" Max said to Rosetta. "Work will do her good. I won't have to support her—only give her a place to live," he said while knowing he would give Susanna anything she asked for.

"Why am I responsible?" Rosetta asked.

"I thought we were talking about the boxes. I already settled that. If it's Xavier you're worried about, hey, I'm in the middle. Susanna and her ex have been fighting from the day they met. When they got married, didn't I bring Father Robert all the way down from Miami, rent the main dining room at the Pier House, and pay for everything?" he said emphatically.

"You look tired. Maybe you should rest until we go to the party at Michael's restaurant tonight."

"Rosetta," Max shook his head. "We've been over all of this earlier. I'm fine, just fine. Leave me alone. I've gotta get ready."

CHAPTER 18

BRENT L. LIVINGSTON III KNEW his wife Ellie was still alive. He could sense it, feel it in his bones. Instinctively, he knew Ellie as well as a captain knows the sea—his true mistress. And of course that was ridiculous. Only women use their intuition. Any man worth his piss does not go into action without proof positive. But then Brent had never been on a serious hunt before.

Women never leave him. He leaves them—always has, always will—except for Ellie, who jumped overboard into the midnight sea in the middle of one of those damned hurricanes, killing herself. Or so he thought. Now that there was even the slightest possibility she was alive, he would not allow her to be the exception.

Stupid broad. No one jumps overboard during a storm who has any sense. So when the latest detective, Steve Myers, who came highly recommended, called and said, "Last night, your ex-wife was asleep on a bench outside the Fontainebleau Hotel," Brent was not the least bit surprised, only shocked to hear of her appearance. She was a woman with a fantastic figure, who fit a bikini perfectly, yet she dressed formally whenever they went anywhere because she did not want to draw attention to what she came by naturally.

Myers was an ex-cop, ex-police beat reporter. You name it, he'd done it. Within weeks of being hired, he located the condo in South Beach where Ellie had stayed and just as quickly put in a wiretap.

When Myers claimed to recognize Ellie, Brent thought the private detective must be out of his mind, or else he wanted to race forward and collect his check but somehow got his wires crossed. The last two years had been nothing but dead ends. Truth: she jumped into the stormy waters with nothing on her person—no IDs, no money.

Her health was shot, and she'd been drinking and taking those pills she was addicted to. She was out of her mind and on such a high. If she somehow survived, God forbid, she could actually be that bag lady in the park. Or worse, she could have pulled herself together and was going to the police to tell her story.

Eventually Brent gave away all of Ellie's clothes. By the next storm, some young, sexy thing with a body that would not quit was on his boat in a different skimpy bikini. He romanticized what their travels together would be like. He left out the part non-sailors know until they actually experience first-hand what sailing requires—all hands aboard must work. This includes extra duty as the seasonal hurricanes appear.

When he allowed his mind to wander, he often wondered what happened to Megan. She wasn't like the usual boat babes. With her curiosity and youthful enthusiasm, did she finish law school and by now was practicing corporate law in Manhattan.

As the granddaughter of the grand dame of Miami, Claire Wellesley, Megan was certainly in his class. It was no wonder, after mad, wild sex for a month, that she left at the first opportunity. His orange juice filled with shots of vodka in the morning turned into almost pure vodka by sunset, and he was back to his old routine, a new, sexy lady at his disposal or not.

"Yep, in the park," Myers said. "Your ex-wife went to sleep on a park bench. Must have borrowed a phone. Next day she ended up at some condos in the high-priced section of South Beach."

"Should I go there?" Brent asked.

"I wouldn't. She used the house phone to call someone in California. That's where she's headed."

"I could identify her. Maybe even talk to her."

"Not a good idea. At least not yet."

The bitch, Brent thought. I will find you, and when I do, this time I will drown you.

He did not need to figure out how to get her on the boat. That was the simple part. Once she was aboard, he would tie her down and keep her below, which was the real trick.

If she was alive—and now he was sure she was—she would be in a weakened condition and scared.

She would beg him to take her back.

The real question was how she had supported herself in the first months of her disappearance.

⊰⊱

Rosetta trailed after her husband into the bedroom and watched as he rustled through the closet for fresh gear, his urgency more about rushing out of the house than organizing himself for the next trip.

Or as her mother used to say, "No doubt, he's got other fish to fry!" That phrase stuck with Rosetta ever since her mother said it the year she and Max were newlyweds. Her mother was referring to Max's disappearing acts.

In his day, he was a too-handsome boatman with a roving eye, and Rosetta's mother was positive her little girl was not going to have an easy time of it with this man of hers.

Lately, her husband's excuses were to see Mabel Browne, a divorced white woman who was head librarian at the local library. The library hung pictures of the large catches that once were common occurrences in the waterways of the Keys.

That Miss Browne was her husband's latest choice was made certain in Rosetta's mind by the tribute to local fishermen, with Max as the center authority. So obvious it was sickening. She was toying with someone else's husband. Why did it have to be her husband?

Word around town said Miss Mabel Browne may look official, but she flirted with whomever she wanted, had her fill, and then went on to the next one. She had fiery red hair and hands as smooth as silk. Her skin was white as a puff cloud. In fact, being from Chicago, she probably had never sat in the sun one whole day in her entire life. This was definitely a turn-on since Conch women who worked as day laborers while their husbands fished for a living had wrinkly, dry skin as tough as leather.

The truck finally packed, Max was ready to go. However, he needed to lie down. Nothing was specifically wrong, but he felt unusually tired and was still out of sorts. A year and a half ago he'd had a minor heart attack. Ever since then his family acted like a mother hawk over her young.

Before being released from the hospital, the doctor wrote out several prescriptions and ordered Max to join a health club, eat more nutritious foods, and drink less alcohol, none of which he followed.

"It's your heart!" Rosetta gasped the last time Max felt this vague, all-over achy feeling. "Call the doctor before you leave! He will make you stay home."

Max did not listen now. And he did not listen the night he landed in ICU. When he woke, the family was all around his bed. No one said a word. They only exchanged I-told-you-so! looks.

Now as Rosetta followed Max down the hall where he planned to take a short nap, she said, "You look awfully tired. Maybe you should cancel this trip."

"Rosetta, for the second time," he responded in disgust, "I had early morning customers. Then I cleaned the boat. I'm tired. At sixty-plus-one, it's a natural phenomenon."

"We are not so young any more, are we?" she said soothingly, anticipating his agreement. "Randy used to help. Then Jose. Get Jose. He can miss a day of school. Especially if you ask him."

"No one is skipping anything because of me. Not if I can help it. Leave me alone. I need a little extra rest is all. You aren't dressed for the party?"

His lips were pasty, his mouth almost glued to his teeth.

"I wanted to stay with you."

"I told you, I'm out for a long one. I need all the energy I can muster." Max was lying straight out, his legs crossed, Rosetta at his side. He rolled away from her and sat up.

Rosetta jumped out of bed. Smoothing out her dress, she asked, "Muster? That's a new word."

Rosetta!" Max barked. "None of us stays the same. I read the word in one of those yachting magazines Alvarez keeps around. Muster means to get going."

Max realized how much Rosetta wanted to please him, to do for him all the days of her life, but if he did not keep up this inane banter he would lose his composure and scream at her again.

At the same time, he was visualizing her throat, cut and bleeding. Rather than the usual babbling from her mouth—the mouth he once desired—instead blood would be gushing out.

Rosetta did not deserve his wrath, and he knew it. The fact that he had not truly loved her for years was not her fault.

"I'm getting my John Wayne boots on and I'm ridin' high tonight, woman. Now rustle me up some eggs!" Max teased her.

"You want eggs before you go?" Rosetta asked, staring at him in disbelief. She did not understand him these days. Forgetting dates, names, and not discussing his plans were only a few of the latest annoyances.

What was her husband hiding these days? Usually she could tell something was up with his mood changes. He was either taking up with someone new, or he was being dumped. Or he could simply be getting older and a little more senile, his path leading to Alzheimer's a little quicker than hers.

"No, no," Max plopped back down onto the side of the bed. Slowly he leaned on his elbow to look Rosetta's way. "Honey, I'm playin' with you."

"Like pass the mustard?" she asked, brushing her dress as if there were crumbs on it.

"Yes, dear. Like pass the mustard." Max stopped talking, honoring how Rosetta had been such a good and faithful woman all these years while he was a first class jerk who acted as if he was fancy free and could do whatever he wanted. For sure he should discontinue this constant confusion.

"What about the dinner tonight at Michael's restaurant?" Rosetta asked.

"Tell Susanna to take you," Max urged, scraping the bills and change off the highboy.

"I want to watch *Jeopardy*. I'm too depressed to go. Did Susanna give you the news about nursing school?" she asked, her hand on the doorknob.

"She did not!" Max stopped following her and stood dead in his tracks.

"Yes. She plans to stay at the bank for six months. Then go into the nursing program at Miami General. After she's pinned, she wants to return home for a higher-paying job. She asked me to take care of Xavier for a whole year!"

"She hasn't talked to me about any of this!" Max said.

"I'll be dead by then." Rosetta held tightly to the door. Facing it, she asked, "Why can't she get a small place for herself and Xavier? Hire a baby sitter? I love my family, but not this. Not this. Remember Tomas?"

"Tomas's death was not your fault. His death was ruled accidental. Rebecca thought you …"

"That was five years ago. I was younger then. I had more energy," Rosetta sighed. "Mother was alive. She could help. She took the little ones in the stroller every day. I'm older now. The same thing could happen again."

"I'll talk to her. When I get back," Max clarified his promise, "and don't go calling me from the restaurant if you two start arguing again. Where's Jose? Did you ask him over for dinner?"

"Always."

"And?"

"He's studying at Ariel's."

"Invite him and Ariel and Ariel's mother to the party. He's a big help. Get Susanna to pick everybody up," Max mumbled, his face turning ashen.

"My sewing group meets every Sunday morning. Do you know what that daughter of yours told me? 'It's not important.' To her own mother. 'It's not important.' Imagine that! This time I stood up for myself. 'My plans are just as important as yours!' I told her. Does she listen? No. There is more, my Maxy."

"More?"

"Yes, Poppie. She's talking to that rotten, no-good ex-husband of hers."

"Christ. Let me discuss all of this after the trip. When Rebecca had her first baby, you insisted on no sitters. What's the difference now, except you and Susanna don't get along very well since she returned home?"

Breathing for Max was becoming laborious. Suddenly the feeling of a steel plate plastered on his chest caused him torturous pain.

CHAPTER 19

A SET OF CLEAN CLOTHES, Max's second pair of fishing boots for the day, and a bag of tools from the garage were at the back door. He returned to the kitchen to say good-bye.

Baby Xavier was sitting in his high chair, banging on the small tabletop, his short, fat legs twitching and kicking. Food was all over his face, and he was laughing. As Max passed by, Xavier put his arms out and screamed, "Poppie! Poppie!"

"Jesus. Where's your mother? Susanna!" Max yelled, plopping down into the nearest chair. "Your kid ..."

Susanna came rushing out of the kitchen, drying her hands with a cloth. "Excuse me, Poppie," she said. "Your grandson has a name. It's Xavier Tomas Ruiz. I was cooking broccoli and cauliflower. If you recall, we are vegetarians."

"That is not your father's concern," Rosetta's tone was scornful.

"Separate pans, separate food. This all takes time, Poppie," Susanna reminded him while pulling another Corona out of the fridge for her father.

Max popped the top and allowed the chilled liquid from the sweaty bottle to slide down his throat. "Are you okay?" he asked Susanna.

"Couldn't be better," she snapped, absent-mindedly running her fingers through Xavier's hair and rolling her eyes.

"Have you two been at it again?"

"She doesn't understand." They were referring to Rosetta, Susanna's mother.

"Rosetta!" Max yelled to his wife, who was folding clothes on the dining room table. "I changed my mind. Pack me a lunch. Susanna will take me to the bank and then to Garrison. There's only so much of the two of you I can handle. Don't expect me home before 2 p.m. tomorrow."

"Where will you stay?" Rosetta asked, surprised.

"On the boat as usual. We return tomorrow around ten." He turned to Susanna. "I'll call you when we dock. Pick me up after I wash down the boat."

"Not tonight?" Susanna moaned. "You're expected at Michael's for dessert. He's low on customers. I thought you'd take Xavier for two or three hours. If you're not home, I have no sitter. The baby cries all night when you're gone."

"Take both Xavier and your mother with you. Use the truck."

"Talk about spoiling my fun. Okay, I'll take care of my own child."

"And your mother?"

"If she decides she wants to come along, I'll pick her up on the way," Susanna replied with a shrug.

"Can the two of you make it through the night without killing each other?" he asked, looking sternly from one to the other.

Mother glanced in the general direction of her daughter. Each nodded in agreement.

Susanna and her father went to the South Coast National Bank. He wanted to make a deposit, and it would give her an opportunity to flirt with Enrico, who was the handsomest man she had ever seen. He had a full head of wavy, dark brown hair and a flash of gray hair on the right side of his temple. He was tall—very tall. Next to her five feet without heels, he was truly a foot and a half taller. Aware of his height, Enrico always stepped back, especially when talking to short people. She found that fascinating and pleasing. Most people who stood next to her, if they were taller than she, crowded her in. Enrico's way made her feel as though he had respect for her presence—a neat trick for sales purposes.

"Hey, Enrico. I came to check on the competition," Susanna said, flirting with him while her father went to the entrance for safe-deposit box users.

"Good to see you again today," he said with a smile.

One of the officers at Susanna's bank told her that Enrico had been sent down from the flagship office in Miami ostensibly to work as its senior manager. He was also to audit the books and keep an eye on a potential manager who had impressive credits but no connections in town.

If everything was satisfactory, within six months his redheaded assistant, Denise, would take over. Enrico would then return to Miami as their senior operating officer. Key West was his last stop before officially becoming a higher-up.

Susanna wasn't listening to her father's latest story, but she knew it was going on for far too long.

"Dad, just sign the card," she said as she handed Enrico the key.

"I'll walk you over to see Denise. She's in charge of that department."

"You don't need to go," Max said gently to his daughter. "You can …"

"I know. Wait over there."

"What about your other box, sir?" Denise asked.

Max said nothing. He kept on walking—closer to marching—until they reached the other side of the bank.

Out of his daughter's hearing range, Max spoke loudly, "Thank God my daughter can't hear you or I would have you fired! My personal business is not your concern or anybody else's. Didn't you take a pledge not to share information with anyone but the actual person who banks with you?"

"Yes, sir," she replied, apologetically. "I thought your daughter …"

"I think I'll talk to Enrico right now. Have you fired. You are plain stupid. Ignorant. Who allowed you to work for a bank?"

Enrico came to the desk where Max was. "Anything the matter, sir?"

Max looked at his daughter, still sitting in the chair at reception as she thumbed through a brochure on investments. Hesitating, he opened his mouth and then closed it, his mood changing when he saw the girl he had been yelling at was in tears.

"Can I assist you in any way Mr. Hernandez?"

"It was only a misunderstanding. Nothing serious."

"Anything I can correct?"

"It has been resolved to my satisfaction."

While inside the private room with his safe-deposit box, Max took out envelope number sixteen and stuffed it into the deep pocket of his fisherman's pants. He closed the metal box, gave it back to the clerk, and as was his custom, he tapped his pants twice before he went over to sit next to his daughter.

"Ready to go?" he asked.

Susanna knew what was next. Her father would pull out his thin, brown book, flip several pages in, take a pencil from his shirt pocket, put the point to his tongue, and write out some sort of figures in a column. Then he would snap the book closed and tap it twice.

He did just that as she pretended to be reading a magazine.

She also knew, according to her father's will, all proceeds from the two safe-deposit boxes and various checking accounts were to be divided equally between his five children and their mother. Meanwhile, she had a power of attorney over those particular assets.

When they left the bank, Max commented, "Enrico seems like a nice fellow. Is he single?"

Susanna nodded.

"Has he asked you out?"

"We definitely do not travel in the same circles, Poppie."

"What does that mean? He's Cuban, isn't he?" Max snapped.

"Yes, but he's after much more. Word is he has a big job waiting for him in Miami. Assisting at this bank is some kind of training ground. The redhead you were talking to? The bank wants to give her a fair shot at running the operations."

"The one I yelled at?"

"Poppie! You didn't!" Susanna gasped.

"Sure did. She blabbed my personal business in front of everybody. Why don't you apply for a manager's job? You already sound like one."

"Education to begin with. I'm not a CPA, nor do I care to be one. I'll work at my job until life settles down."

Ready to turn right and head for the marina, Susanna asked her father, "You sure you want to walk to Garrison? What about your tools in the back of the truck? Your clothes and things?"

"Put my bag back in the house. I packed like I was going to Europe or something," he chuckled, changing the subject. "It's going to be a beautiful night."

"Are you sure? All the loonies, Goths, and goons come out this weekend of the full moon. A harvest moon four times a year, and they're everywhere," she replied, knowing how much he liked being out on the water when the whitecaps are lit by nature's night-lights.

"Earlier, Mother and I chased some teenagers off our property. They were driving a mama 250 Ford pickup truck. The goons were all dressed in black, ready for nightfall. They looked really scary. Remember when we were kids? How we'd come home screaming after playing in the cemetery?"

"I remember," he smiled. "You okay?" he asked.

"For the tenth time, yes. It's your health that is at issue here. We worry about you. Be extra careful. That's all we wish. I want you at my baby Xavier's high school graduation to see firsthand the family legacy you're always talking about."

"Thank you," he said modestly. "Remember your mother's part too. Are you getting sentimental on me?" he asked.

"It's the truth."

"I ... we're surprised you noticed," Max responded. "Or, are you trying to butter me up?"

"No, Poppie. I love you is all," Susanna sighed.

"Any calls?"

Susanna paused for a long moment before answering. She hated lying to her father. "Any calls" referred to ex-husband Mario Ruiz. "So far, we're all clear."

"You need any money?" he asked.

"If I did, I personally know the go-to guy, and I can sign on your accounts. Get whatever I want," she smiled in a satisfying, secure manner.

"You sure?" he hesitated.

"I'm sure," she replied, blowing him a kiss and watching until her father was out of sight.

CHAPTER 20

BRENT LEANED BACK IN HIS captain's chair. He was thumbing through the bimonthly *Yachting* magazine. Bemused, he went to the ad section at the back of the magazine. He might try another one of those ads. Meeting women directly, his luck had not been so good.

When he and Ellie were married, he thought his new bride was actually in love with him. At the female's average height of five foot six and weight of 120 pounds, she wowed him right away, and everything she said sounded like she was his soul mate. That she had the current hairdo of long, luxurious hair down past her shoulders and flashing dark eyes only added to his attraction to her.

On one of their many trips in the Caribbean they visited her old haunt—where they had actually met—and his Ellie told him her whole story. He—cautious Brent L. Livingston, with a name to live up to—was the jerk from her rebound.

Once he learned that, all the romance went out of his dreams of how their life would be different from the previous ten years, when he picked up whatever thumbed a ride from the boat docks—the boat babes lusting after a free ride and willing to pay any price for the privilege of living like the rich. Ellie had been one once, only it did not show. She was already in love with someone else and had just been dumped.

And yes, maybe it gave him another excuse to drink again, but this time the amount of liquor he carried aboard and drank all of was extraordinary. He had fallen in love. Nobody does that to Brent L. Livingston III, head of the Livingston Trust, which gives away millions a year, thanks to his father and his grandfather, and gets away with it.

"Will it always take seven calls to reach you when it concerns our son?" Paulette asked her ex-husband.

"And you want?" Chris asked.

"To talk to Billie. Have you talked to him lately?"

"Yesterday, as a matter of fact."

"About the divorce?"

"No. He's thinking of coming back after his summer classes. Misses his friends, who are all at UCLA."

"Really? He didn't say a word to me."

"He can't talk to you."

Paulette wanted to say, that was none of his business. Instead, she said, "I see. And when is he expected? He has another two classes I paid for."

"The paperwork for UCLA is already in the works."

"Is he staying with you?"

"Nope. You have the house. He wants to bring his buddies over to for the weekend. During the week he'll live on campus."

Oh, joy, she thought.

"Great!" she replied as enthusiastically as possible. "I appreciate the information."

Paulette always shook after a family confrontation. Or was she the problem? She was once the center of the family dynamics, and now she was the last to know what's going on! What to do about that? How to go along with the flow? Those were only a few of the thoughts going through her mind as she paced the empty apartment, wondering if she ought to catch a flight immediately and take charge of what she had desperately fought for in court and won.

She could stay a week and fly home, or she could stay the planned three months. This would take some thought and a call to Kathleen.

Meanwhile, the next day she had a date to go to the White House Reef, see Hemingway's chair, where he wrote *The Old Man and the Sea*, have a late lunch with Flower, then go to the dressmakers to see the dress she was wearing to her birthday-anniversary party on Saturday night.

CHAPTER 21

~∾⌀∽∾~

THE ENVELOPE BULGING FROM THE lower pocket of Maxwell Hernandez's fisherman pants was for Ariel Costas.

All his life he worked for symmetry, workable systems, and order. When he and daughter Susanna went to the first bank where Maxwell had been putting cash away for years, taking anything out would have been an impulsive act. And here he was dying to give it to someone he had no business even being around.

Max wouldn't dare offer Mabel, the librarian, anything other than taking her to dinner up the coast and having passionate sex later at her house. If he'd made any offer of monetary value, she would have clobbered him, even gone so far as to break off their relationship.

What he really wanted was to impress her, let her know that he may not have a college education or be in a profession others admired, but he was definitely rich.

On the other hand, Ariel Costas made him feel young again The thought of Ariel made Max light-headed. He knew her from her childhood on. Rented her mother a house next door for real cheap.

When Ariel became a teenager, he was shocked at how beautiful she had become. She was a waif of a girl, small, even petite, with brown hair. As she matured and became a senior in high school, he became a crazy man with an insane crush who knew better.

No matter what, whether crazy in love or crazy in lust, he did not care. He went out of his way to be wherever she was. And if she was not home, many times he would constantly call her cell or drive around until he found her, knowing full well they both could face dire consequences.

Ariel's graduation from Key West High School was this year, and Max wanted to further her education, give her a fresh start. Thirty-five thousand was not very much. Hopefully, it was enough to make it out of Key West before she hooked up with someone from the neighborhood who had nothing going for him and never would.

Heading for the cemetery, all Max could see in front of him was her smile and her youthful, sexy body. At times, she even took to teasing him.

Burning through his pants was envelope number sixteen, combined with the five thousand the two Cuban boys paid him earlier in the day. Was that money from the first or the second bank? He could not remember.

First he had a stop to make.

He went over to the next block and around the corner to the library to see if Miss Browne was on duty. She was.

"Doin' okay?" he asked.

"Sure. And you?" she replied. Her serious face was on as she continued stamping due dates on small white sheets of paper.

"Fine. Just fine. Goin' on a trip this evening. Wanna come along? We'll be back in a coupla days."

"Sorry. Call me next week when you get back. I haven't heard from you in a while. Go on about your business. I have to work!" she finally released a smile.

"Keep that bed of yours warm. I'll be back!" he said, imitating Arnold Schwarzenegger.

Should Max go past Ariel's house? Or shouldn't he? There was so little time. His passengers would arrive within the hour, but he needed to see her in the worst way before his departure to give her this envelope. Maybe he should turn around, put the money in the safe on the boat, and return it to the bank after this upcoming trip.

All he would do, he promised himself, was see her, hand her the envelope, no strings attached, and be out of there. What harm was there in that?

Cutting across several blocks, Max returned to the south end of Petronia, where his family residence was. The house was dark and empty, the truck gone.

He tried Ariel's cell number once more. Still no answer.

He ran to the corner of Olivia and Frances, a route his family never traveled. Max's heart beat heavily in his chest as the sweat dripped down his back, his clean shirt sopping wet.

He hesitated at the corner driveway.

Stepping forward, Max saw a light glowing over the kitchen table in Ariel's house across the street. Two people were sitting opposite each other.

It was Jose Rodriquez and his Ariel at her kitchen table.

Jose was a nice kid and all, but he'd been in so much trouble, A real scrapper. When his father returned to town and put Jose to work, he pretty well straightened out. However he did not deserve to even sit at the same table as his Ariel.

In fact, it was his wife, Rosetta, who rented the house her mother left her to Jose and his mother. He and Ariel had the same kind of family issues: mothers with good jobs, but alcohol and too many men were their downfall.

Too dangerous, he speculated as he stared through the window.

Max was always disturbed whenever Jose and Ariel were together.

All of a sudden Rosetta's voice reverberated in Max's ear with the reminder that what faced him in retirement was a place where she could keep an eye on him—sitting in the rocking chair on the back porch, the one gathering dust.

"Marriage is forever. For breakfast, lunch, and dinner, but never for retirement," one of his mother's friends once said in front of Max. Here it was all these years later, and finally he understood what that old fool meant: Now he was the old fool, trying to avoid his inevitable future, one filled with more days of endless boredom.

Ariel answered her cell phone. "Are you free?" Max asked.

"It's too late," she whispered, glancing over at Jose who was fitting his civics book into his backpack.

"You have company?"

"Not exactly. It's Jose, and he's going home to bed where you should be."

"Not tonight, honey bun. Tonight I have a charter. Meet me for just a few minutes? Say hello. I haven't seen you in weeks. The usual spot?"

Ariel was to wait for Max at the unlocked back gate of one of the oldest cemeteries in the country. If he was late, she was to go to the Spanish section and sit on the familiar piece of coral that honored his ancestors.

CHAPTER 22

~~∽∽∽∞∝∝∝∝∽~~

ARIEL HATED WALKING THROUGH THE cemetery, especially on a weekend like this one. It was the harvest moon, and the goons were already out, waiting behind the trees, hoping for ghosts as other goons showed up.

It had rained late that afternoon, which meant everything would be wet. This included the back entrance where a new foundation had been poured, yet sand and mud still covered the ground whenever there was the least bit of rain. She was wearing her newest shooties, but to take them off meant tearing her feet up on the exposed sharp edges of the coral rock below.

She tentatively backed away from the streetlights and went into the dark.

Actually, she was very proud of her new shooties—they were quite fashionable—as she was also proud of her new hairdo. She had let her naturally curly, light brown hair grow quite long, and now it was layered, thanks to one of the students who was anxiously waiting to graduate, as was Ariel, so her friend could go to beauty school.

Finally settled on the top of a shelf carved from coral rock, she sat on the ledge, her legs swinging freely. Here on the ledge where she lost her virginity.

Waiting on top of the hard surface never bothered her before when she was in need of someone to talk to. During those times, Ariel was filled with a sense of urgency.

This visit was the last one. She was wrong. This was wrong. And she had to try and make it right. She must face reality and tell Max she was pregnant with his child and then go on home and hope he would finally leave her alone.

Max was the one who always listened, was always there and patient. He never cut her off or dissed her even though he had five children and a myriad of health problems. She felt as though he was like a father. What girl in her right mind would have sex with her father?

Ariel's conversations with Max were usually about her mother's destructive behavior, about how, if alcohol had not been her mother's driving force, Ariel might have grown up as a normal girl with friends her own age to confide in.

When Ariel was eight years old, she confessed to Max: "Mother has a new gun!" She gave him her hand like any child of eight would do. "She said she was going to kill Daddy with the gun in her dresser!"

"Where is your brother?"

"Upstairs. I was upstairs helping him with his homework when Mother came home. She really, really scared me. She started screaming at me, talking like she does all the time: How much she never wanted me. How I ruined her life. What about Daniel? What about him? Doesn't he get in trouble too?"

"Your brother isn't defiant like you are," Max had said.

That was all such a long time ago, and now look what a mess she was in.

The last time Ariel and Max sat on the ledge of his family's plot, she pulled away from his touch.

"Honey, I get it. But I can't keep coming here like this only to be turned away."

Ariel should have stayed away after that. But he was her friend, and she did not understand. Most of the girls had sex with plenty of the guys by the time they were eighteen. She hadn't, and that birthday had come and gone months ago.

Now at almost three months pregnant, Ariel had very few weeks left to decide whether to abort the fetus or not. This important decision she was making on her own.

She was a good Catholic girl. Once she thought of asking Father Shanahan what to do. She tried, in a roundabout way, but it didn't matter. She had barely phrased her question before stiffness surrounded him like a closed steel trap door. She already knew what his answer would be: duty, responsibility, and right action. None of it to her benefit. How naïve of her to think otherwise.

The only solution was to have an abortion in South Miami like the other girls.

Or she must marry someone before beginning to show. Keep her baby in order to avoid the trip into hell's fiery furnace. If she was involved with someone else, there would still be time to see Father Shanahan and promise to be a good Catholic, marry properly, produce many more offspring, and raise them in the Catholic faith.

Was that what she really wanted?

If she aborted her fetus as soon as possible, there would be no harm, no foul, and she could go on with her normal life and her future plans, unencumbered by a huge mistake.

CHAPTER 23

MAX WAITED AT THE GATE. No Ariel was waiting for him as instructed.

He needed her to show up. There was the new will and divorce papers to discuss—how, over the years, all five of his kids were given what they expected to inherit, which included such items as educations, cars, down payments on houses, and various loans that had never been repaid, thus telling all of them so Ariel would not feel guilty.

In person he could explain to Ariel how his gift to her was "purely from the heart."

On the other hand, he was not completely stupid. Max could not stand the idea of his Ariel married to someone else and still having access to his hard-earned cash, so, as a man who left nothing to chance, if the answer was a flat-out no, his estate would be distributed equally between his wife and their five kids.

With no Ariel at the entrance, Max walked quickly through the graveyard and gradually came alive when he spotted her—on top of his family's interment center!

Light as a feather and gleefully, Ariel jumped down and ran to him. Dressed in a gown made of white gossamer, her small, thin figure so youthful and appealing, the scene almost broke his heart.

"Let's go back up," he said through the frog in his throat. "You're so beautiful. Let me enjoy your face in the moonlight."

Max reached for her as a sharp pain went down his left arm, numbing his fingers.

Ariel did not notice the erratic motions as Max was flung sideways by the jarring bolt that shot through his arm. He yelped, but she did not alter her pace.

When he caught up with her at the top of the steps, he said, tilting her chin upward, "Kiss me."

"I can't. We have to talk." She tried not to giggle and act stupid. This was serious, and he needed to know she had something important to say. "And no sex," she added.

"Honey, sex is the only way between a man and a woman."

Ariel kissed him, all right, but she was holding back, and Max wasn't sure he could wait. Time was against him, and even with Ariel right there, he felt as tired as he had earlier in the evening.

"I brought some money," he said.

"What money?" she asked, pushing herself further away from him.

"The envelope in my pocket. We talked about it, remember?"

"I don't feel right about any of this."

"All right then. I'll lock the envelope on the boat for another time. But I have it right here, right now." He paused before continuing. "If you don't want it, at least look in the cabinet above the safe where I have a surprise for you. Two surprises. One is inside a small black velvet box. Under the box is a large envelope addressed to me. Will you at least look at that?"

"Yes."

Ariel had never taken money directly from Maxy before. Once in a while she accepted a prepaid credit card to buy clothes like the gown she wore tonight, or to pay for school lunches, or go out with her friends on a Friday night.

"I see you're wearing those slave shoes again," Max teased. "Don't fall over any dead bodies with those things on."

"Oh, gross. They're not slave shoes. They're shooties."

"You are absolutely right," he said, her melodic voice pouring warmth over his body.

"I … I can't stay long." She pecked his cheek as she wrapped her small, thin arms around his neck. "Is everything all right at home?"

"Wait, wait!" He laughed for what seemed like the first time in weeks. His heart connected to her gaiety as her youthfulness pumped fresh blood into his worn-out, old arteries. He was not going to remind her how she was the one who was staying away. At least he had acquired a bit of sense along the way.

"One question at a time," he said, laughing. Suddenly he added: "Will you marry me once you've gone off and done what you want?"

"That's impossible!" she shrieked, sliding backward into the dark and bending her legs up underneath her, ready to bolt. "I came here to tell you I ... I have something to tell you." She wrestled free of the grip his hand had on her arm and pulled herself further back into the shadows.

"No talk," he said, choking up. "Let's make love."

"Are you kidding? My back really hurts when I lay on this rock," she moaned, forcefully freeing herself. Calming down, she said, "Tell you what. When you come in from this charter, let's rent a hotel room. Right on Roosevelt at the Holiday Inn. No one will see us. We could spend the whole day together. Make love, feed each other. Watch movies. How about that?" she said to him deceptively.

"If you say so. Sure. Why not?"

"Can I come with you?" she asked suddenly, unexpectedly.

"Now? This trip?" Max replied, surprised, especially after her latest comments of wanting to end things between them.

"You have another woman?" Ariel asked.

"You know I love only you. Won't you be missed? Your mother ..."

"She's at Miami General for the rest of the week. Some kind of seminar," she said, volunteering an explanation. "Well, can I come with you or not?"

Ariel had to go on the trip. Chicken that she was, she hadn't told him yet what he should know about her condition.

"Your choice," Max shrugged, withholding his enthusiasm. "You're sure of your mother's schedule? We're not back until tomorrow, late afternoon some time. What about school?"

"Tomorrow is Sunday. Like anyone cares when I miss a day of school," she added.

"All right," he said. He struggled to get up and straighten his pants.

"Oh, good!" She began dancing awkwardly, trying to steady herself in her new shooties. "That means we'll stay overnight at the Holiday Inn!"

When the light of the moon no longer blocked the rain clouds, his angel asked, "Can we have a special dinner too?"

"We arrive too late."

"How about breakfast tomorrow morning?"

"Too early. This is not a pleasure trip," he was clear. "Strictly business."

"You're no fun," she pouted, slapping him lightly on the shoulder. "Okay, okay. I'm just glad to get out of here. You're an answer to my prayers, you know that? My knight in shining armor."

He doubted that, but replied, "Thanks, babe."

Distracted by her twitting about, in order to stop her, he held firmly to her shoulders. "If you're serious, we have to hurry!"

Ariel walked slowly, dragging herself behind him. Taking off her shooties so they were not an excuse for her hesitancy, she still remained two steps to the back. He didn't seem to notice. This was not going to be one of her better experiences. Why had she even made the suggestion?

CHAPTER 24

TRAFFIC ON ROOSEVELT BOULEVARD WAS backed up as tourists poured into Key West for the weekend. Horns were blasting and headlights flashed brightly, blowing sand into Max and Ariel's eyes as they made their way to the Garrison Bight Marina where the Ramblin' Rose was moored.

Unnecessarily, Max worried about the people milling about. Then he worried that his daughter might drive by in his truck with his wife Rosetta sitting beside her. Then he remembered how Susanna and Rosetta should already be at Michael's restaurant.

"You look preoccupied," Ariel observed.

"No … well … a little," Max replied.

"Is your charter waiting for you?" Ariel asked.

"Depends. If we're late, they're waiting. If we're early, I can settle in the way I like."

"Mmm, maybe there's time," she said, teasing him.

"You would." He kissed the top of her head.

"Yes, maybe I would," she said, laughing.

With no one to report to for one whole evening, Ariel's bare feet skipped lightly over the sidewalk, her new shooties off her feet and in her hand.

At the marina and trudging along the wooden dock, Max was at the front with Ariel close behind.

Two Cuban boys were leaning against Max's boat, six-packs in each hand. Behind them was a big man, older and stronger, holding onto the handles of a red cart with a black fifty-five-gallon drum resting on its lip.

The two boys shook hands with Max.

"What's this?" Max referred to the black drum as he took the envelope in payment for the extra cargo from the bigger man.

Cash had become a boat captain's method of trade for services since the 2009 recession. These days a credit card charge can be canceled between the time of the charge and returning to port. Thus no payment for the cost of crew, gas, and other expenditures is covered. Cash obviously solves that problem.

"Another drum—same size—on the way," the oversize man grunted. "People waiting in Islamorada. Said they cleared this with you."

Max mumbled a negative comment, definitely unhappy about having Ariel on board. She was the last person he wanted to witness his involvement in illegal business dealings, but when she asked and was in his presence, how could he resist?

After boarding the captain's boat and settling into their surroundings, the smaller, younger, dark-haired, curly-headed boy took special notice of the pretty girl standing at the door frame of the main cabin. "She coming with?" he asked Max. "She's not part of the deal."

"Neither were your cousins'—or was it your older brother's?—drums," was Max's quick retort.

"Maybe." He sucked air in between his teeth. "You took the money, didn't you?"

Much as Ariel tried to deny her interest, she actually kind of liked the curly-headed brother. He was thin and no taller than she was—the one who looked her up and down several times, enjoying the view. Once Max was behind the wheel, she could break away for a while. They could talk.

Before the giant wheeled the second drum on board, Max told Ariel, "Go across the street and buy some new clothes. Stay around but out of sight. I don't want anyone getting ideas."

"I didn't prepare," she moaned. "No comb, no brush. No toothbrush! And my clothes on board? They're too small or too old."

"I said go over there and buy some clothes. Get what you need. Some kind of T-shirt to cover yourself."

"I want something better," she moaned.

"Are you trying to tempt me?" he asked, surprised. "If so, you had one hell of a way of showing it back there, dressed like that."

Max saw the younger man's eyes wander when Ariel had on a scanty top. The last thing he needed was some kind of skirmish in the middle of the night. He went deep into his pocket and took out a handful of twenty dollar bills. "Go on now. The gift shop must have something decent."

"Yeah," she said, scrunching up her face. "I'll have Key West across my breasts."

"Stop complaining. After this trip I'll buy you whatever you want."

"Why do I have to hide?"

"Can we talk about this later?"

When Ariel returned, dressed in shorts and a loose white T-shirt with Key West written across her chest, Max winked his approval. Turning to the young men, he asked, "You boys ready?"

After the nod to take off, he made small talk. "You boys fresh in from Cuba? My family has lived in Key West for three generations. We ..."

"You ready or not?" the third man standing near the drums stepped forward.

Faking his enthusiasm, Max replied, "Ho, ho, ho, and a bottle of rum! That's how ready I am!"

Still in Max's right pocket was the thirty thousand dollars in envelope number sixteen that he'd withdrawn from the bank. He also had five thousand in cash from the boys, given to him earlier in payment for the trip. Then there was an extra two thousand for the drums— seven thousand dollars more for his Ariel.

Solid blackness was everywhere as the Ramblin' Rose departed the Garrison Bight Marina. A heavy blanket of low clouds hid the reflection of the moon. This meant they were working off the lights on the boat, the floodlights reflecting calmness on the blackened sea. Max started the first engine and, because of the load, pressed the start button to the reserve engine.

Suddenly exhausted, Max's vision was blurred. The burning heat under his skin was making it difficult to maneuver the wheel.

The trip to Islamorada was expected to take three to four hours. Once the Ramblin' Rose was past the protective reef and into the flow of Intracoastal waterways, Max was counting on the guidance of the harvest moon, its reflection whipping across the ocean as far as the naked eye could see, an uneventful journey with passengers and cargo delivered safe and sound his goal.

He called Ariel over to the captain's chair. Most of his kids, but especially Jose and Ariel, could be trusted to take over.

"Get us out past the reef. I'll be back by then. I'm going below," Max explained. "I know you can get through the inlet. Watch out for quagmires and rocks."

"Yes!" she answered gingerly. "Can do!"

Ariel moved into the power seat, put the gears in reverse, and moved out of the slip like a pro. The thirty foot skiff shifted forward and glided smoothly and effortlessly beyond the seven-mile reef into the more turbulent waters of the Atlantic.

CHAPTER 25

AFTER TURNING OVER THE WHEEL to Ariel, Max sat at the captain's table and map station, the ride as smooth and calm as if they were riding on top of glass.

Taking out his small, well-worn brown leather book, he wrote about today's trip to the bank on the outside of envelope number sixteen:

Disturbing. My numbers seem to be out of sync. Finally completed envelope #16. All for Ariel under certain circumstances stated in the divorce papers and new will. All four locations have sixteen envelopes, minus one less at South Shore Bank. One envelope short. Very disturbing.

Max returned the envelope to the inside of the safe, placing it behind the number sixteen that had no writing.

Looking through some papers in the drawer below the safe, Max spotted a framed photo of Allyson Jackson as the young girl he once knew. She was sitting alongside him in his bright white and turquoise Ford convertible back in the day. She had long, luxurious, blonde hair. In those days he would do almost anything for the right woman who gave him what he wanted of them. She was the only one who asked to participate in his business. The sex, Allyson insisted, was separate from work. Additionally, she was a good organizer and bookkeeper.

Then one day she left Key West without saying a word, not even a good-bye.

For the ten years of their romance, she ran his business. She taught him how to hold back tips and cash payments and how to set up his private accounts. And she told him what he had to spend and how to cut corners. After she left so suddenly, unannounced, at the same time the economy tanked, forcing him to cut his fleet from four fully equipped, ready-for-hire fishing vessels down to the remaining one he captained today.

If Allyson was here right now, if he was still driving that convertible, she would have all the answers. This time he would listen like he should have from the beginning.

Reaching into the cabinet above to check on the large envelope from his attorney containing divorce papers and his new, fully executed will and a set of signature bank cards underneath, he was ready to return to the wheel.

Pausing, he clicked open the small black velvet case. He smiled inwardly and returned the box to its original location on top of the new will.

As he reached the staircase, the fire that spit through his veins and numbed his arm knocked the breath out of him.

He tried to shout out for help. Nothing came out of his pasty, dry mouth.

Max's digitalis was at the bottom of the cabinet under the sink in the smaller bathroom. He dragged himself there. The expiration date was last year. He placed several tablets under his tongue, expecting the pills to stop his pain.

Next, he took an OxyContin tablet out of a plastic bag hidden under the clean, folded towels in the storage cabinet. He made the sign of the cross, praying one pill would block this constant overall feeling of malaise he'd carried around for several days.

Hugging the thin wood railing and grabbing on with his hands, he lifted himself up the stairs one foot at a time. Finally reaching the galley, he reopened the kitchen cabinet, went into the doors behind the pipes, and returned the little brown leather book, his "money bible" as Julie Jackson called it, to its original location.

CHAPTER 26

LOOKING HAPPY AND IN CONTROL, Ariel was at the wheel while Max stood at the top of the staircase.

"Hey there! This is so-o-o fun!" She glanced over for Max's approval. "Can I ..." Seeing the vacant look in his eyes and his unsteady stance, she asked, "You okay? What is it?"

Panting, he replied, "Nothing you need to wrap your pretty head around. I'll take over now."

Concerned, she knew better than to argue. She had never been around him when he had sweat so profusely. Hesitating, she relinquished the captain's chair. "You sure?"

"Positive. Now take a break."

Moving to the bow of the boat, Ariel rested one hand low in the water. When she spread her fingers wide, the ocean's spray wet her Key West T-shirt. As her nipples rose, the young man with the curly hair unashamedly stared down at them. "You his?" he nodded over to the captain's chair.

"Sometimes," she replied, patting the seat closer to her as he slid over.

He sat there for a moment, beer in one hand, cigarette in the other, and his arms resting on the back of the seat. "Two questions: Does he always watch straight ahead like that? If he does, will you go downstairs with me? Have some wild sex, share a bottle of whiskey?"

That's three questions," she said, her laugh throaty and loud. "Answer to question number one: Yes, unless I'm in one of the seats at the front of the boat looking for quagmires, rocks, or other obstructions so our asses aren't thrown overboard. About question number two: I'm pregnant. You wanna take on that responsibility? Before we get to question number three," she asked.

"Hey, I'm married," he said, flashing his hands up in self-defense and jumping up out of the seat. Changing his stance, he went from a cool dude, definitely interested in the woman sitting in front of him, to a defenseless young man, realizing he had stepped into quicksand and might not get out.

"Good. Then don't go fuckin' up your life."

Recovering, he replied, "Yeah. Like you're gonna tell me some lame story about the two of you. Like it's going to make me care." A new attitude was also plastered on his face. Pausing for but a second, he turned his middle finger in the air and said, "Besides, I'm married. Have a good life."

Max set the gears on autopilot. She seemed happiest at eight with a course of north and three percent east. Coming over to Ariel, he asked, "What was that all about?"

"He wants to have sex with me, but he's married."

"What did you say?"

"Guess."

"That's no answer," Max stammered, scenarios beginning to form. "Did you see him walk away or what?"

"Sure, babe. I'm just a little worried about having you on board. Boys like that …"

"Sex is my choice, not yours and not theirs. So no worries," she said, smiling up at him and offering him her hand.

Max kissed it and, after rechecking the gauges, motioned for her to take over the captain's chair again. "Back in a few minutes."

"No prob," she said, grinning and grabbing at another opportunity to feel an exhilarating moment of total control.

As Max studied Ariel behind the wheel, she was in a world of her own where she was free to experience a release from her life of oppression at home.

When Max returned with the bottle of digitalis in his front pocket, he did not want to alarm Ariel, so he put it behind the steering wheel. He took over without releasing autopilot. As the clouds opened up, the full moon guided them for the next several hours. The moon was far above the water. The whitecaps set a rhythm that reassured him a great peace was on the horizon. The feeling he had was one of reassurance that somehow everything was going to work itself out.

"Over there," the older boy said, directing Max to shore. "See that Juniper tree? Next to it."

Max cut the engines and glided inland, scraping the bottom of his boat, which made a grinding sound. Suddenly, three men appeared out of nowhere. They jumped on the boat and began rotating two fifty-five-gallon drums from side to side. From the trunk bed, a crane lowered a heavy chain with a wide-mouthed clamp at its end. The clamp tightened around first one drum and then the other, each landing onto the flat bed of the dark green Chevy truck.

"Meet the boys at your motel. Six in the morning." The boxer-size third traveler nodded before taking off. The two young passengers were already in the back seat of the truck.

"What ...?" Ariel said, in shock, as Max held her back from the group.

"Stay," he commanded. "We'll see them tomorrow. Not sleep with them tonight."

After several minutes of sliding back and forth in the sand from the weight of the two barrels, the truck thrust forward.

Once the truck was out of sight, Max called for a cab, which arrived within minutes. "Holiday Isle Hotel," he told the Haitian cabbie.

CHAPTER 27

ELLIE LIVINGSTON WAS ON FLIGHT 640 to LAX. She had no place to stay. Since when had that ever stopped her? She tried to leave a message for Paulette, but her calls did not go through. After several more tries, she thought, *Oh well. I'll call from her house phone. Give her the good news she now has a free house sitter.*

Ellie's thoughts were on Brent L. Livingston III, lah-de-dah, her unofficial ex-husband, who was probably out on the Atlantic Ocean somewhere, trolling along in his fifty-eight-foot catamaran, persuading yet another boat babe that she could be luxuriating on his boat, free of charge. Then, if things worked out, she could help him spend the proceeds from a two-million-dollar double indemnity life insurance policy taken out on his wife, who accidentally drowned at sea during the last hurricane.

Brent was actually stalking Ellie. She wasn't just being paranoid. With all his money and connections, why hadn't he confronted her?

Since getting sober and giving up the pills, she remembered more than she wished to about jumping overboard during the eye of the storm. On a buzz for days before that, Ellie had this out-of-touch feeling. She lost track of how many pills she took or how many drinks she'd inhaled during their last trip. Instead of staying alert, Brent stayed drunk and passed out before dark, leaving her to make sure they weren't stuck out on a sandbank somewhere.

On her last trip, Ellie tried to fight back. It was almost too late. She was down to her last OxyContin tablet the night she jumped. Earlier in the day, she had challenged his manhood by being specific about his performance as a lover.

Accusing him, but telling the truth, she said, "You can't get it up without being blasted!"

She went too far and laughed too loudly. He knocked her across the room, swearing, "Bitch! If I could throw you overboard, I would!"

This latest argument was over the fact that he did not go into the boat hold as ordered by the Coast Guard. Their drinking and drugging at this point was out of hand.

He was Gunga Din. He would fight like he had in the past, only this storm was one of the worst, and they knew it.

It was certain she would die if she jumped into the angry sea in the middle of a category 3 hurricane. That was exactly what she wanted. There was no value to life once she learned the love of her life, Todd Evers, had been in a brawl the night he died. Beaten up after hours, he was buried at sea by three strangers to the island.

She wept for her loss, but it was Todd's last words, said directly to her face, that spoke the truth of their relationship: "I want you to know I love you. But my family needs me." His eyes glazed over as he spoke the words that cut through her like a saw blade, chopping her in half.

She could only stare at him in disbelief. He became annoyed. "Don't you get it? I'm going home to my wife and two boys," he said. "We're leaving for Houston tomorrow. We have family and friends there. It's where we belong. Together. Without you. Now get going."

When Ellie and Brent were in port the next time to see Stan, they were married. Ellie asked Stan once more: "Tell me what happened to Todd."

The story was the same. "I'm really sorry, Ellie. I know how you felt," he added.

Ellie still did not believe a word of it. That's why she was going to Houston—to find the answer for herself once and for all.

If the story proved to be true, she would kill herself. Her dying prayer had already been mailed to Mama Mae. Her only wish was to meet her beloved on the other side, his arms wide open, where he would say: "I have been waiting for you, my beloved."

From LAX, Ellie took the Van Nuys Fly-Away to the central station and caught a turnaround ride to Ventura Boulevard in Sherman Oaks, where she caught a cab.

"You want me to drop you here? I think not," the cabbie said. They were parked on Mulholland Drive, two houses away from Paulette's home. "This here is a fancy neighborhood, but there are bad incidents going on. Not like the old days," he said. "But here, in the dark? No, ma'am."

He turned the meter off and sat with his arms crossed. "You take me to where you really want to go or we sit here all night."

Ellie got out of the cab, paid him, and started walking uphill.

"You're crazy, you know that?" the driver yelled out the window.

"Go on now!" Ellie turned around to face the cabbie. "I paid you. I know what I'm doing."

She stood her ground, and as he pulled away, darkness consumed her.

There was a security system in place, so she fumbled her way to the back of the house where she went under the porch until she located a secret door. There were no locks or other identifying marks, and if you did not know the opening was there, you would pass right by it.

"Great!" Ellie sighed. She pushed the door inward, found a light switch, closed the door, and went up to the kitchen just as Paulette had told her about years ago. It was an entrance used by her husband or son whenever they lost their keys or forgot the front door code.

Ellie heard voices, which turned out to be a television set running on low volume above her. Climbing a set of wooden stairs, she reached the kitchen and began to relax. She found the master bath where she showered and dressed in one of Paulette's nightgowns.

She went back into the kitchen and opened the refrigerator. Nothing was there that she could eat: meats, chicken, steaks, hamburgers. No fresh vegetables, yogurt, or orange juice.

While settling down to watch the lights of the San Fernando Valley from the living room, the doorbell rang.

CHAPTER 28

ELLIE WAITED IN THE KITCHEN with the lights off.

The bell rang a second time and a third. "Hey, you in there! Let us in! I'm Billie. My dad lives just a block away, and he will be up here in five minutes! He will call the cops and get you kicked out for sure."

Ellie ran back to the kitchen and shut off the lights, wrapped her robe tightly around her, and put her bare feet up on the table facing the couch, the view no longer of interest.

Soon she heard the ripping of tires out of the driveway and down the road. And soon she climbed the stairs and fell fast asleep in the master bed.

"Kathleen Moore."

"This is Dr. Marshall, Paulette's ex-husband. My son just finished telling me the most amazing tale. He went to the house on Mulholland Drive and couldn't get in. Not only was someone in the house, that stranger would not let my son in even after he identified himself."

"Do you know what time it is?" Kathleen asked.

"Later than you think. If I find out she leased the place, I hope you know what that means."

"Duly noted," Kathleen said.

"Hear this. If I don't have a clarification on all of this before I go into surgery at 9 a.m., I will call the cops, and I will have papers from a judge to throw whoever that intruder is out of my house!"

"Good night, Dr. Marshall," Kathleen said as she slammed the phone down.

Ellie tried several more times to reach Paulette. On the last call, she answered. "Can I get back to you? I'm at Higgs Beach on the pier watching the spectacular sunset and this guy and his marbles," she said.

"No! Wait! It's important. It's a good thing I'm here. Guess where I am!" Ellie said lightly.

"How are you?" Paulette asked. Paulette was distracted, watching the sunset as a young man with tattoos over his nearly naked body had set out various-size stones in a circle toward the sun. When he finished, he sat cross-legged and he began to chant.

"I'm in your house, and three kids tried to break in. Good thing I was here! I chased them away."

"Where? In LA?" Paulette asked, shocked. "How? Why?" *Oh, my God*, she thought, *that means anyone could break in!*

"What time?"

"About nine. It felt like midnight it was so dark up here. Love the lights down below. Cool."

"Wha ... I don't understand. I said if you were coming to LA. Certainly I did not have to tell you to call me first for my permission. That's a given ... I would have thought."

"I saved your place from real thieves," Ellie responded proudly. "Some kids mumbled something like they had a key to the door. I had double locked the front door so they couldn't get in. They left after I told them I would call the cops."

"You are actually in my house?" Paulette withheld her accusations and a scream with the realization that she was powerless. The only option was to call Kathleen—or the police.

First, she called Kathleen. The phone went to the answering machine, and her cell phone was shut off. It was early morning, and Paulette reached Kathleen.

"I heard," Kathleen said. "Your ex called me around three thirty this morning to tell me someone was in your house. Your son and two of his friends had a key, but the door was bolted from the inside. They couldn't reason with the woman, so Billie called his dad who called me."

"Three thirty? You're kidding, right? I called you earlier. I left a message."

"You did? We were at dinner. Well, he got us up in the hours when going back to sleep was impossible. You haven't rented the place, have you? That would void your agreement, and Chris would have that house before you could get on a flight to LAX to pick up your things!"

"Please don't yell," Paulette said. "I have no idea what to do. How to get that woman out."

"How well do you know this person? Is she a close friend of yours?"

"I barely know her! You know the story. We've known each other since we were kids. Her family is very, very rich, even by Palm Beach standards. They live in Miami now. Her mother is high society. Ellie ran away at eleven and has been on the run ever since. Calls about every five years or so."

"You did say if she came to LA she could stay there?"

"Not exactly. Wouldn't you call and ask the owner first?"

"Yes, but I don't think either one of us believes this is a normal person. I'll call you back as soon as I can. By then she will be on a plane to somewhere else, taking advantage of someone else."

It was 6:30 a.m., and a cappuccino con leche from Starbucks was on her desk.

"Kathleen Moore here."

"This is Ellie. Ellie Wellesley Johnson Livingston. I …"

"I know who you are. I could have you arrested at this very moment and put in jail!"

"Don't bother. In one hour a car is picking me up and taking me to LAX. My next stop is Houston, Texas."

Ellie knew her goal, the reason for her very existence. She would find her lover, Todd Evers, and they would create the same life they once shared on Cat Island before he suddenly felt a sense of guilt and went back to his wife and two boys, who were in Houston somewhere, living with her parents.

"Do you have any idea, or even care, what trouble you caused Paulette? She could lose the rights to her house because of you. How did you get in? The kid with the key? That was Paulette and Chris's son, Billie. He and a few friends came to stay overnight. They had a key and permission," Kathleen emphasized.

Ignoring the threat and innuendos, Ellie explained about the use of Paulette's car. "I went down for groceries and some gas. Did you know her tank was almost empty?"

Kathleen exploded. "You foolish bitch. You think you can intrude like this onto someone else's property and not face consequences? You have no idea how violated we all feel."

Ellie's laugh was a nervous one.

"Is this how you live your life? Behind the walls of everyone else's successes? Like a deep, dark shadow in the night?"

"Very well put," Ellie replied, admitting, "seems to be the way my life has turned out."

"Nothing about your problem is Paulette's problem or mine. Go to Houston or wherever. We could not care less. I will be at the house in one hour with the security service manager, who will check everything. You better be gone. I mean every plate washed, every bed made. Like you'd never even been there!"

Ellie said nothing.

"Well?" Kathleen asked. "Yes or no?"

"One hour?" Ellie asked.

"Yes. One hour!"

"Agreed. Now can you calm down? Where are the boys now?"

"You care? ... Their son, Bill, and his two friends are on their way to Utah this very minute."

"Driving?"

"What difference is it to you?" Kathleen asked.

"I want to see my mother," Ellie said. "She has given away my property to the city of Miami. At least, according to the newspaper. Do I have any rights to sue her?"

No one had ever raised Kathleen's blood pressure this high before. The set of balls this woman carried around was amazing. Her sense of entitlement was in total ignorance of the rights of others. And all because once upon a time she was rich? If this woman hadn't gotten caught by Paulette's son, she would still be living off a productive individual who worked hard for her rewards.

Angered at the thought of how one misstep by a virtual stranger could cause the loss of everything Paulette had worked so very hard for, Kathleen said, "So now you want to sue your mother?"

"If I have to, I will."

"The only way to find out is to talk to your mother one on one. Or find an attorney who will file a lawsuit. It definitely will not be me! This is a question only the courts can settle. When was the last time you talked to your mother?"

The call disconnected.

The next call Kathleen received was from Chris on his private home phone. To avoid the possibility of the having to file a police report and avoid publicity, she took the call. Kathleen expected him to say he was coming right over to the Casa, his lawyer at his side, a petition in his hand, authorizing occupancy and signed by a judge.

"If this matter isn't settled by the end of my first surgery, the sheriff will be given papers to take over occupancy by default," Chris said. "If that happens, no one but my new family will be allowed in. Paulette sure has a weird way of paying me back. I always thought she was pretty bright—smart, actually. What she's done only hurts her, and real bad."

"I'll have Paulette call you and explain the special circumstances."

"There are no special circumstances," he yelled into the speaker.

The treadmill's noise stopped and Kathleen volunteered: "I am going to the premises within the hour."

"With the cops, I hope," Chris commented.

"I don't think that will be necessary. The police are aware a burglar may have been on the property last night. The first thing Paulette will do is fire the security service, and we'll go from there.... Is that all?" Kathleen asked, holding her breath, seeing subpoenas and a new court hearing before her, all issued by a different judge, who would not be as lenient once he learned Paulette had left the premises.

CHAPTER 29

DOUG AND FLOWER MITCHELL WERE the only truly happily married couple left in the entire world that Paulette knew.

Together for fifteen years, they lived across the street from Higgs Beach, two blocks from Paulette's new apartment she had rented online for the summer.

The Mitchells' two-story nautical style home rested on a precious half-acre lot a block from the Atlantic Ocean, its waves held back by the barrier reef that runs for approximately seven miles up the coast from just south of Key West to almost Marathon. The house was painted light gray and had an overhanging porch that led to the front door. Hung along the outside porch were loose fishing nets with rusty anchors nailed to the outside wallboards. Dead, stuffed sea animals were mounted on all four exterior walls.

The public tennis courts directly across the street were available to his family and other local residents. For the planned festivities, all three courts would light up for Flower's eighteen-year-old daughter, Alyssa, and her friends, who would dance to their kind of music while the older crowd would rock to Island music and the soothing new-age sounds of Yanni.

Paulette went over to kiss Doug on the cheek. He did not look her way, only pointed up the stairs where Flower was in their bedroom, getting dressed.

When Flower heard Paulette, she yelled down, "We're up here, darling, doing my hair. Come on up!"

Flower had a bottle of champagne on ice. She offered Paulette a drink.

"Not right now," Paulette replied. "I'm still in recovery from all that's happened in the last few days." She drank hardly at all, and while her personal life was in this state of flux, drinking was really out of the question. No new habits needed!

"I hope by the time the party starts, you'll imbibe," Flower laughed. "When we went for the fitting, you were right there with me."

"I also carried a gigantic headache for two days. Wine, champagne, and so many of the liquors have too much sugar." Paulette changed the subject. "Your dress is absolutely perfect. You'll put the rest of us to shame. You and that dress. All I can say is *per*-fect!"

"Remember Alexander Pope's poem, *The Rape of the Lock*, where the women who were married had one big curl down their back? Your hair reminds me of that poem," Paulette said.

"You would get literary on me. But yes, isn't it fun to look this way? Doug hasn't seen my dress yet. He is going to… I was going to say something nasty, but I won't. Correction! He is really going to enjoy the view, shall we say."

Paulette sat on the bed as Flower slipped into the top and then pulled on the long skirt and held out the fabric with both hands and swung around. "Check out these shoes. Would you believe they're Sketchers?"

"I'm sure no one will see your feet!" Paulette laughed, adding, "I think I will take that glass of champagne after all!"

Ariel lay awake at the furthest corner of the bed she shared with Max at the Caribbean Motel in Islamorada. It was 3 a.m., and he was finally snoring.

She put on her Key West T-shirt and new, strategically torn jeans. She opened the heavy front door and slid her backpack out onto the sidewalk. Inside once again, she closed the door and was standing ramrod straight.

Leave while you can, she heard a voice from inside warn her. Even so, she stood at attention and waited. Nothing. With no movement and a sound coming from Max like someone was choking, each moment felt like an eternity. His chest went up and down, up and down, his mouth gasping for air.

Ariel tiptoed to the closet where his fisherman's pants hung on a hook. Deeply and as quickly as a pickpocket, she grabbed a wad of hundred dollar bills. Seven thousand dollars in cash! She stuffed the wad into her bra and tiptoed to the exit door.

Another wait. Nothing. No movement; only the echo of her own heavy breathing pounding in her ear.

Reconsidering, she pulled the money out of her bra and decided to return two thousand dollars to his pants pocket. Five thousand would not nick him all that much, especially after the way she had previously turned down a much larger sum of money tied to conditions she could not accept.

This was enough for the abortion. If her idea worked, she could also have a great weekend in a fancy-schmancy hotel.

Exiting once more, she slid close to the outside walls, feeling like a lowly toad, knowing Max would never give her any money ever again for anything. But then why should he? She was the worst bitch on the face of the earth. Max was the father of this … this fetus she was carrying, a fetus whose fate she had not yet decided.

No more waiting. If Max came after her, he wouldn't know how to find her anyway. She was always good at hiding. When her mother came home drunk; when her father arrived and her parents had big fights and threw things at each other; when she took long walks in the middle of the night trying to figure out her life and how to escape it—no one ever had any luck in locating her.

Suicide was an alternative.

After all, what did she have to live for? She had no future, and her past belonged to a woman who had stolen her daughter's chances for a clean record. This occurred when a neighbor called about a brawl at their house. The police record had Ariel's name on it! She could never be free of all her family's sins and transgressions, nor could she be forgiven for the ones she was about to commit. So there you have it: a lose-lose situation.

Thank goodness she was so smart in school, getting straight As without much effort. She and her counselor had filled out several applications for scholarships, ones that would allow her to leave town for a legitimate reason.

Ariel looked back at their motel room three doors away. If Max came out in the next thirty seconds, she'd be toast, her legs too weak to run away. That did not happen. She slinked past the vending machines where there was reception on her cell phone, and she called Jose.

Jose was the only logical choice. They had known each other since they were little and began taking trips on Max's boats along with his kids. As they grew up and their mothers became less and less attentive, she and Jose were free to do whatever they wanted.

They were buddies then, before grades, ambitions, and other opinions got in the way. She could trust him, call on him. He put his feelings out there when he asked her to the prom even before the date was set.

"I don't know, really. I don't know if I'll have a dress," she said. The truth was she never thought of Jose in that way. More than that, was he thinking in that way, or was it because he had so few friends in school and Ariel was a convenience? The only reason he would graduate was Jose knew Max would be so disappointed if he didn't.

"Hello," he answered groggily.

"Hey there, it's Ariel. Can you come get me?"

"What are you doing up at this hour? Where are you? When I left, you were going home to bed."

"No questions, please," she whispered. "I'm in trouble. Real trouble." After giving him directions as to where she was, she pleaded, "One to one and a half hours, right? I can count on you? You won't disappoint me?"

"I'll be there," he said. "Questions come later. You can count on it."

"Okay, but hurry."

While waiting for Jose, Ariel left her possessions behind the No Vacancy sign at the front of the motel, her thoughts drawn back to the boat with a singular purpose.

Did she have the courage to return to the Ramblin' Rose and take what had been offered her? Max said he'd put the thirty thousand dollars back in the safe, after holding it for several days, just in case she changed her mind about his offer.

Before Ariel lost her courage through second guessing, she climbed aboard and immediately went below to the safe, reasoning that he had offered that money to her twice before. If he told the truth and this wasn't a trap, the envelope was still inside the safe she had been given access to years ago. Reasoning that he was the father of the fetus, she mumbled: "Max would understand what I am doing. Desperate people do desperate things, right? I'm damned desperate, and he knows why!" At the exact same second, her Catholic conscience made her wish she felt better about all of this.

Ariel's hands shook as she tried to unlock the safe. Her right arm was stiff, her hands sweating. After a second try, she absolutely knew she'd forgotten the combination. Wasn't that God's signal she was sinning?

Suddenly she was strong and defiant, daring her inner voice to tell her what she could and could not do. "So what?" she said out loud. "So frickin' what?"

After a second try, she gave up and went upstairs to the main cabin. Behind a set of pipes under the sink was the little brown book she'd known about since she was a kid—the combination to the safe written at the top of the second page.

With her brain all scrambled, a voice loomed out from somewhere deep inside. It was arguing back. "Do not take this money! Go right on home! No worries and no pay back. Think of your future!"

Ariel reasoned in return: "If I want to go to school and keep this baby, I have to take it to survive. Okay," she bargained, "but I will not be greedy."

Ariel checked the notebook. Of course the combination was correct. She was not that dense. She had been too nervous to get it right.

She paused. She should be honoring Max by not stealing from him.

With the release of that thought, her Catholic upbringing began to do a real number on her. Being a good Catholic girl, she would have to go to confession, or she would never be forgiven for her actions. The priest would then give her a penance he felt fit the crime. *Oh, God, I'll be on my knees for the rest of my life*, she thought. She would figure out all the angles later: figure out what was sinful and what she had honestly earned. She might try to reason and rationalize, but only the Holy Father above and the church had taught her how wrong was wrong and right was right—with no gray in the middle.

Defiance was cemented into her very soul. No one could make her life move forward except her, and that was exactly what she was going to do. With that resolve, suddenly, what seemed like a bolt of lightning went through her when she realized she would do anything to keep her baby.

Finally inside the safe, Ariel hesitated. Since the time she was very little, she knew about all this money; about how methodical Max was about his savings; about how he kept track of every penny. Not once did she think any of it would ever be hers—not once. And here she was stealing from him like a common thief.

She thought bitterly she had no reason to worry about the outside world if someone right here and now, someone on the inside, was the thief. And where was the rightful owner? Asleep soundly in his room, without a thought that anyone, especially someone he knew, was robbing him.

CHAPTER 30

ARIEL DROPPED HER INNER DIALOGUE as she reasserted her promise to take only what she was convinced Max had previously offered her.

Losing interest in the old leather book, she slid it into a narrow space between the safe and the cabinet. She took out the top envelope and snatched it tightly to her chest. Her heart was beating in her throat as she checked the envelope. It was envelope number sixteen. She would take that one and nothing more.

Why did she flip to the next envelope? It was also number sixteen. Which one did he promise her? She must keep the right one. Maybe Max was confused or something. She clutched the one she had slipped out of the box, putting the other one back inside. This made all the envelopes even the way Max liked them to be.

Waiting the longest, most indecisive moment of her life, she closed the safe and slipped the envelope into her back pocket.

Now what was the problem?

Ariel thought about how trusting Max was. After all his hard work, all someone had to do was scoop up these envelopes in one quick moment. It was not right. Suddenly, Ariel was riddled with compassion for him—an emotion she could ill afford or all would be lost.

Momentarily, she lost her nerve. Not her nerve, she decided, but as she paused to step outside her own problems, she saw Max's disappointment. What in any way was right or honest about stealing from a benevolent friend?

Relieved the choice was made, and with the envelope tucked in at her waist, she must escape while she could, but her curiosity was aroused by what Max told her was in the cabinet above.

"It's a big surprise," he had said. She hated waiting for surprises. Somehow, peeking inside assuaged her guilt. Strange reasoning, she knew, but then all of this was nothing like the real person: Everything was surreal.

On top of a big manila envelope was a small black box. She put it aside to first look inside the large manila envelope dated two days ago. Inside were dissolution of marriage papers, a will, and several blue cards. She skimmed through the documents. "After we marry, he gives me everything? What about his kids? … Holy shh-it," she said out loud.

She could not possibly agree to any of this. Horrors follow all ill-gotten means, and that certainly would be true in her case.

She wondered who Max discussed this with. Hopefully not her mother or, God forbid, her brother Daniel! Max could not know she was pregnant! No one knew. The doctor who gave her the test promised her file was private and sealed once she left the office. Forced to face Max and Rosetta at the same time about the money and the fetus, what would she do? Would Max pull her aside and threaten to tell her mother if she didn't return his money? Whatever remained after the abortion and a short but lavish vacation on South Beach, Max would just have to accept what was left and let her go.

Surely he would never send her to jail!

He could also deny he was the father of her unborn child.

What would Rosetta—poor, put-upon Rosetta—have to say? "Oh God," Ariel cried out as her overactive imagination worked its number on her. She must stop and pull herself into the present moment. Leave the boat unseen. If Max woke, he would be looking for her. If he looked long enough, he would find her and know exactly what she had done!

But aha! If she escaped first, she would become untraceable! She and her baby!

Yes, she could take the money, but no, she could never marry Max! He may be strong enough to ignore the gossip and not care about being shunned by the neighborhood. Didn't he understand? She planned to return to Key West after college and traveling. She did not want the very people who already looked down on her because of her mother's actions to form an even more damaging image of her because of her involvement with Max. Key West was home and always would be.

Tears were streaming down Ariel's face as she saw no positive future in front of her, only condemnation for what she had done. She was still going to peek inside the fuzzy black box.

She did, and in the center of the case was a shiny two- or three-carat yellow diamond ring set in fourteen-carat gold. A very big diamond. Tiny little white diamonds went all the way around the band.

She definitely would be insane to snatch that! Shame covered her. She created all this! Max must be insane. She must be insane!

She slid the ring off its holder and tried it on. How beautiful it was on the third finger of her left hand. Now that she had seen how perfectly it fit her, she longed to keep it, especially after passing up all those envelopes, reasoning that the ring had been cut to her size, after all. Therefore, it must be for her. She reasoned that someday she might have to sell it to feed the baby.

Suddenly everything was too much.

She tossed the empty box onto one of the two sets of bunk beds behind her and slipped the ring into the small pocket at the top of her jeans.

The divorce papers she could do nothing about, but the new will she could. Quickly, she went upstairs and looked behind the door and below a layer of dust. There was Max's old will: not the one he told her about last night, dated the day before, but the one she knew about for years that left everything to his family—just as it should be.

What to do?

Back downstairs at the cabinet above the safe, she opened the new envelope and took out the new will, along with the divorce papers. Up the stairs again at the sink, she put the new will and the divorce papers inside the old envelope.

Next, she ran back downstairs to put the old will in the new envelope. The old will was now safely inside the new envelope in the cabinet above the safe. She did not stop to check out the small cards inside.

Should she go back downstairs and open the safe again? She couldn't. Already she was too nervous to concentrate. Her hands and her mind were too jumpy.

Returning to the kitchen, she dusted herself off. Did she do it right?

After the trip to Miami, she would give him what was left of the seven thousand dollars, also envelope number sixteen, with the full amount of thirty thousand dollars inside.

After wiping her hands clean of the dust, she secured the secret panels and the cabinet doors and hurried off the Ramblin' Rose. Then she went to the front of the motel to sit near the No Vacancy sign, hoping Jose would soon rescue her.

Chapter 31

It was near dusk the night of the Mitchell celebration. Paulette had stopped by earlier to visit with Flower, gone home, and, as suggested, put something Key West on.

Doug pointed upstairs and said, "She's just about ready. Wait 'til you see the vision walking down those stairs and the surprise we have for her!" he said excitedly, proudly.

At five foot six, Doug was a man no taller than Paulette in her bare feet. He had short, cropped hair, custom cut, not like her last visit when his curly brown hair was shoulder length.

"You look sharp," Paulette said. "And sexy. You're really in shape. Both of you. Are you turning tires at one of those CrossFit centers instead of lifting boring old weights?"

"Something like that. Actually, owning and operating a boat, taking passengers out to the various reefs, and cleaning up afterward takes a great deal of effort." He changed the subject. "Hey, take a look up the stairs. Flower is going to descend—note the word *descend*, not come down the stairs—in a few minutes. I'll bet she looks like a knockout," he said, winking.

She slipped away up the stairs as more guests arrived through the wide-open double doors. The two sides folded open and the smell of real down home southern cooking filled the air.

Flower was at her dressing table, about to take a long brush to her preset hair.

"What are you doing?" Paulette gasped.

"No use pretending. Doug's all worked up. He's been on the phone all day with other issues. We can't keep up this pretense."

"Pretense? What Pretense?" Paulette asked, shocked at Flower's sudden change of attitude. "Earlier we were sharing champagne. This time no headache," she said to cheer Flower up. "I see you finished the bottle. Go into the bathroom and splash some cold water on your face!"

"I am not going anywhere. You go on downstairs. As soon as I pull myself together, I'll do what Doug wants."

"I thought you wanted the party too," Paulette said.

"You are so naïve," Flower scoffed. "It's not about the party. Now go on. I'll be better sooner than later."

Paulette left Flower reluctantly, given the state she was in. She looked over the food, great foodie that she was, ready to taste real deep-fried chicken, barbecued pork ribs, and freshly fried fish cooked the good ole Southern way—most of it cooked in the same iron skillets as the corn bread that was already cut and lying to the side.

She filled a small plate with a variety of dips and spicy sauces and then went after the deep fried mini fritters with conch fish in the center. Baked potatoes and basmati rice were covered with deveined and grilled shrimp. The grill was the center of everyone's attention. More fresh shrimp coated with lemon butter and other seasonings were being checked constantly by the head chef, hired away from a local restaurant for the night. Yanni and good food. What could be better?

Her cell phone rang. It was Chief Detective Allan McKenna. "I'm calling about the robbery and possible murder you witnessed in Key Largo … on your way down to Key West?"

"Yes, yes. It's a very special night. I'm at a party. Aren't you working awfully late? Can you call me on Monday morning? Monday afternoon would even be better."

"The Mitchell house," McKenna commented.

"How did you know? I mean, about the party?"

"Small town. Big events."

"Come and join us for a drink," Paulette said enthusiastically. "It's Flower's birthday and their wedding anniversary."

He let the invitation drop. "I have some photos I'd like you to take a look at. Early tomorrow morning if not tonight."

Paulette hesitated. "How about first thing Monday morning? Doug says it's not too likely I'll see anything of my stolen possessions. I'll be putting in my claims soon. What's the hurry? And about the incident in Key Largo, I don't remember much, really. The last thing I want is for hopes to be raised that I can seriously identify anyone. And so far as a police line-up is concerned, there's no way."

"Let me determine that. Many times new details surface when possible suspects are on the other side of the glass. For right now, I have a set of photos I would like you to look at."

"All right. Tomorrow around two then?" she suggested, wondering why the detective was in such a big hurry.

"Two it is," he agreed.

Soon the house was filled with couples doing the same. Other guests were sitting on the steps, smoking, drinking, eating, and laughing. The women were dressed in colorful skirts and loose silk shirts, their hair reminiscent of the sixties era: long and curly and wildly flying everywhere.

The under-thirty crowd was cheeky and up to date with their fashion. The women wore seven-inch heels with two-inch platforms and carried themselves skillfully as they cautiously maneuvered the stairs. Others wore identifying symbols of their youth, which included small tattoos on their ankles and butterflies on their upper, exposed shoulders.

The men's island attire, mostly Harvey T-shirts or open shirts with famous club names, sports teams, or fishing sites displayed on their backs. Their pants were cutoffs.

The lavender-colored tablecloths that covered the small, round tables arranged in the center of the Mitchells' open living room accented the light gray coloring of her walls and furniture. Flower always had a flair for decorating, Paulette thought, and tonight she had outdone herself.

The centerpieces on the tables consisted of small, round soy candles balanced inside shells, surrounded by circular holders containing gardenias. Overhead, balloons bounced inside fishing nets.

The weather was exceptional: no humidity and seventy-five degrees with a slight breeze. "Perfect ambiance" as Flower would say. If only there was nothing wrong with Flower.

CHAPTER 32

MOMENTS AFTER WHAT PAULETTE THOUGHT was an outburst from nerves, Flower glided down the winding staircase in a flowing, floor-length skirt of lavender chiffon, her blouse a formfitting beaded top that accentuated her athletic body with surprisingly overpowering, full, and natural breasts. Her skin was luminescent, her cheeks flush, the tears of earlier covered by extra layers of mascara.

Her long hair, beginning to turn a pleasing gray at the hairline, was, for tonight, swept to one side in an old-fashioned, strikingly attractive style she did not ruin with her hairbrush. Small ringlets framed her face, and one large curl went down the middle of her back.

When Doug saw Flower float down the staircase, his face held this "I can't believe she's mine" grin. He whistled as he gently took her hand. Next, he waved to the caterers, who were dressed in a dark shade of purple with white dress pants, and they released the balloons from the nets.

"You look more beautiful and sexier than the day we first met," Doug said, looking her over from the floor-length tip of her skirt to the top of her head. "Happy anniversary, darling. It's been the best fifteen years of my life. And happy birthday."

Aglow from all the attention, Flower pursed her lips in his direction.

"See up there!" Flower was standing next to Paulette and several other guests. "Doug made all those decorations when we lived elsewhere," she whispered as an aside. "Up there! Up there!" She pointed to the stuffed fish, anchors, hooks, and extra nets attached to the ceiling.

"Elsewhere" meant the small apartment they once shared with her daughter and his three sons for more time than either one of them wished to admit. Trying to succeed in a town like Key West was nearly impossible as they told Paulette at the time. "Nearly" being the operative word they clung to until their situation suddenly turned around, the result of work from one big business client in Miami.

When Flower told Paulette this story, Paulette had said, "Must be some sort of big client for you to be able to afford all of this." Flower quickly turned away, and Paulette pursued the matter no further.

Flower also told her how the decision to move permanently to Key West was not an easy one, but to remain in Miami was out of the question. Doug's ex-wife was certifiable and doing her very best—and succeeding—to turn his three boys against their father as the battle for their custody raged on.

"It was an impossible situation," Flower admitted. "When the same neighbors who witnessed the abuse and neglect firsthand were cross-examined in court, they couldn't remember what they saw and heard. After that, it only got worse."

An hour into the party, Doug seemed to have no reaction to anything personal that was upsetting Flower. He only exuded pride and pleasure. "Ugh!" Paulette moaned. "I really want to go to bed. Jet lag. I was so looking forward to all of this: meeting new people, meeting your friends. I don't know. LA blues is all. Not your fault."

"No one here is all that social, really. We force ourselves here in the Keys to be social animals. That's how we survive living on the rock. Otherwise we turn into these hermits. Island fever runs rampant around here. Go diving. Get a boat. Maybe Flower can hook you up with a group who do mall crawls once a month in Miami. There are some really good sales."

"These ribs?" Paulette changed the subject. "They are fantastic. Let me settle in, and I might take you up on some of that. Right now ..." she laughed, ready to dig in while thinking that riding for three hours up to Miami to shop and three hours home was the last thing she wanted to do. She was the type who hit the stores every six months or so and bought what she liked whether it was on sale or not.

Paulette and Doug walked slowly back to the party.

"The decorations are incredible. Flower could start her own business if she wanted to," Doug bragged, adding, "She gets like that every time we're into a problem. Spends more money and overdoes everything."

Paulette said nothing, waiting for Doug to continue.

"Let me entertain you," he said, shaking off the last topic. "I'll explain my—our connection to each person."

There were fellow boaters, seasonal residents, and shop owners—all on Duval Street—several firefighters, two policemen and their wives, and the principal of the local high school with his new wife.

Doug took Paulette's hand. "I want you to meet Mario Dominquez. He's the principal of Key West High School. Lovely man; a Conch. But a social one. Back in the day, he was a linebacker for Florida State."

"Mario and Andrea, this is Paulette. I was anxious for you to connect," Doug said as he looked past them to the opposite side of the room and nodded. "Paulette is in from LA for a visit. She's rented an apartment for the summer. Selfishly, I'd love for her to move here. Maybe you have something at the school? She's a crackerjack therapist with enough degrees and awards to fill a wall. She also has the courage to work with gang kids. Bless her heart."

Mario Dominguez was six feet tall by five feet wide. Paulette couldn't help but notice how buff he was as he bounced from side to side like an athlete in constant preparation for the next challenge.

To Paulette, Mario appeared to be ill-fitted for the classy and serene Grace Kelly lookalike standing at his side, who was as slender as he was broad. Paulette thought they were an adorable couple, and she could tell Mario worshipped the ground she walked on.

"We don't have many gang-related issues here," Mario told Doug. "Drug runners, but not gangs."

"She claims she actually likes kids. Teenagers at that. 'You treat 'em right', she says, 'and they'll reciprocate.' She's been teacher of the year and was voted the most valuable employee by her school district twice in a row. But she's here now."

Switching his drink from his right to his left hand and wiping the dampness from his glass on the side of his pants, Mario said, "Quite an introduction. I'm impressed. We get a lot of qualified teachers down here on vacation. We usually end up putting them to work."

Stepping forward, he landed on the top of Paulette's shoe. "I'm sorry. That's just like me." The man in his late forties chuckled. "I'm always embarrassed by my awkwardness. My wife has finally gotten used to my bull-in-the-china-shop ways, if you know what I mean. Tell me about working in LA."

"Guards, gates, and guns at a school in the ghetto. However, the kids were great," Paulette began. Realizing this was neither the place nor the time to continue such a discussion, she concluded, "That's about it."

"No, no. This sounds intriguing," he insisted, his feet still set in the mode of a tiger.

Paulette went on about the middle school experience until Mario's eyes glazed over. "One of our counselors is out. She might be out for the entire year," he mused. "So far we're sure about the next three months. Call my office Monday. Let's see what can be worked out. So many students are signed up for summer school."

"I really came for a vacation. A getaway from LA for the summer. My ears are still ringing from all the screaming teenagers and the constant bell system."

"Teachers are teachers. If you stay for the summer session and things work out, obtain a leave of absence from your district. A holiday would be right around the corner, and you could visit your family and friends then," he pointed out. "My bet is you'll come back for the next semester. They all come back."

Paulette was shaking her head. She was determined to be on a vacation, and it was not to counsel teenagers or teach psychology classes.

"You and Mario seemed to hit it off," Doug said when he came over to Paulette, who was waiting at the bar for a Diet Coke. "Ah, there's Enrico Armando. Let's catch up with him and offer him a drink. He's my banker. See the babe next to him? Her name is Denise."

The handsomest man Paulette had seen in a long time stood before her. He was over six feet tall, probably six two or three. He was thin, his back straight as an arrow. It was his eyes that attracted her. They were sparkling brown to match his hair, which had two small gray patches beginning to grow in at each temple.

Earlier Paulette had noticed that he and the woman he arrived with, now known to Paulette as Denise, were the only two in street clothes.

"What happened to your Hawaiian shirt?" Paulette asked, smiling.

"With apologies," Enrico replied. "My partner Denise over there and I just finished a late meeting. No time to change."

Paulette liked his official yet friendly voice, the way he leaned slightly forward as he spoke, and how he buttoned the middle button of his jacket. Silly, but it was a mannerism that intrigued her. She also liked that he had a full head of hair with no signs of thinning. Also how closely he shaved—none of this one-day shadow so popular these days.

After introductions, Doug said as an aside to Enrico: "Can you make a trip to Miami next week? Saturday, specifically? Take your friend with you," he nodded in Denise's direction.

"She can't go with. The half-day Saturdays are her responsibility."

"You two involved? I hear rumors."

"Really? Not at all. She is living with her aunt, who runs the library. She has her own little cottage in the back on Flagler, a block away from our branch."

"So?"

"Her goal is to transfer here to take over my job, and I will return to Miami. She would follow me to Miami if the bank gives the Key West job to someone else." Enrico thought out loud. "I suppose I could do a turnaround on the same day."

"Call me. We'll work out the details," Doug said. "I have one more delivery, which should erase our losses. You okay with that?"

Enrico nodded yes, and then shook Doug's hand. Next he bowed in Paulette's direction, and then he disappeared.

Paulette wondered what that was all about and was about to ask Doug, except a flurry of activity surrounded the latest guests, who were arriving at the front entrance.

CHAPTER 33

PAULETTE DECIDED TO FOLLOW THOSE going to the pier alongside Higgs Beach to admire Doug's new pencil boat.

"You like her?" Doug was at the entrance. "Naming her Tender Trappings seemed to fit. Wait 'til tomorrow."

"Because?" Paulette asked, always interested in tidbits.

"I'll show you what she can really do tomorrow after the brunch. Here, try these. Best ribs in town." He handed Paulette a full plate from the table set up at the launch. "Add the special sauce if you want to burn your mouth." He laughed out loud. "We have some real down home cookin' here. Pulled pork is big these days, also corn tortes, beans, and rice. Anything your little heart desires … except what you really want, huh? … Right. I'm sorry. Guaranteed, you'll learn how to make your own fun once you jump this first hurdle. Upward and onward!" he said, thrusting his fist into the air.

"I know this much about you," Doug continued. "You are not the kind of person who would intentionally keep an ex-husband from his happiness. Why not take your share of the house money and start a new life?" he asked Paulette.

"The court awarded the Casa to me. At least temporarily."

"Take his offer. Move on," he urged. "All the grief, anger, and brokenheartedness you'll go through is not worth the extra bucks. I speak from wisdom. I wish I had given up on my boys sooner than I did. Even today they're afraid of me because of the poison my ex put into their heads. I've never been that torn up since.

"So many couples say their breakup began at the undertaking of a huge project."

"It wasn't the house," Paulette admitted for the first time to anyone. "We simply fell into the old cliché of marrying too young. We were so close then. Now …"

"Why be so sad? Maybe that's all the time you were supposed to be together." Doug gave her a close hug with an arm around her shoulders. "So he wants to start another family. Are you willing to change diapers?"

Paulette chuckled. "Once was definitely enough!"

"Well, he is."

"Surely, you jest. He won't have to change a single one," Paulette said with emphasis.

"That's none of your business now, is it?" Doug said. "Unless you want to stay in the middle of a situation from which you have been removed. It's over, cous'. Good thing 'cause you're young enough, healthy enough, pretty enough, and in great shape. I mean it. Reinvent yourself. Write a whole new chapter in your life. You may never know when it occurs, but someday he will wake up and realize his mistake. Then you can pity this woman who is stuck with his child."

"And two kids of her own. Too bad; so sad," Paulette said in a sarcastic voice that was so easy to find lately.

"Give it time." Doug repeated: "Time," as he wiped the surprised look off his face.

"Men find another match so easily," Paulette complained.

"Is that really what you want? Hey, where is that upbeat, positive person I knew when we were kids and lived in the same neighborhood all those years ago?"

"What I want is a second PhD. Maybe open a private practice. In the meantime, where did I end up? Working at a gang school and getting so involved in their needs that I felt guilty about my privileged life. Even before the divorce, I gave everything I spent money on a second thought. I recycle and I cut corners all the time."

"You loved those kids, bleeding heart that you are."

"Yeah, well, that's why I see no romances ahead."

"You want to go back to school? Do it! But give the fun of the single life a chance. Other women claim they're happier than they've ever been. Enough!" Doug stopped talking and added, "Let's par-*ty!*"

CHAPTER 34

~∞∞∞~

ALL EIGHT OF THE NEWLY-ARRIVED and very late guests were dressed in white robes. The young women and men made a circle around their leader, a man in his later years who also wore white, his hair wrapped in a turban. His pepper gray beard was waxed and braided tightly to his chin.

As he walked with purpose to the center of the room, the guru's white gown brushed loosely against his body and exposed what looked like black ballet slippers below.

Ziam Elms had entered.

Doug moved closer to his wife and brought Paulette along with him. As the last of the group came up the front steps, someone whispered in a reverential tone, "That's the great Ziam."

"Everyone, please meet Ziam Elms," Flower announced. "We have offered him a center here in Key West. So far he has declined. He believes yoga masters are plentiful in this area. Maybe we can convince him otherwise."

Flower turned to Paulette. "He is my master teacher," she said worshipfully. "He is from India and is making the rounds in the States before he heads for Europe."

Doug grinned and said to the guest standing next to him: "Flower convinced Ziam to visit the center I support on Roosevelt. Costs me a pretty penny. So what? If it keeps my wife happy, so be it."

"Miss Flower, be well." The guru bent low. "Remember that each day is a new arising, a new beginning. On the yearly celebration of your birth, the sun rises to greet you, to kiss your lips, and to surround you with special gifts beyond your imagination: of joy, good health, and happiness."

Flower bent low as well, replying, "The same to you, dear friend. The hotel is to your liking?"

"Why, yes. It was not necessary to offer my staff such superior lodgings. The accommodations go well beyond our expectations."

Ziam hesitated and stared directly at Paulette, who was casually observing the group until his energy drew her attention directly to him. The guru's eyes were tired eyes—wise eyes. They were very dark brown with yellow lines in his irises. As Ziam continued to search Paulette's face, he made her feel self-conscious. Yet she held her own against an intriguingly fierce force emanating from his very presence. Finally, she looked at the creases surrounding his eyes and saw kindness and the lure of mysticism.

"This is my cousin. Actually Doug's cousin," Flower said nervously as she pulled at her wedding ring and ran it around her finger. "She's in for a visit from LA."

"Most pleasant greetings." The guru placed his hands in the prayer position and bent slightly in Paulette's direction. As he did so, it was as if he could see inside of her.

Paulette did the same.

Ziam eased slightly forward and gently touched the tip of Paulette's shoulder. "Tell me, what is your purpose here? It does not seem a happy one. Your aura is orange but it should be yellow."

"Sir, I have no idea," Paulette said, embarrassed and chuckling nervously.

"Oh, not 'sir.' Others speak to me in such a manner."

Paulette looked to the young girls standing in attendance at his sides before she replied. "I am here as a woman seeking truth—at the very least, my own truth. In our country the woman is overshadowed first by her parents, then by her husband, and last by her children. When none of these people are supportive or any longer around, a woman is forced to look elsewhere to offer what she has to give. Searching inside myself seems as good a place as any for me to start."

"In my country, this is never the case. We all work together as one."

"How many children do you have in your household?"

"Three well-educated sons. Two are Fulbright scholarship graduates in engineering. They have traveled extensively throughout the world as ambassadors of good will for our country."

The guru continued, "Thanks be to our hostess, we are here for several more sessions. Are you able to make an appointment to see me at the center before we depart? There are many books, music—ways to assist you on your journey."

"I'll talk to Flower. See when she's going."

The guru paused. Seeing this as a signal that their conversation was at an end, his group closed in on him. He waved them away. Slowly and respectfully, they returned to their former open-ended semicircle.

"You are a very old soul. Many lifetimes, much wisdom," Ziam observed as he went back into his deep, thoughtful state by rubbing his chin and looking into the distance. "It is time you widened your vistas by sharing your knowledge and displaying the goodness within your heart center for the benefit of all mankind."

"She sure will," Flower said, coming forward and wrapping an arm around Paulette's shoulder. "Won't you, dear heart? This is a teacher to the young, and she has been for years," Flower proudly told her master teacher. "Come. There are so many more for us to meet."

"After you resolve certain aspects of your life, we shall meet again," Ziam said to Paulette as he bowed low. "Soon we must retire for prayer."

This signal his circle understood. As his followers enclosed their leader, they retreated into the night.

CHAPTER 35

DOUG RETURNED TO HIS PARTY after dropping Paulette at her rental apartment. The alleyways were of concern. Kids and vagrants stayed in the high bushes and engaged in dangerous antics and worse to those apartments with front and rear doors.

At midnight the police arrived. Flower had previously excused herself and was preparing for bed while ten or so guests were scattered about the premises.

Two officers, fully suited and carrying weapons, headed for Doug, who was seated at the bar. One of the officers thrust a warrant at Doug as he opened his mouth to ask for one. A local judge had been awakened earlier for his signature on a search warrant, not only for the house, but for Mitchell's new bullet boat.

The tip came from an anonymous caller who reported that Doug Mitchell had an unregistered gun in the house. There was more.

The caller said: "If you look around, you'll find kilos of drugs in the front closet under the staircase in the living room. Several kilos are also stored in the hull of that new boat of his. I hear tell he and his partners are taking off at 2 a.m. The goods go to his cartel in Islamorada, at the east side of the small air strip."

"Against the wall," one of the officers said to Doug, forcing him to turn around and put his forehead on the wall. To the second officer, he said: "Check the kitchen staff and anyone around. Frisk 'em."

"What's this all about?" Doug struggled to turn around. "This is my home. What are you doing here?"

"Read the warrant," the officer in charge urged.

Doug figured he must have been under surveillance for months. Tonight of all nights for them to show up.

The two officers tore the front hall closet apart. One of them looked inside an unmarked box under a box of canned tomatoes. It was filled with little white plastic bags.

The officer phoned downtown. "Nothing on the boat," he told the captain. "We found packets in the closet. The rest of the house is clean."

Doug watched as three big evidence bags were taken from his home. Within minutes of removing the bags, one of the officers said, "Take 'em downtown. Book 'em for possession and trafficking."

"How …? Who signed the warrant? Sons of bitches, you cannot do this," Doug yelled at the two officers who stood waiting, their hands on their hips, their holsters showing gun handles in full view.

"Watch me," the officer said as he twisted Doug's arm around until his wrists were held close together and plastic stripping put on them.

Doug kept wrestling and resisting. He thought this could not be happening now. Three years of clear sailing, and suddenly on this primo night of celebration, the cops come out of nowhere to take him away—and in front of his guests?

The officers gathered in the kitchen. One of the policemen took a shrimp off the platter.

"Don't you put that in your mouth!" Doug shouted. "That is private property, and you have no rights here. You are not a guest!"

One look from the boss, and the young cop dropped the shrimp.

"You've got to be kidding," said the one guest remaining at the bar, who was requested to accompany his host to the downtown station. It was banker Enrico Armando, there to enjoy his last drink before leaving. Apprehensive about the goings-on, he did not know whether to continue talking or fade into the background and slip out the back way. No such luck. The police did not cuff him, but neither did they set him free.

"Call my lawyer!" Doug yelled up to Flower, who was undressing in their bedroom, the door ajar. "And bring the checkbook."

CHAPTER 36

IT WAS NEARLY 4 A.M., AND Ariel could not sit still.

She called Jose's cell phone to cancel the trip. In two hours, Max was expected to take the two Cubans back to the Garrison with Ariel on board as well. The pressure was too much, the timing too close.

Jose's cell rang and rang. He must have stopped for gas. She would try again in five minutes. Now the line was busy. Who was he talking to? He was not contacting her mother, was he? Stupid idea. He didn't even know her mother was at a workshop.

"Hi, Jose, it's Ariel," she said to the message machine. "If you haven't left yet, don't come. See you in class on Monday. Everything is fine. I can handle this. Thanks."

Even though she'd left word, she knew to wait at the motel. If Jose did not see her out front, he'd come knocking on the motel room door for sure. Jose was like that. How would he know which room? She'd been dumb enough to tell him.

Slowly, she dragged her bag out of the shrubs and went to sit closer to the entranceway so no one would hear him pull up on the Florida pea rocks chipped from coral and covering the driveway.

He had better hurry. It was nearly 5 a.m., and they would be cutting it close.

If Jose listened to her message and turned around, she would walk to the bus stop, end up in Miami, and have that abortion.

She learned about the steps of an abortion in a nursing preparatory class. Yes, she could do it because, if she was alone, taking on a baby would not make any sense. She had things to do, places to go.

On the other hand, if Jose came around and fit into her plan B, everything would eventually work itself out. They would have sex, and within a reasonable amount of time she would announce her pregnancy. He would never trace the dates. He just was not that kinda guy.

At 5 a.m., exactly one hour after her call, Jose pulled up to the motel's No Vacancy sign. Ariel came running out from the darkness created by the overhangs of the wide turquoise-colored eaves. Projecting cool and casual while shaking all over, her body as cold as ice against the warm air of early morning, she walked slowly and hesitated in front of the lights of Jose's car.

He rolled down the window. "I got your message. How'd you get all the way up here?" he asked.

"You got here mighty fast," she replied. "Lucky there were no cops around at this hour."

"Your mother is going to fry your ass," Jose said, sighing, looking straight ahead as Ariel closed the passenger door.

He was sure that if Ariel could see his face, she could read his mind. How he wanted to touch her, make love to her, possess her. But this was Ariel, his childhood friend, his best friend that he wanted to seduce. Jose turned the wheel for a U-turn back to Key West.

"Wanna go to South Beach? Rent a really nice room overlooking the ocean? Go in the water? Eat in one of those fancy outside cafes?"

"Are you crazy?" Jose replied. "I'm taking you home where you belong. What about your mother?"

"She's in Miami for the weekend, 'til Tuesday some time, I think. Didn't I tell you? Please don't ask me anything else." Her voice was soft and whimpering, her shoulders bent.

Jose calmed down. "Who's paying? You?"

When Ariel nodded, he whistled until he was out of breath. "What rich sugar daddy gave you that kind of dough?"

"For your information, I have money of my own, and I can spend it any way I want."

"I told you to stay away from that old man. He wants you in the worst way that only a rich, old man can afford, and Max is far from rich."

"I did it as a favor. He said he didn't want to make the trip alone," Ariel explained.

"Then go back with him!" Jose spouted angrily.

Ariel reached over and turned the radio up loud. "I did not sleep with anyone, if that's what you're implying," she said haughtily.

Jose continued to stare into the distance.

"There was this kid on board pushing himself against me. He tried to lock me in his bedroom. He's going back to Garrison with Max. I didn't want to deal with that either."

"And Max stood by? I don't believe you," Jose said, shaking his head. "Why didn't you call me? Right then. From the boat."

"I tried. There was no reception out there. At least not on my cheap phone. I don't have an iPhone like you. Besides, Max was in the captain's seat. He can't hear nothing going on below."

"Why didn't you tell him? I can't believe Max wouldn't jump in to protect you. You sure? … Bastard." Jose lit a cigarette as the anger rose up to his neck.

Max was Jose's idol, an image he carried since early childhood. Max always did the right and honorable thing. Sure, he kidded around about women like all the old men his age did, but he certainly was of the highest moral character. He wouldn't harm Ariel, and he wouldn't allow anyone else to, either.

"He was already nervous about the trip."

"Why?"

"How would I know?"

"And you went for what reason?"

"The ride. To get outta Key West. I've done it plenty of times." Ariel sighed heavily. She was exhausted and tired of the quiz going on with Jose.

"Sure, when we were twelve. We're eighteen now. It's too dangerous."

"Since when are you responsible for me?"

"Since the moment I met you."

"Oh, Jose, how sweet."

"Don't do that. Don't you ever do that again!"

"What?" Ariel asked in pure innocence.

"Patronize me."

"I … I'm sorry," she stammered. She changed the subject, gulping before she continued. "Do we need gas?"

"Not yet. Why? You got money?"

"Yes, and plenty for a motel room in South Beach, too. Let's have some fun. Forget … things," she said, her voice filled with the type of female wile no man could resist.

Jose mellowed but still had questions. "Where did you get that kind of stash? Not from Max, I hope."

"Yes, Max. He paid me in cash."

"None of this makes any sense," Jose admitted.

Watching his facial muscles tighten into a solid bulge at the jaw line, Ariel became afraid. The dimmed lights on the dashboard provided enough light to see an outline of his face: the pointed Adam's apple everyone made fun of at school, his slightly overlapping front tooth, and his handsomeness. Yes, if she went ahead with her plan, she had made the right choice.

"Who gives a rat's ass where I am?" Jose said with a harrumph. "I live alone most of the time. Have for a long time. If it wasn't for Max and his family—now I don't know what to think."

Ariel attempted to loosen Jose's tight grip on her hand, which should have been on the steering wheel. "Jose," she said softly. "Let it go. Now … do you need gas or not?"

"I can't. Not something this monumental … Gas?"

Ariel reached over and turned the radio off. "Most of what is in my pocket is my own cash. From work. Savings," she lied to him. "So no worries. Okay?"

"What about your mother?"

"I told you. She's miles from South Beach. Anyway, she hates the beach."

Jose could not rid himself of wandering questions: the type from his own situation that turned into major trouble in his not-too-distant past.

He looked sideways at Ariel and wondered what made her so tense back there, what nerve he had touched. Questions he could let go of, but the Max thing would linger until it was resolved.

Chapter 37

Ariel signed her mother's name to the credit card. When they checked out, she would pay in cash, and the charge would go away.

The doorman unpacked the car. They were escorted to a room at the end of a private walkway of the Omni Hotel, a line of small palm trees lit by sets of multicolored LEDs leading the way. In front of them were several pools, one an infinity pool, another with a fountain in the center. Colored lights surrounded palm trees. Lush green bushes and in-season flowering plants were at the entrance to the pool suites.

Jose whispered to Ariel, "This place is expensive ... *real* expensive, and we're hardly dressed for it. Have you been to places like this before?" he asked, looking around, wide-eyed.

"No, but isn't this fun?"

After changing clothes, they were ready for a late afternoon luncheon out on the terrace of the hotel.

"You look fabulous and so do I," Jose joked. "You sure know how to pick 'em," he said with a whistle. "You're payin', right?"

As the waiter seated them at one of the big windows facing the ocean, Ariel winked. "I got this covered," and added, "I'm starving."

After being seated, Ariel excused herself to the bathroom where she took out three one hundred dollar bills from inside her bra.

If she wasn't totally worried, she could enjoy all of this. However, in her suitcase in the hotel room, in full sight, was Max's thirty thousand dollars, tucked into a Kotex bag. *Lame move*, she thought. What if the maid came in to turn down the covers and boom!—there was this wad of money facing her? Even so, she dared not rush into the room without raising more questions.

The light meal out in the fresh air gave Ariel the breather she needed to take all of this in.

Ariel was nauseous—not because of the fetus growing inside of her, but from the cold, hard reality of how many lives would be changed by her decision to keep her baby.

Upon paying for the meal in cash and showing him the receipt, Jose was in shock. Recovering, he said, "You're something else."

Taking Jose's hand as they walked the pathway from the dining room directly to their front door, she veered him to the pool. "Let's put our feet in. You first?"

God, I want to throw up, she thought, the words rushing out like a flash of light from her toes to her stomach and up to the middle of her forehead, giving her a brain freeze.

Chapter 38

Strolling past several wading pools filled with guests and swirling salt water, they kept going until they found one that was not occupied. "You comin' in?" She began covering her legs with the warm water as she looked up at him and splashed his shoes.

"Bad sport," she said as she kept splashing and he kept dodging the water.

"I am not!" he said adamantly. "Come to the room. I'll show you what a bad sport I am." His body's pulse and motion became less rigid and friendlier.

Ariel liked the change in his voice, his tone, the relaxation of his body. "Mmm," she said, smiling up at him from her position on the pool coping at ground level.

"So you wanna go to the room?"

She offered Jose her hand and he helped her out of the shallow pool. They walked closely together to the room, hands touching breasts, hips and belt buckles.

"Isn't this terrific?" Ariel asked as she bounced on the king-size bed. "We can see the ocean and everything! How about a big dinner tonight at one of those fancy patio restaurants across from Muscle Beach?"

"You know about that stuff?"

"Some … You think they'll ask for our IDs if we order wine?"

"No wine for me. I'm on probation, remember?"

"Who is going to catch you way up here?" she asked.

The linens smelled so sweet, like gentle lilac. These sensual sensations distracted Ariel and caused her to lose her trend of thought and control over her emotions. The sheets were crisp and clean, not at all like the ones at the motel with Max where they were clean but cheap.

Here, the room was obviously Zen centered. The bed rested away from the wall and was closer to the center of the room. Covered in one hundred percent pure white Egyptian sheets with so many pillows, she felt like a queen.

She scooted back against the all-white linen spread to the headboard as the ocean breezes danced through the curtains. The loveliness of the flowers and the smell of Jose's body nearly melted her final reserve.

Ariel longed to excuse herself to the bathroom, scoop down, move the clothes around, and hide the money she had left uncovered. But she could not.

Her surprising and sudden desire for Jose frightened her.

"Come here," she said ever so gently, her money's safety fading away. "Let me hold you. Come and cup my breasts and then kiss me," she whispered. As she spoke these words, she kept offering up her body until he began to respond.

When Jose moved his hands slowly and sexily all over her body, Ariel's mood changed. She forgot herself and her pretense and responded to his maleness. She wanted to wait for him and hoped they would experience a sense of flying high together.

Their first time had to be memorable: long and lazy, sensual and fulfilling.

Jose leaned his head on her shoulder, his hands slowly rising up to do what he was told—feel her breasts and enjoy them. No problem there.

CHAPTER 39

~∞∞∞∞~

THE HEAT FROM ARIEL'S FINGERS as she lazily stroked his hair caused Jose to unexpectedly pull away. Obviously, it was his turn to make a move. He placed himself against her thigh. She did not react. The only sign of change was that she had begun to take shorter breaths, the rise and fall of her chest in sharp contrast to the holding of her breath in the beginning.

Ariel slid down, leaving her comfortable spot. She paused long enough to ask, "Are you sure we're ready?"

"Lead the way, babe. Lead the way."

Ariel gently kissed his face. She knew her butterfly kisses were arousing him to the point that soon there would be no turning back. She moved to his neck and, for only a second, ran her lips ever so softly over his shoulder.

Jose's nipples hardened, and as they did, she looked up at him and smiled. He moaned as she held his balls and rotated her hands. She could tell he had not been with anyone lately.

Slowly she rolled to tuck herself under his arm. Soon Jose turned her on her back. Gently, sweetly, and finally forcefully, he held her down until she rose up under him and began rotating her hips.

As Ariel moaned, the sound was one he had never heard before. It momentarily shocked him. The result was to arouse him further.

Once she had satisfied him, it was his turn to do the same for her. "Wait!" she said.

Jose felt the strain of waiting for a second release. As hard as he tried, he could not stop. Tearing at her as if he were climbing a mountain to avoid an attack by a mountain lion, her reaction was to whimper, digging her nails into his back and begging him, "Please, don't. Do not stop!"

Finally spent, they rolled over onto their backs, remaining silent until Ariel breathed out the word: "Wow!"

His outstretched arm gave her the opportunity to nestle her shoulder. Jose was finished. "That was really special, wasn't it?"

She kept his moisture inside. "Don't go. I need you to stay," she whispered, suddenly open and vulnerable.

"I doubt that." His throat was full of phlegm, his brain foggy.

"Come here," she said. He rolled toward her.

"We can't go back, can we? Especially after this," he said with no regret in his voice. "And that's another wow!"

"I do not want to go back to Key West. Not ever."

"That's not what I mean," he said softly, brushing a dampened curl away from her face.

"I always thought that was a woman's line," she said. Catching herself, she chuckled slightly.

"Maybe so, but we should be thinking seriously about our futures, not being here like this."

"Oh no?" she purred. "We both agreed."

"This was, without a doubt, the best sexual experience I've ever had," Jose said with great gusto. "Even surpassing the night Susanna dragged me into the closet and sat on top of me."

Ariel's eyes widened. "I never knew that. You never told me. How old were you?"

"Nine or so. For sure I should not have told you. It just slipped out. Max said women never forget stuff like that. Are you my woman now?" he asked as he held Ariel in place.

She smiled. "If that's how you want it."

At that moment Jose was so handsome with his features softened. Before, when all the girls told her how good-looking he was, she'd say, "Jose?" Now she saw what they saw: smooth, rich, light brown skin, dark hair, dimples, a man's nose and facial features—no longer the boy she once knew.

His body was tight and athletic from playing baseball. In fact, he was so good he could qualify for tryouts in the minor leagues and get out of Key West. Max thought so, too. In fact, he told Jose he would pay for all the expenses if Jose would go to trials following graduation.

The thought made Ariel very sad because now he never would.

CHAPTER 40

PAULETTE WAS READY TO FIND a small market for supplies. She'd been told there were quite a few on Duval.

Her garden apartment included a separate bedroom and bath, kitchen, and dining room. She also had a living room with a full porch—a real luxury for apartment dwellers in Key West. At the back door was a rock-filled alleyway with low-hanging palm trees.

Out of the bushes surrounding her front door jumped Chief of Detectives Allan McKenna.

"I thought we were meeting later," Paulette began. Astonished, she asked, "How did you know I was here? The rental agency told me the paint wouldn't dry until later today," she said as an explanation while forcing an automatic smile in order to hide her annoyance.

"I was sitting on the stoop waiting for some movement," the detective admitted, "only to discover you left the Mitchells' home early last night. The landlord is a contact—a good friend of mine. Thought I could catch you here."

"You want more information on your case, right? Come on in." Paulette pulled out her keys and opened the front door. "There isn't any furniture to speak of. Soon I'll make this a real home."

Settled on a hard, wooden chair opposite the witness, Detective McKenna spread out on a small table. He presented several photos of the Flamingo Terrace Motel, a two-story 1950s motel with outside air-conditioners, a motel in need of major repairs. On the grounds were old, crooked palm trees, bent by numerous hurricanes. Rocks, shells, and pebbles with weeds growing intermittently substituted for a lawn. The pool was closed.

"Yes, that's the motel," Paulette said, grimacing. She thumbed through the photographs.

McKenna held her signed statement in his hand. "We hope you can supply us with some answers. You stated here there were two men. One raced up the southern set of stairs and knocked on the door to room 211. A moment later he came rushing down the other set of stairs at the north side of the building. Waiting in a black Dodge Charger was a second male. He handed the perpetrator what looked like a hammer, which you later discovered was a gun.

"The perpetrator then ran back up the same set of stairs and broke in through the glass sliding doors. A few minutes later you heard two shots. The same man exited the room through the front door, ran down the same set of stairs at the north end of the motel, jumped into the black car with dark windows, and then drove away."

"That's right."

"Those are the exact words from your signed statement," he commented, pulling out a set of photographs.

"So I did. I couldn't see much. I told the officer that. The sun was setting and the car stirred up so much dust."

"It was five o'clock."

"So it was. I've been quite distressed with personal issues lately, so really, I didn't pay close enough attention. All I know is it was damned hot and I wanted out of my courtroom suit. Did you find my purse?"

"Not yet. I'm sorry for your loss, but any time you're in a resort area you must be careful to carry your valuables on your person at all times. I have some photos here. See if you recognize anyone."

"I was standing too far away. On the other side of the street."

"I'm aware of that. Please give these a closer study if you will."

Hesitating, she handed the photos back, saying, "These are computer composites. They're not very clear."

"A matter we're working on. I've been on the job a month. Buying the latest equipment is definitely on my to-do list."

"Where are you from?" Paulette looked up.

"Cincinnati."

"You like it here?"

"I'm settling in."

Paulette smiled. From her limited experience, most cops do not seem to respond openly and directly to personal questions. It was a nice change to hear a detective speak informally.

She flipped through the photos more carefully.

The view of a large man wearing a white Cuban shirt struck her as a possibility. He also wore a straw hat like the man she saw. "Here. He might be one of them. But I couldn't swear to anything. Certainly not in a court of law, if it ever came to that."

"I, or one of my men, will be in touch as new developments arise," he said, getting up. "Coffee some other time?" he said absently as he put his papers in order, waited a moment, and then dashed out the front door.

Chapter 41

Leaving the rest of the glitzy, touristy Duval Street for later, Paulette decided to take Doug and Flower up on their coffee invitation. She walked past the Casa Marina to the back side of the city's tennis courts and onto the small roadway leading to Higgs Beach. She turned left at Flower and Doug's house. Everything on the outside had been cleaned up, including the tennis courts where a bunch of teenagers had burst the balloons and turned over food tables.

Paulette knocked on the front door. No one answered. The door was unlocked, so she went inside. Flower was dressed in a house robe, her hair unbraided and uncombed. She was behind the kitchen counter, pouring coffee into a silver carafe. For a long while she stared at the carafe and did not speak.

"Doug's sound asleep upstairs," Flower said as she put the sugar in between the two cups. "I'm so very glad you came to visit us. Even happier you're staying ... for a while." Flower spoke softly but in a staccato manner. "Whenever you come to visit, could you do me and Doug a huge favor? Call or text one of us first? I mean, what if we were in the middle of something where we needed our privacy? Doug always has some kind of important papers laying about. Stuff even I don't know much about. I wouldn't want him to think ..."

"I ... I'm sorry. I was going to sit outside and wait a while longer for you to get up, but the door was unlocked," Paulette said awkwardly. "I was ... going to visit, pick up a few more of my things. Go my new home. Unpack."

"My point exactly. This morning is very precious to us. Private hours. Could we meet at the Pier House at 2 p.m. as planned? No hard feelings?"

"None taken," Paulette replied, the comfort of her pose in the chair turned into a straight, stiffened walk to the front door. How could her attitude—and maybe Doug's—change so drastically from yesterday, especially after how eager they were to allow her to stay in their home until she found a place?

"Remember. Two o'clock. Wear something casual and Key West looking."

CHAPTER 42

MAX WOKE WITH A START. It was 4:12 a.m., forty-eight minutes before the alarm. He rolled to his side, reaching for Ariel. When he realized she was not there, he snapped to attention and flew out of bed. Checking the room, it was obvious she was gone. No notice? No note? Kids these days.

Maybe she was at the pool. It was too early, and the water was too cold for such a delicate person.

He pulled on his pants and checked his pockets. Two thousand dollars. What happened to the other five thousand?

A second later there was a knock at the door.

Expecting it to be Ariel, Max stood back from the door as the older of the two original passengers stepped inside. "You ready? Gotta go now or we hit sunrise. Too many people hangin' around."

"Give me a minute."

Max slammed the door and called Ariel's cell. It was off.

He left word that he was desperate to know her whereabouts. "Taking off like that isn't right." At the end, he sighed heavily into the small instrument. "When I get home, I'll ask you the hows and whys. Right now, I just need to know you're safe."

He thought about the money missing from his work pants as he fingered the two thousand dollars but could not bring himself to think Ariel took the rest from his pockets when she could have had so much more. Any afternoon after school she could have taken it all.

Was the money why it was so urgent she come along? Otherwise, it made no sense.

Max's reaction was to race to the boat. He worried about his safe. That money took him a lifetime to save, much of which he also realized somewhere along the way he was losing track of. However, he must first think of his customers and get them underway.

An hour into the return trip to Garrison Bight Marina, Max was hungry. "I'm pulling into Bahia Honda," he told them. "Takes less than half an hour. You boys must be hungry."

They nodded, thinking of their plan to disappear before the boss returned to Key West. They had found a guy with a fishing boat who promised to return them to Cuba once they completed their assignment for big brother. They were also holding onto two bags of their boss's money inside a suitcase, stored at a bed and breakfast on Duval Street in a holding closet, with their names on the tag.

The cell phone number they wrote on the tag belonged to the boss. In case anything happened, he would still get his money—unless the boys had time to pick the suitcase up before sailing off to Cuba in a hired speedboat.

Cell phone reception on the water was so bad they were unable to reach their boss. Until they knew when and where they were to be picked up, they would hide out on the west side of Key West, next to the Truman Annex, or get lost in the crowd on Duval Street.

With several miles yet to go before reaching Bahia Honda, Max put the boat on autopilot. Unsteady on his feet, his tongue felt thick, and he was unusually thirsty. Not sure what time it was, whether early morning or early evening, he went to the sideboard, sweat pouring profusely from his scalp and running down his cheeks. His left arm was numb again. This time painful pinpricks were poking out from below the surface of his skin.

Where were those nitroglycerin tablets? In back of the steering wheel is what he remembered.

Unable to climb into the captain's chair, he called to the two young boys, who were whooping it up and slapping each other's knees. They could not hear him.

Even so, he yelled, "Help!"

He could have another heart attack, and if they did not hear him, he was a goner.

The doctor had said never to go on his for-hire boat without capable men on board who had been trained in first aid. He couldn't afford that. So far he hired kids from the high school. He paid them a minimum wage and it worked out.

Ariel was gone. She could have helped. He wondered what happened. She would never have abandoned him like this.

Oh, my God, I am going to die if these boys don't come soon. His headache was not only pounding now, it had taken over his whole brain so that his vision was distorted.

He was on the floor by the steering wheel, and his legs could not move. He struggled, but there was no response. He used his voice. He could not speak. If only he had kept those nitro pills in his shirt like the doctor told him to—a year ago.

"Help!" Max yelled through a throat completely closed.

Slowly pulling himself up from the floor next to the captain's chair where he went to reach for his pills, he was finally at the captain's chair.

One of the boys grabbed Max before he fell again.

"Over here, dude," the boy told his partner. "I think the captain is sick."

"Check his pockets," his brother said. "He put our money in there."

Slowly, reluctantly, he came over to assist in getting the captain back up again.

They dragged Max's retching body to the bench at the far end of the bow of the boat.

"He's sick or somethin'," the other boy confirmed, trying to keep the captain's body steady as the old man gagged and spit up phlegm and stomach water. "Can't we help him?"

"How? I'm not a damned doctor!"

The younger boy took two thousand dollars from the captain's pocket and held it between his fingers. Then he stuffed the bills into his own pocket and asked his brother, "You know how to steer this thing?"

"It's running, but I wouldn't know what's next. You?"

"Hell, I'm seasick. Like the old man—out of control."

They stared at each other in a panic. "Throw him overboard," one of them said. "We swim away. Find downtown and wait 'til night. Go to the hotel's locker room and pick up our suitcase. Get lost in the crowd. We have an additional two thousand dollars in case we have to stay overnight."

Pointing to where early beach walkers were at the calm shoreline searching for shells and driftwood, the older brother yelled, "Turn the key off! Throw it overboard!" He put his head to the captain's chest. "Nothin'. He's a goner."

Meanwhile, his little brother was puking all over the floor and onto the captain's shoes.

"Get the fuck up! We have to throw him overboard before people see us."

Together, they dragged the captain's body to the edge of the boat.

"Wait! The money. Put the money back in his pocket."

"You're fuckin' kidding, right?"

They twisted the body around but could not reach into his pants pocket.

"Stuff it into his damned shirt. Get rid of it! If we're caught, we're dead meat."

"Yuck! There's puke everywhere! You do it!"

The older brother touched the slime and pieces of undigested food like it was nothing and stuffed the hundred-dollar bills into Max's shirt. From the stairs at the side, they tried to drop the body into the water.

One brother held the captain by the armpits as the other grabbed under his knees. When one of the captain's shoes fell off, the younger brother dipped down and threw it overboard.

"Whh-aat? You idiot! Now they have your fingerprints! I can't believe what you just did! Fuckin' idiot!"

They said nothing more as they struggled with the limp body, finally tossing him over the side into the water. The fiberglass flashing ripped the captain's shirt and scraped the boys' arms.

"Guaranteed. He lands face up. Then we're free! We jump overboard ... No. Hands up! Quick! If someone comes aboard, do *not* speak English! Do *not* talk to them unless you have to. And *never* laugh. Got it?"

Following the rising tide, the Ramblin' Rose slowly drifted toward the inlet at Bahia Honda. In unison, they made the sign of the cross, not looking at each again as the boat continued to drift.

Max's body landed face down in the water.

Max felt the sting of wet upon his face. Below there was a cave with a light at the end—so pleasing, so inviting. Did they know him? Sure, it was the light of death from the earth to wherever the light was leading, and he was willing to go. First he must say good-bye, but there was no one around he knew, yet he was not afraid. The water was warm and slowly wrapped him in a blanket. He did not resist. The waves above were filled with sand, and all he wanted to do was lie back down and watch upward. Such a wonderful feeling: His whole body was covered, and he was sinking into the blanket, the warmest he had ever been. Now, now, he was more comfortable and felt freer that he ever had. And he smiled. And he wiggled. And he felt the blanket, but there was no bottom, and it was … wonderful.

Chapter 43

The captain on the glass-bottom boat, making his first run for the day out to White House Reef, radioed to park headquarters.

"In front of us we have a body, face down in the water. There are two people—they look like kids—waving for help. Call it in. Over and out."

Red and blue lights flashed inside and on top of two all-black Dodge Chargers with hemi engines. The hot cars belonged to the Key West Police Department, and they were speeding over the Overseas Highway at ninety miles an hour. Tourists were pulling over to the shoreline allowing them to race past.

Tall Tom Jamison, the first officer on site, signaled to his partner to take a position at the far end of the concrete abutment. At the same time, Tom scrambled up the three-foot sand embankment to reach the Atlantic Ocean, where a fishing boat was stalled approximately a quarter of a mile from shore. On board were two males, their hands in the air.

"I'll call headquarters," Tom hollered to his partner below. "You call the coast guard. Send a diver. Quick! Tell 'em the vic is face down in the water! … Wait! … Wait! … It's … I think it's Maxwell Hernandez's boat! Yes! The Ramblin' Rose! The vic is … he's two hundred yards farther out at the neck of the harbor. Get here quickly!" Tom repeated. "Also notify the tugboat service and book a haul to the Garrison Bight Marina."

Hanging up, Tall Tom said, "Oh, my God, not Max! We … a few nights ago … we went fishing."

After taking a sharp right-hand turn into the entrance of the Bahia Honda State Park, the two police vehicles with Monroe County decals on the sides came screeching to a halt at the end of the concrete boat ramp. Close behind them was a white ambulance belonging to the city of Key West.

A second team of officers arrived. Tom motioned for one of them to go across the walkway of the broken bridge to the other side of the park. The other officer was to crouch forward at bayside, behind the small sand hill, and ask the beachgoers to leave in an orderly fashion.

Meanwhile, beachgoers on the other side of the sandbank who had gathered under the old, broken, and disconnected railroad bridge that, in the days of Henry Flagler, was the main artery into Key West were craning to see the body on the other side of the boat.

Within minutes two divers arrived by patrol boat. Suited up and ready to enter the water, the first diver wet his mask, dove in, and swam against the early morning tide. Ready to administer CPR, he turned the lifeless body over from its face-down position and checked the victim's pulse.

"No pulse," he yelled to his supervisor.

"Is there a heartbeat?"

"Nope."

"Try CPR anyway," the senior diver yelled back.

Holding the victim's body as still as possible, he placed a breathing apparatus on the victim's chest. The next step was to thrust a long blue tube down his throat. A minute later the diver pulled his mask off, shaking his head. "No need for the tube," he shouted. "It's a DOA."

The senior diver swirled the boat closer to the scene. Before jumping in, he asked, "No go, huh?"

"No, sir. No chance."

Taking the gear away from the victim's face, the diver hooked the crook of his arm around the man's neck and began frog kicking toward the landing dock. Dragging the lifeless body to safety, the weight felt like two thousand pounds of concrete.

Dread always comes with a dead pull. Rescue, resuscitation, and timing are basic skills required of the job. The real victory over death was accomplished when the vic was released from the hospital and went home to family.

As the body was dragged from the water, Tom ran around the docking area yelling, "I know that man! I know him!" Moving to where the lifeless body was stretched out on the concrete, he told everyone within earshot, "This is Captain Maxwell Hernandez, a great man … We … I just saw him. We fished. Talked …"

"Hey, Tom, could you help us here? Put up the tape?" one of the divers asked as the crowd began to close in on the crime scene.

"Oh! Sorry. This man was … everything to me when I was a kid. He took me in. I lived with them through high school. He was my baseball coach …"

Notifying the family would come next. Even though the possibility of seeing Max's youngest daughter Susanna gave Tom a rise, he definitely did not want to break the news to Rosetta, Max's wife of forty-plus years.

Tom had been in love with Susanna ever since tenth grade when he first became a full-time member of the family. But she was determined to marry into money. Recently divorced from the son of a reported drug lord, no ordinary cop's life and salary would satisfy her even though they were raised in the same household and graduated from Key West High School the same year.

CHAPTER 44

RETIRING CAPTAIN HAUSER GAVE HIS last word of advice as his new replacement prepared to leave for the Bahia Honda site.

The new captain, Allan McKenna, was the most outstanding candidate for his replacement. He was new. He did not know the politics of the town. Maybe he could clean the place up. Like most cops, his private life was a mess. Having had two divorces and two sons somewhere along the line, the new captain was by himself and adamant during the interviewing process that he was up to the task. "Looks like what I did for Culver City. Just talk to them down there."

"We did, and the job is yours," Hauser was pleased to say.

On this, one of McKenna's first assignments without Hauser behind him to give him the skinny and specific direction, Hauser said from his squeaky chair, "You gotta make this one look like a serious arrest, a top priority. The town's been ripe for an outbreak for more than a year. Certain forces have been holding them back. One of my reasons for hiring a young fellow like you to head the department is that you run faster than I do. Maybe the vic is Captain Hernandez like Tall Tom says. Maybe not. Be prepared either way.

"And whatever you do, keep the details away from the damned reporters. Those bloodsuckers pretend to be your best buddy. Once your case ain't newsworthy, they don't know your name 'til the next time. Cases like this? Could be some rich guy comes into port and can't steer his boat worth a damn. Meanwhile, down below he has his hidden treasure who needs a way to escape. Makes 'em scared shitless to call for help."

McKenna shot Hauser a quizzical look.

"In case you don't know," Hauser said and paused, "the story's an old one. A hidden treasure is someone those guys don't want found. I'm talkin' about women inside their big boats and keeping them out of sight when the family comes around. In private we call 'em free agents. Or boat babes. You might see BB in a few of the files somewhere in initials at the bottom. It certainly ain't Bridgett Bardot." He released a belly laugh that flushed his face.

"On the other hand, it could be Captain Maxy, and that would be a different story."

Hauser's look from across the desk sprouted an implication that his new recruit might have more learning ahead than he could handle about how this city's crime world operates.

Allan McKenna recognized the tone. The old man may not have noticed, but Allan had plenty of experience along with a quick instinct about any new place he went to, if not in Key West yet, then soon … soon.

At twenty-two, McKenna was one of the youngest graduates from the academy. His first assignment was in a squad car, working the streets of downtown LA, patrolling Culver City, located near LAX, and then the area south of Beverly Hills. Most deaths out on the water, whether accidental or with intent, never hit the news unless the incident involved residents from Beverly Hills, Bel-Air, Brentwood, or some other rich neighborhood. Then floodlights, cameras, and reporters came out of the woodwork.

When McKenna left LA for Cincinnati, the area was cleaning out the gangs, drunks, and everyday homeless who survived in the empty factories being turned into highly sought-after lofts.

He had learned as an observer of Key West's more visible people that it was a place where quirky people lived in a happily insane place. Key West was a playground for adults who happened to love sun, fun, the water, and never having to grow up. Therefore, keeping law and order on nature's playground had its own set of rules.

"So this sea captain is well-known?" Allan asked Hauser on the way out.

"Yep. Once a close buddy of mine."

"Once?"

There seemed to be no response coming until Hauser finally said, "You'll hear it sooner or later, I suppose. At one time we were best friends. We parted ways under difficult terms never to be resolved. And that's all I have to say on that matter."

CHAPTER 45

TALL TOM JAMISON WAS ON the line to Captain McKenna. "We need a haul for the Ramblin' Rose to Garrison. Unless we find a key."

"There's no key on board? You checked the entire boat? Secret hiding spaces and such?"

"Yep. Nothing." The cops standing by agreed.

"The victim may have had it in his pocket. Not any longer, sir."

"Give me five minutes," McKenna said.

Arriving and assessing the situation, McKenna went aboard the Ramblin' Rose, trusting the officers on site to continue at the site where the body was brought out of the water.

McKenna motioned to officers inside the second car that had arrived on the scene. "Come with me," he said. "Grill the boys again. They say they don't speak English. I don't believe it for a minute. Wait here. Handcuff them and I'll go below."

On the way he said to the two suspects, "Last chance to see daylight. Did either of you two boys take the key to the ignition?"

The pair shrugged their shoulders and grinned. "Key? What key?"

"To start the engine on this goddamned boat, a-holes."

"Hold them here. Take them to headquarters when we're finished."

Below, McKenna quickly looked around, storing a mental picture. The usual boat parts, spare oil cans, and various pieces of fishing gear overcrowded the small space. Boxes of aged records lined the hall, their bottoms water stained. Thrown on the bunks were dirty clothes and new rags mixed with oil-stained ones.

He opened a rusty cabinet full of clean, unused clothes. Cleaners for the fishing gear and other supplies rested on the bottom shelf. Nothing odd or unusual.

On a wall to the right was a safe at eye level. *Not a good idea*, he thought. *In plain sight is downright crazy and careless.*

The victim's safe was protected by a side key and a combination lock in the center of the safe. It was a cheaper model and recently installed. McKenna thought that drug runners work differently: Cleaner. Bigger.

On the floor was a key ring with two matching keys attached. Putting on gloves and testing the keys, he found one released the extra lock on the safe, which was not locked, and the other was a duplicate.

"Get Tom to see the daughter who lives at home. Give her permission to go behind the line and enter the safe to check its contents, nothing more," he wrote on his pad.

Back on the deck, McKenna checked with one of the officers who stood at the land base observing the divers.

"We have a shoe, but that's about it. We bagged it into evidence."

"No key?"

"Not in his shirt pockets or his pants. Found a few thousand dollars inside his shirt. Anything else we find will be on the evidence sheet as well."

"Make certain the area is blocked off ASAP. No one, including the family, comes aboard. No one," McKenna emphasized. "We're already in corruption mode."

Returning to the docking area, McKenna said to the two officers standing by: "The death of the old fisherman? There's a real possibility he wanted to have it over in a spot he loved best. If that's true, all this drama and expense is a waste of taxpayers' money."

"Accidents happen, yes sir. But not to this guy. He was a big shot in the fishing industry for a lotta years," Leon "Scooter" Lyle informed his new boss. "Ole Max was past his prime but with a reputation that sparkled. In the good ole days, the captain had a fleet of three or four large fishing vessels. I hear tell his family was responsible for bringing in the priest over at St. Mark's. Five kids and a whole bunch of grandkids. Some local kids with no family. A sports coach, scoutmaster."

McKenna had seen it all before at Marina del Rey in LA—suicides and murders made to appear accidental; heart attacks and strokes—all resulting in the victim falling overboard. If the vic was famous, elaborate details were in the *LA Times*. Otherwise, the body was added to a statistical list and forgotten.

The big deal here in Key West was that because it was a small town, local criminal acts were discussed and their cases resolved by those willing to accept secondhand information as gospel when in truth the actual parties involved were the only ones who knew the situation. Too often even they were not sure of what they witnessed.

"How did this happen?" McKenna asked as he got into the face of the older of the two boys.

"We know nada dis, man," the older one responded as his younger companion eagerly nodded his head in agreement. "No speaka de English," he explained. "Nada. Nothin'."

"So I heard. Yeah, yeah. What wonderful accents. Did you check their paperwork?" McKenna asked the officers as he turned away to answer his cell phone.

When his new boss finished, Scooter commented, "They may be illegals. Probably brothers. They have no passports, no driver's licenses. A few bucks in their pockets. Little doubt they were entering Key West illegally. Or reentering."

Looking at each other, the possible suspects began to laugh.

"What's so damned funny?" Scooter jumped in front of McKenna, ready to strike with force. His deepest desire was to throw them overboard with an "Oops!" and never look back. And he was the man to do it. A man on probation with the department because of excessive violence, he was five feet eleven, 210 pounds of muscle, with quick response. To gain control of his erupting temper, whenever he ran into idiots like these two, Scooter kept the remarks coming, which stopped the impulse to smack them from the start. "Smart like little foxes, aren't you boys?"

They both shrugged, wide grins glued to their faces. "See, we got this uncle. His son, Hernandez, Dennis? He's our cousin. Our uncle was buried in town. Call our Miami lawyer. He says we's in our uncle's will. Told us he owned property on Roosevelt Boulevard. We have rights."

"How long ago did this uncle of yours die?"

"Last month," one brother said while the other one jumped in: "Last year."

"Yeah, just like every family. Where there's a will, there's always family." McKenna spoke from experience.

The others present stifled their chuckles. Meanwhile, the thought that either one of these lowlifes had any of Max's blood running through their veins was a threat to their sensibilities. They may not have been the receiver of any of the sea captain's kindnesses like those who knew him better, but this type of irony, should it be true, was just plain mean.

"We's no relations to the captain here," the boys shook their heads in agreement.

"Thank God," McKenna heard in the background. One of the officers began: "You have the right to an attorney. You may call one once we are back at the station. And that's the end of the story for you two boys. Your rights have been read. Now let's vamoose."

"Wait! No jail!" The next words volunteered were spoken as clearly as any born and bred English speaker: "He jumped. Just like that. Boom!"

"Now you speak up … How long ago?" McKenna asked.

"Coupla hours," the older boy replied with a disinterested shrug.

"And neither one of you went in after him?"

"We don't swim," the leader said, the other one nodding in agreement.

"Not even when a man's life is at stake?"

"We know him? The lawyer say jump, we jump. The lawyer say call 911, we call 911. First, we gotta know our rights."

"Know this. If the deceased did not die of natural causes, you will both end up facing murder charges and long trials attached to many, many years in jail," McKenna threatened. "What time did you leave Islamorada?"

After a nod from his older brother, the younger boy told McKenna, "We drifted for hours. We're tellin' ya he jumped. Just like that," he snapped his fingers.

"What time did you leave Islamorada?" he asked again.

"Six? Okay, maybe six."

"Don't you remember? We left early when the captain came banging on the door. Said the girl was gone. Did we see her?"

"Girl? What girl?" McKenna asked.

"Maybe his daughter."

"Dressed like a honey bun, no way," the curly-haired younger boy hissed.

"When did she come on board?"

"She was already there. She knew her way around, I can tell ya. Once he started the engine, she took over, steered for hours."

"Did you catch her name?"

"Allyson, Alexandra? Wants to be a nurse."

"You learned all of that and you can't remember her name?"

"Might be pregnant." The curly-haired boy took a giant step forward, wishing instantly he could pull back.

"What happened to your arms? The scratches, those bruises?"

"That? We tried to fish," they chuckled as they jostled each other.

"Have the doc check them out. Take samples. Then we have DNA. Call Tom back. Ask him to write out a request to open files. Officer Thomas Jamison is to follow through with me on this one. Are we done here?" McKenna asked Scooter and Ted Drew, Scooter's partner.

"All clear, sir."

"You got us wrong. We come to America through channels. Here with money to spread peace and love. No jail! No jail! We have connections!"

"Key West definitely does not need any more of that! Book 'em," McKenna said, not heeding their pleas. "Let legal do their job. Discover who these characters are, how they got here, and what their business in Key West was all about."

McKenna nodded for the officers to take the suspects downtown for booking. "Give 'em their one call and keep 'em locked up until someone comes to rescue 'em. When you're done here, call Islamorada and tell them to be on the lookout. Either way, if their connections are solid, they'll be bailed out before the ink dries. The most they might have to stay is overnight."

McKenna may not have known all the ins and outs of the underground in the town yet, but here's what he did know: If bail was posted within hours of incarceration, the suspects are more than likely supported by a professional drug ring, probably out of Islamorada, where the majority of Columbian contraband leaders traffic.

"If these kids are part of a drug ring," Scooter volunteered, "the bigger operators set up chop shops on the outer islands. Maybe that's where they were headed. Got sidetracked by the captain, who pulled a strange one."

"Sure, and then they repackage the kilos and cut them into small packets. The goods are then taken to Miami, either by plane or boat, where their docking space is rented from private citizens," Drew piped in. "Ordinary cars head for another Miami location where workers mark the packages and send them to prearranged locations."

"Sounds well organized to me," McKenna commented.

"Hey, it's been going on for years. *Years*," Scooter said.

"You know what to do?" McKenna looked from one officer to the other. "Good. See you in town."

Upon returning to the shore, they sent the body of Captain Maxwell Hernandez to the morgue. "Is the CSI team on the way?" the new captain asked?

"We should have answers by tomorrow," their new boss replied.

Gently, one of the officers at shore told his superior: "This isn't LA, sir. Harry Vernon processes fingerprints and reviews photos from the scene within forty-eight hours, if he can. Depends on how many cases he has. An autopsy around here takes at least seventy-two hours."

"So this is it then?" McKenna said under his breath. Meanwhile, his suspicions were based on little proof that the victim was pushed overboard. If the victim voluntarily jumped off his own boat, he was hoping his team would uncover further clues and answer the question: Why would a successful, well-respected fisherman do such a thing?

A man works hard, long hours, raises a family, becomes an outstanding citizen in his community, and all he has to show for it is a small, falling-apart fishing boat—his body floating out at sea, his face down in the water, dead. And no one gives a damn about rescuing him.

"Sorry, sir," Harry Vernon said, interrupting McKenna's train of thought. "The boat has been fingerprinted and samples sent to the lab," he reported to the chief.

"That was quick. Thank you for coming in. See you Monday," McKenna said. That was the signal Vernon had his boss's permission to race back to his reverie among the mangroves.

McKenna understood only too well how so many drinkers began their journey as functioning alcoholics with good jobs and bright futures, hoping to share their potential with family and friends. Harry was aging more quickly than most and swore he would be dead by now if, a few years ago, he hadn't "become a friend of Bill's" (the signal in AA that locates another alcoholic on his road to recovery).

Vernon's kidneys could not filter out his liquor fast enough, so his kidneys were shot. And there was no promise of a replacement for either of his gray and withering pair. Not now and not in the future. He was beyond the age limit for any such list.

Harry Vernon was walking down his final road. The divorce and leaving two teenage daughters behind was a far easier ride in Key West than in Boston.

CHAPTER 46

LEON "SCOOTER" LYLE AND HIS partner Ted Drew were on the front deck of the Ramblin' Rose. Scooter was walking up and down and threatening the two suspects tied to the wire. "I'm tellin' you right here and now the man you boys killed—the victim? He was a member of this community, Key West, you hear? Which means I will personally see you both rot in jail forever if either one of youse did this."

"Hey, Scooter, let up," Ted Drew said. Drew's caution came from the fact that he was aware of his partner Scooter's unnecessary roughness. Scooter was currently on probation after spending six months cleaning up at a drug rehab facility. He had returned to the job only two weeks ago.

Drew, on the other hand, never took a drop of alcohol. A family man and churchgoer, his wife expected their third baby. Unlike his partner, Drew did not go out beyond the department's requirements and never used force unless absolutely necessary. A smaller man, he knew his power and his place within his role as a cop. This was his first time off the track, and to be honest, he was frightened to death of being caught, but the thrill of doing his first illegal act was one of the most exciting things he'd ever experienced.

"One of 'em speaks no English. The other you've got ready to shit in his pants," Drew said. "Besides, down there"—he glanced at the entryway leading to the cabin below—"we have work to do when the head honcho vacates the premises."

Scooter gave a salute and backed away. "Turn to the side," he ordered the suspects, checking the two plastic strips. On each boy, he tightened the strips and cut off the excess with a pocket knife.

When the coast was clear, Scooter and Drew went below to the safe. Scooter turned the key to the left and listened for a click. On his third twirl to the right there was no click. After two more attempts, Scooter figured he'd have to send Drew for a torch in the trunk of Scooter's car parked at the station. Which was not very smart. If anything was missing, they would be the first ones to be called in, and an investigation would ensue. And cops never go easy on their own. They both knew McKenna had been below and without a doubt would remember that the safe was in perfect condition.

Scooter said, "Get the kit. Make sure the sensor is there. Click, click, click."

From the looks of the door to the safe, the mechanical dial lock at the center of the door was still in use instead of the more current digital dials. However, the center handle had been recently disengaged, and whoever did it opened the safe. Also, there were fingerprints everywhere, lifted by both Harry and Scooter.

Drew returned with a stethoscope.

"What the hell. This isn't a trick to cheat me, is it?" Scooter asked, hot tempered enough to take over.

"This is the best I can do for now. But lookie here." Drew took out a small chip the size of the ones inserted into cell phones. "Listen to the sound through the stethoscope. If it works, we're in!" Twirling the dial three turns, Drew waited for the click.

Nothing.

Stopping as the dial went around once again, he said to Scooter, "Holy crap! The combination must be digitized by the guy."

"Which means?"

"He kept the original door on for appearances. Damned smart—or neurotic for a wreck like this."

Pushing Drew aside, Scooter loosened his fingers, cracked his knuckles, and put the stethoscope up to the lock for the first click. "Those new gadgets can't match a good set of ears," Scooter bragged. "I can't hear the TV, but let me listen to music and I'm there! Pop!"

The third turn and he was in.

Scooter opened the first envelope. Inside were hundred-dollar bills, maybe twenty, thirty thousand dollars worth. He made a quick count of how many, and if the money was approximately the same in each one he opened, he had his hands on close to six hundred thousand smackaroos!

Whistling, Scooter told his partner, "Let's get outta here," as he stuffed ten of the envelopes inside his shirt.

"What's in there?" Drew asked.

"Close to a hundred grand," Scooter told his partner. "Let's get outta here."

"Gimme one of 'em!"

"Trust, man. Do you trust me?" Scooter waited. With no response, he explained, "We'll meet up later and split the cash. 'Til then we'll stick it in the usual spot. I'll burn the envelopes and we're home free. Talk tonight, partner," he winked.

"Deal! Fifty thousand? Wow! I'm retirin', and that's a fact." Drew laughed with excitement as he began jumping around.

"Not so fast," Scooter warned.

"This here is the biggest haul—ever! What about you?" Drew asked.

Scooter said nothing, but Drew knew it was. Otherwise, why had Scooter kissed every politician's ass in town to save his job as an underpaid cop?

"Gotta hurry," Drew warned. "We've been here more than half an hour. The others might get suspicious and want to know what's up. Hey, you okay?" he added as an aside. "Those cash register signs. Are they blinding your eyes?"

"Your concern touches my heart," Scooter said sarcastically. Going through his head was what a clean haul this was. No confiscated drugs were involved in the deal. It was all pure profit—unless they got caught.

With drugs, the usual first step was to cut and package the goods. Profits were high, but the wait could be as much as six months. This time he and his so-called partner would have their hands on monies that were not traceable.

The only person who might have any idea of the amount of cash stored in the box was the daughter who still lived at home. If necessary, he could take care of that little problem.

"Tell 'em the place was a mess," Scooter said about the extended time they were below. "We don't know much about this McKenna fellow, but I do know he does not want any changes right away."

"How are you so sure?"

"The Captain? He said so. We're buddies. He promised we'd go drinkin' when he retires."

"Shouldn't we take a few of those bills and leave them in the safe? Just in case?" Drew asked.

"Good idea, partner. Now get the two suspects into the car. I'm right behind you."

As Drew left, Scooter took out several hundred dollar bills and laid them at the bottom of the safe. He closed the safe and took off his gloves, leaving them inside out and attached to his belt.

The boys were in the patrol car and heading back to headquarters. "We have to make a stop. You boys want a soda or somethin'?" Scooter asked.

Drew swung around, surprised and with his mouth open. "Wha ... the ...?"

"We have a stop to make," Scooter repeated. "Have a bite of lunch, sit in the shade. It's about that time, isn't it?"

"I suppose so."

They arrived at the first convenience store on the left-hand side of US 1. After putting sodas and sandwiches on a wooden picnic table behind the store, each officer brought out one of the prisoners from the patrol car.

They cut their bindings, then strapped each one back in by tying plastic stripping through the slats in the table as Drew commented under his breath, "Good thing this table is cemented down."

The four of them ate in silence, and then came the usual bathroom routine.

Scooter—the bag man, the one with the money from the safe—walked a short distance away to a group of palm trees. The tree with its trunk curved so low it touched water was what he wanted. He looked around and then walked onto the trunk of the tree at the point the bent trunk turned upward. On the far side and unrecognizable by any neighbors who might go nosing around, he slipped the envelopes into a hole in the trunk, scooped up a handful of seaweed, and stuffed it tightly into the opening. Then he rinsed off his hands in the murky water and returned to the table.

It was time to report in at the station.

Scooter and Ted waited until Harry turned in his report before giving theirs. With McKenna's attention shifted to them, Scooter said,

"We searched everywhere for the combination, boss. Searched a second time. Found nothing."

"Touching nothing, I hope," McKenna stated.

Scooter produced a pair of blue, see-through plastic gloves hooked inside a small loop at his right hip. With twenty years of experience, if he wasn't on probation, a question like that would cause words between him and this new guy. So far his view of McKenna was that he was nothing more than a detective with more degrees than experience who caught a lucky break, nothing more.

"Was the safe open or closed?" McKenna asked.

"Closed, sir. I took several sets of prints off before Harry arrived. Harry has the prints."

CHAPTER 47

LIKE SHE DID EVERY DAY of her adult life, Rosetta Hernandez, wife of Captain Maxwell Hernandez, went to St. Mark's Catholic Church for early morning prayer service. After the 7 a.m. ritual, the routine was to enter the confessional booth and admit to Father Shanahan her major sin: how depressed she was since her youngest daughter Susanna returned home.

Today she was not going to speak to the priest behind the wire mesh. He would only order fifty Hail Marys for even thinking about not serving others, especially her own family.

"All is love and love is all." That's what the priest repeated at the end of every service, and she was tired of the whole process. What was she getting out of all of this? If she confessed her true worries to Father Shanahan, his answer would result in fifty extra Hail Marys.

What Rosetta really wanted from the priest was a suggested approach to make her husband and her daughter understand that she may be their wife and mother, but she was no longer their invisible doormat.

The last time she finished with her deepest, more heartfelt confession, she was told to return home and get down on her knees to thank God for her many blessings. The order for Hail Marys was always the same: first the problem, then ten Hail Marys. Each problem after that, added another five. Rosetta must hold the record. In her case, Father Shanahan always ordered fifty Hail Marys adding another ten for every problem confessed after that. Another problem and she would be forced to mop the floors and serve free lunches every day to the poor at the side doors of the church for the rest of her life.

At the end of her penance, Rosetta would be forgiven, only to begin again with the next confession. How did she know about this formula? Her sewing group gossiped about the Church, Catholic guilt, and what it took to be absolved from their sins. Yet no one changed churches or altered their behavior even thought the group decided the penance for many wrongs was too high.

Rosetta decided a long time ago that no priest can absolve anyone of anything. Only God himself, through Jesus Christ, could forgive. And the last thing she needed today was for some priest to tell her what she'd heard for years: "You can put up with anything, Rosetta. You really can. Fifty Hail Marys. See you tomorrow and God bless."

Turning sharply away from those who politely stood in line, Rosetta went to the back of the church, turned, and bent low. She tapped her forehead, her heart region, and both shoulders and went out into the sunshine.

<hr>

After her seventh grandchild was born—and even though Xavier was so easy to raise—there was no way she could tell anyone how seven grandchildren was one beyond her limit. So many times she had to stop and rest. Every day her very bones ached, and she had so little strength to pick him up.

She thought age must be catching up with both of them. Max had not been himself for weeks. They never talked like they used to, asking for suggestions on family matters, discussing their day. These days he was forgetful, didn't keep track of the bills, and never paid them on time even though they had the money. Driving at night was also a challenge. The many fights about Max's driving and his not paying attention to the crazy tourists who drove above the speed limit made her suggest he should give up driving.

Her biggest fear was when he took the Ramblin' Rose out past sunset. For a man who knew the sea as well as he did, at times he became disoriented. The time had come to call a halt. When he returned from his latest trip, she would do the unusual and put her foot down until he actually did what she suggested.

What she wanted from what little time she had left on this earth was to be her own center of attention, meeting her own needs and fulfilling her own pleasures. What they were she was not sure of yet, but if she was alone long enough, she sure could figure it out.

Rosetta was surprised to see Tom ambling toward her, "My, my," she said, "don't you look extra handsome in your uniform! We missed you at the dinner table Sunday."

She went to reach for Tom, to caress his young cheeks, but he kept his distance, and he was not smiling. He did not say, "Thank you, ma'am," and end with a slight bow as was his custom.

She looked into his eyes, memories flashing before her of the oversized, unloved boy whose head tilted downward in the same manner as it was now.

Then she knew.

"Maxy!" she screamed, trying to wrench free of Tom's sturdy hold on her arms. "Something has happened to Max!" She searched his face for a sign that what she was saying out loud was not so.

"No! No! No! Not my Maxy. He's on the boat. Only hurt. Like the last time when they rushed him to St. Anne's with his bad heart. You came to pick me up then, too!"

"I'm sorry, so sorry, Miss Rosetta. He was found next to his boat at the neck of Bahia Honda."

"In the water?"

Tom nodded.

"Bahia?" she searched his face. "What was he doing there? He docks at …"

"I know, I know. Please, Miss Rosetta. Let me walk you on home. Susanna should be there soon."

She released herself from Tom's grasp in total disbelief, ready to collapse.

"No, not Max. Not now when we agreed … It can't be."

"The two passengers said Max jumped overboard. By the time we got there it was too late."

Tom was saddened by how much more he knew and all he had witnessed before he found Rosetta. On the other hand, he was glad she did not hear the sad news from someone else.

"They are wrong! He would never do such a thing. Passengers?"

"Two young boys. Illegals. Cubans."

"They couldn't save him?"

"I don't know, ma'am. Right now I need to take you home. I'm sorry. Is there anything I can do? Personally or as an officer of the court?"

"Yes," she said, sobbing and smoothing out her dress. "Find the truth. He would never jump. Never. He had to be pushed," she asserted. "There, I said it. Now take me home. Last night my Maxwell was alone, out there by himself." Her voice wandered off. "And now ..."

Holding tightly to Tom's arm as her feet moved forward, she allowed him to guide her to the small Hernandez family home on Petronia, one half block from the cemetery, the home where she and Max had lived their entire married lives.

"Where are my children? Susanna? Michael? Rebecca?" she asked. She looked around as if she were seated inside a stranger's house.

"They have been called."

Tom came to his senses when Rosetta repeated, "You find out the truth, you hear? And you come and tell me. Only me. You understand?"

"Is there anything else I can do before I leave?" Tom asked.

"Yes. The truth," she reminded him once again. "Find out the truth. He would never jump. Not my Maxy. He had to be pushed ... Was he safe in Islamorada last night? If not, he would have called. What happened after that?" Her voice faded. "So many lies ... So many lies."

CHAPTER 48

NEWS TRAVELS QUICKLY IN A small town like Key West. Word of the latest tragedy made the rounds before Tom left the Hernandez home on Petronia. When he reached Susanna by phone at the bank, from the sound of her voice, she had been waiting for his call—or someone else's. In fact, she told him she was in the middle of cashing out her drawer. This did not alarm Tom. In his rational police mind, he knew she would take the news calmly and react later.

Tom sat with Miss Rosetta, holding her hand, a box of Kleenex in his other hand. His mind was a blank. He was waiting for Susanna to arrive, and when she did, she walked into the house, threw her purse onto a small table near the entrance, rushed into her mother's arms, and squeezed her close. Taller and much thinner than her mother, all Susanna wanted was to be a child once again and sit on her mother's aproned lap to rock and cry, rock and cry.

At first, Susanna waited in the background, all eyes and ears. Soon she followed Tom outside. "Anything else I should know?" she asked.

"Chief Detective McKenna will call after the services. He needs you to take a look inside the safe and check out the rest of boat. See if anything is missing."

"What about a warrant?"

"He ... we thought that would not be necessary."

"Of course. Somewhere on Poppie's dresser is the combination. I haven't been on the boat in years. When do you want my help?"

"Work it out with Chief McKenna."

"You'll be at the service?"

"Yep," he replied.

What he needed to do, rather than stare at Susanna, was to take advantage of the situation. How was he ever going to make detective if he could not make use of every opportunity to question the very ones who knew the victim so well?

Tom pulled into the parking lot at police headquarters. He parked under one of the few trees that provided shade and sat there with the air conditioning on for some time.

He couldn't help but think of two nights ago, after dinner, when he and Max took the Ramblin' Rose out obstinately to fish, an almost full harvest moon over the Atlantic Ocean to guide them through the mangroves.

It was Max's favorite time of all, at night on the water when he could completely relax and release himself to nature, trusting nature to take care of him as he related to the ebb and flow of life itself.

"The water sure is calm tonight," Max commented. "Time stands still here, and I can feel the wasted energy of the day being drawn out of me. You?" He took two Heinekens out of the cooler.

Max had never been this buddy-buddy with Tom, and Tom was not sure how to answer. "Me? I like the action, the fullness of the day. Noon I guess. When half the day is over and half the day's work is still ahead."

Max seemed pleased by Tom's comment. There was a time when Tom would go fishing with the man who literally picked him up off the streets, a time when Tom had no opinion at all. And so it was there, out on the darkened sea on that particular night, that Max began the talk man-to-man to Tom.

"I know how much you care about Susanna. I see the way you can't help yourself from looking at her in that way. She may be my daughter, but if staying a cop is what you want, she is no one to get involved with. Never change for a woman. It only brings heartache. I know. I've been through it."

Tom remembered how embarrassed he was as Max continued. "My daughter? She yearns for excitement. Seeks out near-criminal acts or acts that take a turn to illegal. She is always at the edge where she hopes never to get caught. Always dramas and problems. Living at the edge is in her blood." He stopped for a moment, then said: "This is not from my family, but from a story told generations ago when the Cubans first came here. You don't want a wife who is in love with her ex-husband. And you sure don't want to marry someone you might have to bail out of jail. You're better than that, Tom."

"I figured it out, sir," Tom replied, "not exactly as you say it, but a long time ago. Being in love is a hopeless situation. It doesn't stop the feelin', does it?" Max bent low and nodded his head in agreement.

Max said, "Maybe it never will. Just remember she is who she is. I think often of Julie Jackson, who worked in my office years ago. She was something else. Efficient, self-sufficient, and when her husband became ill and passed away, she wanted to keep working for me. She had a son. So far as I know, she never married again, just kept working and caring for the next person. Many times I wondered why Susanna could not be a little more like her."

"Isn't she the one who up and left without notice?"

"Besides that," Max said, and they both laughed.

"Women can be irrational like that," Max said, drawing in a long breath of fresh, night air. "She left, and I never did figure out why. Did you?"

"Not when she first left. I was too young. Later on, when you and Rosetta were at odds for so long, I thought maybe you two had an affair."

Max would never compromise the honor of a woman he once loved. "Naw. Women going through the change. Rosetta was in it for twenty years. That was all there was to it. While I endured," he replied as he got up to put the empty bottles in a small recycle bin in the storage room. Returning with two poles set to go, he offered one to Tom. "We came to fish. Let's do it!"

After casting off and settling in the fishing chairs, Max commented on the size of the moon. "A full moon lighting up total darkness. Now that's this fisherman's dream of the perfect time of day."

Then he asked Tom, "When it's time to quit the police force, would you like the Ramblin' Rose? She's in pretty bad shape, but we could dock her at my house and work in the shed or dry-dock her at the marina while you and I work on her together. You can sand and polish her in between your work hours—on long weekends and holidays. Come and go as you please. Once she's in shape again, take my customers. I'll give you a good reference."

"I thank you for that. Fishing with you is about all I ever want to be on the water since baby Tomas died."

Tomas's death was never fully discussed, only referred to now and then. He was the first child of their oldest daughter, Rebecca, and Rosetta had taken care of him from infancy. A slight turning away and the next minute, the baby's face was in the pool. Rosetta panicked.

She called over a neighbor, who called 911, but the child had turned blue and gone limp by then. Eventually, Rebecca had another child. This time it was a girl, but losing a child can never be made up for by having another one. When her second child, Beverly, came along, Rebecca stayed home and as far away from the family as possible without being completely estranged.

Tom was grateful someone recognized his feelings for Susanna. And about the gift of the boat—his acceptance would be unthinkable. The previous use of Max's equipment was one thing, but to own it would mean Max had finally retired, and Max would not want to be anywhere but at sea.

"Too late to change the will now," Max said lightly. "I have a better idea. You're always fixing' cars and foolin' around with wood, creating things. I have twenty, maybe thirty thousand dollars worth of tools: lathes, hammers, drills, a drill press, and various woods. Does that interest you?"

Tom nodded in agreement, a grin on his face.

"Well, good. Drop over soon. I'll show you around, and it's all yours. Just keep the garage door sealed when you're not there. Lots of break-ins lately, I figure mostly by ghosters from out of town. Talk to Jose. Tell him what I said. Give him the boat and you two can make the switch on your own. Keep you both happy."

Neither one caught any fish that night, and as soon as the moon moved on, disappearing in the distance over the horizon and behind the clouds, Max pulled back into the Garrison Bight Marina and dropped Tom at his apartment. That was the last time Tom saw sea Captain Maxwell Hernandez alive.

Why didn't Tom listen more closely to Max's words? To the way he was talking? As if they were never going to see each other again?

CHAPTER 49

It was early Monday morning. Ariel and Jose were sitting inside his father's car, watching their friends cross Flagler Drive in order to enter Key West High School.

The shocking news of Max's drowning was all over the news, so they were prepared for what was ahead: a dreary funeral, Catholic style; condolences all around; and a continuing closeness to the family. Now, instead of Rosetta looking out for them, it would be the other way around.

Next was the investigation. Ariel did not steal anything that Max hadn't already promised her, but eventually the cops would discover she had been on the Ramblin' Rose. It was just a matter of time.

Ariel felt her job was to keep Jose out of all this mess. He came to her rescue, but he was not involved. Let the detectives piece everything together on their own. That's what they got paid for anyway.

"What now?" she asked Jose as he shut the engine off. "I mean, how do we act? What do we do? I sure hope no one at school knows I was on that boat."

"They will, no doubt. Better get your story straight," he told her.

"There is no story to get straight. He asked me to go along like he did so many other times. I went up to Islamorada and changed my mind about coming back with them. You came and got me, and we went to Miami for a coupla days." She shrugged and pretended to be cool while her nerves were working overtime.

She wasn't even on the boat when he went overboard and died. Why or how he did, she hadn't a clue. No idea. He was tired more often lately. She knew that much. Rosetta was the one who said they were both getting up in years and he should not be working. All Ariel knew for sure was that under no conditions could she marry Max.

Jose asked, changing the subject: "Dinner tonight?"

"Where?" Ariel asked.

"On Duval at the Pizza House for calzones. Don't know if I can eat yet, but maybe we should try."

"Thanks for that," she reached over and pecked his cheek. "See you sixth."

"Oh, yeah. I forgot. We're still on for that?"

"Guess so."

Ariel avoided her friends at lunch by staying in Mrs. Trigameyer's room to help grade ninth grade math papers. She was so sweet. Her only comment was to touch vaguely on the tragedy of Max's death. Ariel felt at ease when she did not respond during the pauses in her teacher's conversation. Either way, there was to be no tears and no volunteering of information—certainly not in front of her favorite teacher.

On Monday morning Paulette found herself with a set of keys to a small counseling office off the main building of Key West High School. The principal, Mr. Menendez, had called her late Sunday night, long after the brunch and everyone had said their good-byes.

"I apologize for calling so late," the principal said. "When my wife and I returned home, there was a message from our counselor. Remember I mentioned the situation when we first met?"

"Yes, sir, I do," Paulette replied.

"Now it is serious. If you're available, I'll need you for these last few weeks of school. If you plan to stay for the summer like you say, you can close out the files for the department. Then I would like to offer you the summer session, which is short and sweet and has fewer students."

He outlined the details and continued his sales pitch as Paulette thought about all that extra time she was hoping to have to herself: time to read; go to the beach; run along the sidewalk up US 1, past the Key West International Airport. Study the pine trees and watch the ships sail into port from the Truman Annex.

"I'll be there," she agreed, telling herself she would have the late afternoons and weekends to do all those other things.

This way she would become involved in the community. She could see what effect the life of hippie parents had on their teenage children and whether it was a different point of view than in LA.

She signed in. The proper paperwork would follow. In the meantime, they were trusting her with the confidential records of the at-risk students in the three daily sessions she was now in charge of.

As expected, the files were incomplete. So when she opened the private office and found the desk in total disarray, with unfinished papers scattered everywhere, it was not unexpected.

Paulette had exactly one and a half hours to read the files of those students in her first session. Three of the expected eight students fell into the category of what were called latchkey kids back in the eighties and what has, unfortunately, become part of society's everyday vernacular.

Of the sixth period students, six knew the Hernandez family, and two had been taken in to the Hernandez home at various times when their own home lives overwhelmed them. Her job was to explain the situation about Max and how matters would be taken care of, tell them about the upcoming service, and basically help them to feel comfortable enough to center on some sort of routine in the meantime.

Paulette was assigned an empty classroom by the main office. The first two sessions were uneventful. She started out with "getting to know you" talks. Also high on the agenda was to explain why the last therapist would not be returning for these last two weeks. Finished with that in about ten minutes, she opened the discussion to any questions about Captain Maxwell's death.

"I am new here in Key West, but I'll try and answer your questions," she offered. "I met Captain Hernandez on one of the first days I arrived. What a dear man. I learned so much about the sea and what is underneath it from that one trip to Fort Jefferson. He had the kind of personality that was non-judgmental, and he made me feel very comfortable in his presence."

Meanwhile, the news media was saying the captain's death was a possible murder with two suspects under arrest. One theory was it may have been a suicide, and the long shot was that it was an accident. The two witnesses say the captain jumped overboard. Voluntarily was a stretch, but the media was constantly working overtime on the various theories for obvious reasons.

She told them all, "Do not listen to the media or read the papers. No one has definitive answers, and until they do, the guessing will soon become sensationalism. You do not want to become a part of that out of respect for the captain and his family."

Paulette had a little time to work on school plans before sixth period, her last class of the day and her most important. She filled out her paperwork at the front desk while the secretary told her, "Sixth has mostly at-risk kids. Several were very close to the captain. What a shame. Such a nice man. His family has quite a decent reputation. Rosetta and Maxwell both graduated from this very school as did their five kids. No doubt Miss Rosetta will set up an endowment fund dedicated to her husband."

"Aren't we getting a little ahead here?" Paulette asked kindly. "Who are these special students?"

"Failures. Students that the school's administration hopes will be sparked into trying. Maybe someone from the outside like you will be their lucky charm. Some may be intrigued by your background in the gang schools and all. If they ask, share your stories, your conquests. A couple of them might come around. That's about all we can expect."

"Sounds hopeful." Paulette attempted a smile as her brow crinkled.

CHAPTER 50

PAULETTE EXPECTED EIGHT STUDENTS TO come to her sixth period counseling class. Sally Anderson was the first to arrive. Sally sat in the far corner in one of the two wooden chairs without a desktop. Her backpack was clutched to her chest as she stared at Paulette.

Sally was the only non-Cuban in the class. A bleached blonde and a little on the pudgy side, her underground clothes were solid black. Her bracelets were made of leather with metal spikes that poked out. She had another set of spikes around her neck, a nose ring, and tattoos up her two arms. On her legs from the knees down, she wore heavy combat boots.

An overweight, sweating student with a bright purple head of spiked hair held straight up by jell kicked the classroom door shut. The sweat was streaming down from her scalp. Della Algado said, "Sorry I'm late. When does this goddamned heat stop? Take me back to ..."

"Oh, sit the shit down," Roberto spit out. He was the heavy student tagged Fat Boy by the class who lumbered in after the second bell.

"And who are you to tell me anything?" Della questioned.

"Some of us smoke dope and eat more sweets than others," he replied drolly.

The group laughed nervously while glancing over at their new counselor.

"Okay, everyone, settle down," Paulette said.

"As I was saying," Della continued, "I have no feelings about any of this. I mean, I never even heard of the guy. So why am I here?"

Paulette had everyone's file among the pile of unfinished work sitting on her desk. Motioning to Sally to make room for Roberto in the second wooden chair, as she did so, Paulette took out a blank yellow sheet of paper and had everyone sign in. She would match faces and attitudes to the files later.

It felt to Paulette as if she should move on. It wasn't only Della's comment, but the fact that discussions about Captain Maxwell had probably been discussed earlier in other classes. Because this was the last class of the day, Paulette wanted to leave her distressed students with a feel-good message.

"I think you are all here, both as a group and individually, to communicate with each other and to learn. At the present moment it is your responsibility to listen and support whomever has difficulty sharing with the group."

"Whom-*ev*-er. Cool. Good one!" Roberto responded as he clucked his tongue and pointed a finger at Paulette.

Paulette did not especially like this teenager from the moment he walked in the door. First of all, he was late and proved to be lazy when responding in class. He was otherwise too pulled together and of the highest intelligence, which separated him from the rest of the members, thus allowing his narcissistic traits to grow further into permanent personality flaws. This meant a great deal of work ahead for any counselor up to the task, and Paulette did not plan on being around that long.

Paulette looked past Sally, still the center of the show, to Ariel Costas. Paulette was concerned about the quiet one huddled in a ball and too close to Jose Hernandez. She seemed to wither away in her chair as she held onto her fellow student's arm, her knees underneath her, her dress covering her legs.

Paulette intended to call Ariel out during PE tomorrow to see if she could begin a discussion about Captain Maxwell and her personal loss and to help her move forward into the healing process. This was a great loss for such a young girl, far more painful than for an older person who had more years of experience.

Being an unknown during such a critical period, Paulette had to hold back. She longed to reach out to each one, to comfort and reassure. She wanted to explain as much as she could with the little she knew. But Paulette's background was at a gang school. There the fight was against hard core drug lords who drive by in panel vans to frighten pretty girls and entice young boys who want to go straight. Here the students were part of a diverse community, so the problem was a shadow over the city that would be felt by all its residents for some time to come.

Here in Key West, a teenager had one advantage over the poor in San Fernando, whose parents worked so very hard to support their children and their grandchildren's comfort tool—the cell phone. The San Fernando kids could not leave their community and apply for jobs they wouldn't be hired for anyway. On the other hand, because of the tourism, Key West students could afford expensive clothes; tight-fitting, strategically torn jeans; tattoos; cell phones; and other luxuries paid for through part-time jobs.

In the discussion about Captain Hernandez, she told them about her one trip with him to see Fort Jefferson and how he impressed her as someone unique and special. Also, if they were interested in attending the memorial service, they should stop by the main office.

She closed with: "If you need to talk to anyone, please feel free to come by my office or make an appointment during my two conference periods."

When the bell rang to end the class, Joanna Martinez, the group's leader, remarked: "I thought she was going to use 'with my vast experience' on us. Like the last one. This one seems—I don't know—inexperienced. Too innocent to talk about the Bloods and the Crips." Joanna knew the new counselor was within earshot when she passed along the compliment saying, "Dr. Cruz. Remember her? God save us. This one is prettier than the last one, that's for sure."

"And the one before that," Sally said from the back of the room as she folded up her art pad, zipped up her backpack, and raced out of the room with the rest of the class. "Did you see the two new lovebirds? Bet they have been you-know-what longer than last weekend."

Joanna agreed and went on about the new shoes she bought over the weekend to match her shirt for the motorcycle races on Sunday. "I hope the damned thing doesn't shred. It's to impress Henry," she said, giggling.

CHAPTER 51

THE NEW CHIEF OF DETECTIVES, Allan McKenna, was prepared for Monday roll call at 7 a.m. in the meeting room at police headquarters in downtown Key West.

"As most of you know, sea captain Maxwell Horatio Hernandez died in the waters at the entrance to Bahia Honda. Our job is to prove whether his fall overboard was accidental. Did he jump on purpose? Was he pushed?" McKenna began.

"We have two suspects in custody: Cubans without papers. They are in the holding area right now, waiting for a judge to hear the moving papers of the state and to set bail.

"If the autopsy results determine the victim died of natural causes, all charges against the boys will be dropped. The next step is to check the money inside the boat's safe. If it has not been touched, they will be returned to Cuba."

"What happened to the two bags of money the suspects claim the captain took from them?" Scooter asked.

"Interesting question, Scooter. As you know, since you were one of the officers who went below, so far there's been no trace on the Hernandez boat. I hope this information goes no further than this room." He looked around at his crew of twelve.

The only member missing was Harry Vernon, the coroner and forensics expert. He was in the lab working on autopsy results for Captain Hernandez.

"Ask around about the money. If it isn't found, my guess from experience is it's already on the streets and untraceable.

"Another major issue is the missing IDs on several sets of fingerprints. The unidentified ones must belong to persons with no criminal records. They may belong to teenagers in the neighborhood who sometimes accompanied the captain on his fishing trips. I have Tom looking into it. Tom?"

"Right, sir," Tom replied.

McKenna looked up from his notes before continuing. "Everyone I've spoken to says the captain was an upright citizen. His wife says he often forgot dates, and there were times when he didn't do well while driving at night. Her biggest fear was when he took the boat out after sunset. Unfortunately, we see the results of her worry.

"Tom also has the task of taking the captain's daughter to the boat to check around, including opening the safe to see if any funds are missing, which would then be attributed to our two suspects. I have a feeling the money was tampered with." He reminded Tom, "Don't forget to sign the notebook out of evidence."

"If all the money is still there, a man with over six hundred thousand dollars aboard his fishing boat must have had some special reason for not depositing the funds in the bank," McKenna said as a side comment. "Was it escape money? To my way of thinking, it was odd behavior, especially for this type of fellow.

"Also find out about the relationship between the captain and his wife and their five kids. Is this a close family? I know this is a tall order, Tom.

"A reminder. This is an unofficial look, but a look related to your duties as a police officer. From that perspective, and knowing what the statistics are on the number of family-related murders within the community and society in general—to us who enforce the law and try to maintain peace—happy families are nonexistent."

The group mumbled in agreement and started to move about, ready to be released.

McKenna looked around the room. "Any questions so far? Also, I know it looks like Tom has the most responsibility here—and a delicate one—but other teams are hard at work. Lastly, if we don't have conclusive evidence on his death, I may have to call a team in from Miami. Otherwise, anything that fits into the ordinary customs around here that I should know about but don't, please feel free to fill me in.

"Also remember there are some doors you do not want to open until after the autopsy has been completed. For instance, if the captain's death was accidental, much of the above information is none of our business. Again, depending on the autopsy results, two officers are to go to the high school and review the files of students who were arrested for suspicion of illegal activity but were not incarcerated.

"Otherwise, several students will be in this afternoon on an informal basis for questioning. Stay away from the sensational headlines online and elsewhere. Only the police will have a better picture to report after the autopsy, which should be in by the end of the week. You'll probably hear the results before then. The only good news would be proof that the captain's death was accidental, and that his daughter agrees with the amount of money kept aboard the Ramblin' Rose in the safe. Dismissed."

Scooter met Ted in the locker room.

"We have to go to the tree. Take the money to the boat."

"Why? All of it? Damn," Ted replied.

"Yes, all of it. Didn't you hear Tom's report this morning? And McKenna telling us the daughter knows the exact amount of money on that boat?"

"Yeah, a whole lot more than fifty thousand smackers. Boy, did you fool me."

"I did not lie. When the daughter and Tom get there, they'll find out for themselves. We'll put back exactly what we found: one hundred thousand dollars. They should be real happy. We could go right now."

"You go," Ted urged. "I have other work to do."

"Are you kiddin' me? It better be now. Otherwise some of the other cops will be all over that boat. We aren't the only ones who know about the safe."

"You mean they would like to steal the money the way we did?"

Scooter was emphatic. "I wouldn't put it past any of 'em!"

At the end of their shift, the pair went to the tree where Scooter had stuffed the envelopes into the wide, deep hole. The rest was already in Islamorada in a safe-deposit box.

Scooter scooped up the envelopes and placed the seaweed back in the hole.

"They sure do smell like the stink of dead, wet seaweed," Ted said. "What if ..."

"There will be no what-ifs. We put the money back, and that's it!"

They raced to the boat, went behind the lines, and opened the safe.

"The money is all back, safe and sound," Scooter said without turning away from the safe.

Five more envelopes, chosen at random, were stuffed into his shirt. There definitely would be no sharing of the Islamorada deposit or the money he now had. Still inside the box here was more than three hundred thousand. That was enough for the captain's family. That and all the property he heard the captain owned meant this was a drop in the bucket.

"Big loss to us," he said, motioning to his partner to go upstairs and check to see if the coast was clear.

"Better to return all the money than lose our jobs," Ted said, himself disappointed. "Did you leave a few loose hundred dollars?" he asked Scooter.

"Who cares? But yes, there are thousands more in there than the few hundred you are worried about."

CHAPTER 52

ARIEL LEFT SCHOOL AFTER HER last class of the day.

"Hi, Tom!" She waved at him enthusiastically. "How you been? Not a good question right now, huh?"

"We have to talk. Official business. On the record talk," he said. He was in uniform and standing at the entrance to Key West High School.

"About?"

"Maxwell. We need to go to headquarters to speak with my boss, Allan McKenna, the chief of detectives. Your fingerprints were among the many sets on the boat."

"What?" she asked, sucking in the air of fear. Reconsidering and attempting to act casual, she added, "Big surprise. Right? A whole bunch of us were there at different times."

"That's all I know. He still wants to speak with you. So far on an informal basis."

"Whatever. I'm innocent," she shrugged, "so you should go back to your captain and tell him that"

"You know I can't."

"If you have any fingerprints of mine, they are old, which is exactly what I'd tell your boss."

"I already told him you and I and Jose were on the Ramblin' Rose all the time. Left our handprints everywhere. He wants to talk to you about a fresh set. Ideally, he would like your mother present in case the issue of consent comes up."

"For what?"

"Fingerprinting. Where's your mom?"

"I am eighteen. I can do this myself. Besides she's out of town and she doesn't know I went on that trip," Ariel said emphatically. "Not any part of that trip. She would kill me if she found out. Did you tell your boss how it was?"

"What I could."

"I live at home. I plan to go to college. That should count for something."

"That's why he won't call her. Yet."

Tom knew there were gaps in the information he had thus far and that Ariel was a key to the answers. Tom's worst thought was that Ariel might have taken something of value.

He asked a few more questions and got nothing except vague answers. Ariel would have to talk to the captain, he told her. He wrapped it up with: "I guess that's it. One more question. How did you get home, and why didn't you return with Max?"

"Will you look at us? You have to ask me embarrassing questions, and I … don't know how to answer you. Can I trust you to watch out for me?"

"Within the law and my official judgment, I'll try."

"Good. Then when I'm not so tired—I feel like throwing up right now I'm so tired—I can maybe piece this all together."

Tom flipped his notebook over and said, "I was hoping, informally of course, you knew more about the contents of the safe."

Ariel asked, "Off the record?"

When Tom nodded, she added, "If I said I know more, then what?"

"A summons to court to testify. If it becomes necessary."

"That's what I thought. So I'd never be off the hook. If I tell you or your chief what I know, why can't I stay out of it? I mean if I didn't take the money or anything like that? The whole damned town knows Max kept money on his boat. It's a wonder he hasn't been robbed before this."

"He's been robbed?" Tom asked.

"Who knows? I don't. I'm just sayin'."

"For an eighteen-year-old you're pretty smart about how to act evasively."

"Court battles over support, watching my parents. You should know that. I also testified at their divorce hearing, choosing to stay with my mom so I could be sure my brother was safe. I would be out of school by now, but I'm a November baby. Less than a week over the date according to the rules. Eighteen and three quarters when I graduate."

"Your mother never treated you right."

"Oh, and my father would have? Everyone knows how he never comes around except to harass my mother. You learn ..." Ariel's voice trailed off.

"I'll do my best to protect you."

"You swear—okay? I don't know what's in the safe. I do know there's another will leaving everything to me and nothing for his family. Oh, Tom, you have to promise. About the will, I don't know what that means. I took the new will—oh, this is so private and could get me into *so* much trouble. I did what the drug runners do. I put the old will inside the new envelope back on the shelf above the safe."

Ariel waited for a reaction. There was none. Tom still had his police face on.

"I don't know what the old will said. Honestly, I don't." Ariel's breathing was shallow. "But it sure didn't include me or anything. At least I don't think so. It was all about his family as it should be. I closed the kitchen cabinet. Oh my God," she gasped, putting her hands up on her cheeks. "I left the book ..."

"We found a little brown book. Is that the one? It's kinda falling apart. It's logged in as evidence."

Ariel felt comforted. "The new will is in the cabinet below the sink. The old will is where it's supposed to be—above the safe," she admitted.

"Didn't you think about how someone might look at the date on the envelope?" Tom asked.

"I didn't have time to think about anything except escaping. You don't think someone is going to check, do you?"

"Hard to say. Everything hinges on the autopsy."

"There's more. Oh, God," Ariel began to cry. "Max tried to give me an envelope of money for making the trip with him. Remember the old days and how much he liked company? Someone to talk to? He let me steer the boat into the harbor!"

"Did you take the envelope?"

"Not directly."

Tom sighed heavily, looking away. "Where is the envelope now?"

"I threw it away. The money is at home under my mattress."

"Your mother ..."

"She never goes into my room."

"Once again, how did you leave Islamorada?"

"I caught the 6 a.m. bus to Key West with all the day workers on it. I have to turn myself in, don't I? I was going to, but I had to go to school today. Hang out and hear what was going on. What's your captain like? Can he help me at all?"

"So far he's been a fair man. That's about all I can say about him. Which is to say, he will take circumstances and everything you have to say into consideration. Just be honest with him. That's all he expects."

When Ariel arrived home, there were dirty dishes in the sink and a note from her mother with fifty dollars under it. Addressed to no one, the note read:

1. Buy milk, some eggs. Look around to see what else we need. 2. Laundry to do today. I have no clean uniforms! 3. Your brother is due home tomorrow. Can you make his bed and add his old laundry to today's wash?

Mom

Mulling over the excitement and sadness of the last few days, Ariel wanted to cry, scream, and run around in circles cursing God. How could all of this have happened? Wasn't Jesus on her side? Her only wrong was she had nowhere else to go. She was wrong. That all of this was wrong ran through her mind. Oh, so many complications based on being an adult. Growing up, and ... and ... and ... the rest of it is her bad. She'd made wrong choices she would pay for the rest of her life—her whole life.

CHAPTER 53

THE MEMORIAL SERVICE FOR MAXWELL Hernandez was held at sunset, chosen because the priest was available at that hour, and because Max's family believed it was his favorite time of day.

There were three rows for the family: all five children, the various husbands and wives, and their children in attendance. Susanna was joined by her ex-husband Mario Ruiz. Their son Xavier sat between them, adding more tension between family members. She did this despite the fact that she knew Mario was not welcomed by the family, and at a time like this, even less so.

When the prayers and candlelight service was over, several people came forward to say a few words about the deceased: about his fine character and what their thirty- to fifty-year friendships meant to them.

The local congressman and two of his officials stayed through the reception, reiterating to his widow, Rosetta, how much his contribution to the fishing industry meant to the community. They also reviewed how Max had started the local union, against all odds, and funded the building project himself to its completion.

Paulette was at the service but wished she hadn't come. She wondered why they don't do funerals for divorces. Isn't that a real death as well? She answered herself (a habit she had gotten into a lot lately): It wouldn't work. Too much bitterness, too little sorrow.

She was sitting in between Doug and Flower, the tension between them riddling through her body. Paulette's only consolation was knowing she had not caused it and had no idea what it was about.

"You don't have to come to the reception at the Hernandez house if you don't wish to," Doug said to Paulette as the three of them exited the church.

"I appreciate that," Paulette said. "The last memorial service I was at was for my student who was stabbed."

"I understand," Doug replied. "See you over the weekend?"

"Sure thing," Paulette assured him.

"I have a run to South Beach tomorrow," Flower reminded her. "I should be back by, say, Sunday afternoon. Is that good for you?"

"Perfect. I'll be streaming on Saturday and trying to reach my son on Sunday."

Ariel came into the service after Jose, who was seated with the family in the second row. She sat with several of her girlfriends, who all had Kleenexes in their hands. For many, it was their first funeral.

"I see Jose way down there," Della pointed out.

"I see him," Ariel said sharply as she forced a smile.

"Aren't you ... Weren't you two real close. I mean, at one time?"

"I suppose so."

"Then you should go down there," Della said, yanking at Ariel's arm. "Go. You belong."

With trepidation, Ariel walked down to the fourth row, the row behind Jose, to sit next to Max's other daughter, Rebecca. "I'm so glad you're here," she said to Ariel. "You are so grown-up since the last time we saw each other."

"Thanks," Ariel said. She felt Jose's eyes on her as he turned slightly to the side to face her.

When the service was over, Ariel rode the short distance to the reception with Rebecca and her family.

"We aren't staying too long," Rebecca told Ariel. "If this wasn't about my father ..." She stopped, looked over at her new daughter, and smiled. "These things are too difficult for me. Still."

Ariel had no words of comfort. In fact, she had no idea what to say. Tomas would be almost five by now, and Ariel guessed a mother, at least a good one, never forgets.

The reception for Captain Maxwell was held at his small Conch home on Petronia. Filled to overflow with family, friends, and other important people of the city, food and people were everywhere. After a long prayer, fairly soon everyone was sharing stories, eating, and drinking wine.

Susanna's mom sat silently in a chair in the center of the living room the entire time, looking at no one unless they came over to offer condolences.

Susanna, on the other hand, kept a close eye on the festivities. How could mourners go from crying to laughing so easily? She was even skeptical of her ex's behavior of staying at her side and touching no liquor. She was also thinking about her dad's money. How soon would everyone want to know what was inside the safe-deposit boxes? Then the issue was Who would be in control? Surely not her mother!

She must see her father's attorney ASAP. No doubt Michael would own his restaurant outright, the terms of the will certainly eradicating any debts he may have to the estate. *True or not, good for him*, she thought. She especially liked Michael and was glad they thought alike about most family matters. He was friendly, affable, and a good cook, attributes she had not yet acquired. Also essential was how much his customers liked him.

The rest of Susanna's siblings she took no notice of, except to admit they would all come out of this really well off.

Susanna saw Ariel standing alone at the back side of the living room.

"Ariel!" Susanna said, sounding pleased. "You look terrific. Graduation is what? A week away?"

"Something like that."

"Do you have your dress for the party?"

"Sort of."

"Well, if you want to go to Miami, let me know. I shop in some mighty big stores. It's discount time if you're interested."

"I'll let you know."

As the crowd thinned, Tom took Susanna aside. "Can you come to the boat tomorrow? We need to check out the safe."

"Sure. After work. If Mom takes Xavier."

"I'll pick you up."

"In a patrol car?"

"My car."

"Whew. Otherwise people would talk." Susanna sighed and looked around to see if she could spot where her ex, Mario, had gone to.

"I wish they would," he smiled.

However, Susanna did not smile at Tom's last comment. She was worried what Mario would do should he see her talking to another man.

Jose brought over an extra fruit punch to Ariel. "Sorry for my denial about the baby. Of course it's mine. I take full responsibility."

"That's nice to hear. I may not be pregnant. I only tested with one of those kits. I have an appointment a few days after graduation."

"Will you be my date for the final dance in the auditorium? I promise to behave."

Ariel smiled and agreed. "I know you will," she added.

⊰⊱

Paulette was at the South Shore Bank to cash a personal cashier's check from her LA account. The redhead coming toward her had been at the Mitchell party. She was on her way to assist Paulette when Enrico appeared out of nowhere. "You wish a service or to open an account? It would be my pleasure to serve you."

"You really don't ... I can go to a teller."

"It is my pleasure," he said in an urgent yet ingratiating tone, leading her to his office.

"Sign here, please. I'll okay your cashier's check, and the bank will not have to hold the funds for ten days as is usual for this type of transaction. The faster method is a bank transfer. That way you have your funds the next day."

"The funds are there."

"I'm sure. The bank's procedure is for your protection."

Finished with their business, as Paulette rose to leave, he observed, "You're new in town. We're as good as friends. How about having lunch on Saturday?"

"With you?" Paulette asked. Her eyes moved to the redhead, who was waiting on another customer. "I thought you were otherwise engaged. I don't mean engaged ... *entangled* or seriously involved."

He shook his head and smiled. "Not so. Saturday would be nothing formal. Only to show you some of the sights away from touristy Duval Street."

"Sounds great. You know where I live?"

"It's on the form on my desk." He smiled broadly and shook her hand.

"Ten o'clock Saturday then?"

CHAPTER 54

PAULETTE PHONED KATHLEEN IN LA. "You'll never guess who asked me out! At the bank, I mean I saw him at Doug's party, then the brunch. He's down from the Miami branch."

"Slow down, slow down," Kathleen said. "Tell me, what does he look like? Is he polite? They all are, you know, until you've been to bed with them. Then they want service and turn you into a cook and cleanup gal. After they're tired of using you as a sex slave, they're done with you."

"Kathleen! It's just a date."

"I hate to change the subject, but your son has made his decision. He wants to live on campus at UCLA where his friends are."

"He could stay at the house. We talked about that."

"He may for a few days or on the weekends, maybe bring a few friends. But you know the school is too far from Mulholland, at least in travel time."

"How come you hear all this before me?"

"You chose to leave. Go three thousand miles away and live in another time zone. Shall I go on?"

"No, I get the message. If that's what he wants."

"This is thirdhand information, from hubby, whose client—your ex—is so hungry to live in that house he would do anything to make that happen."

"Anything else?"

"Nothing I can't handle," Kathleen replied moodily. "I'm sending you a couple of papers to sign. They're trying to work around the judge and find one to hear their petition concerning 'best use.' It's a total waste of time."

"Sure scares the hell out of me."

"Don't waste your energy. They can't overturn the judge's decision in a local court, especially if Billie comes home, whether he lives there full time or not—so long as he's still in college. A couple of years down the road, they may have a case, but by then you'll be home and your days of rebellion will be over."

"Really? Is that what you think this is? Rebellion?"

"Call me when your date is over. Let me know how it went. Everything. All the details. I've got to hang up now. I have a divorce hearing tomorrow that's killing my attitude. The woman is twenty-eight with two little ones. A real bad deal. She can't find her husband, and even with the proper papers, she's not likely to see a dime of support."

"I might extend my stay through the summer."

"Why not?" Kathleen agreed. "You have an apartment until school starts here, don't you?"

"Maybe beyond that," Paulette admitted.

Paulette felt an edge, a distance from Kathleen, something Paulette needed to delve into on their next call.

<hr/>

Jose sat under the cabana of Harry's Italian Bar, waiting for Ariel. He forgot how much she meant to him. She always sort of had been there, and without her there was a definite void in his life. He needed her to show up so he could tell her that.

"Two Cokes and two calzones, please," he ordered from the waitress.

The last person yet the only person he wanted to see arrived as he finished the order.

"No alcohol for me," Ariel told the waitress.

"Don't go changin' on me now," Jose said, half-joking.

"Lots of changes are happening so quickly. Graduation. Your dad leaving again. This one should not matter."

"Babe, it does. You okay?"

"Just tired over my life right now. My mother might be asleep on the couch, but when she wakes up, she's ready to scream at me the minute I walk in. No change there."

"The baby? If you are preggers, it sure ain't mine," Jose said matter-of-factly.

"Oh no?"

"For sure. We were together only last weekend, so don't lay that one on me!"

When the waitress brought their order, he took out a twenty-dollar bill. "This time, the meal is on me. It's not the ocean and a king-size bed, but it's me. What I can afford," he said, slapping the money down on the table.

"What was all that about at Max's service, about taking responsibility? The baby is still there. It's not going away but I am!" As the waitress reappeared, Ariel said, "Can you box mine to go?"

Ariel left without her box and ran home. Jose did not come after her. In fact, if he bothered to call, she would not be home any time soon.

Singing "Rock-a-Bye Baby" loudly, Ariel had made her final decision: No more back and forth. "It's just you and me, kid." She hummed the song as she rubbed her tummy. As she sang, she calmed down enough to decide: "Whatever it takes, I will take care of you, love you, and hope you are a girl. Right now I don't think much of men. My fault, maybe, maybe not. What did Miss Paulette say today? 'You attract who you are.' That's why there's a Catholic church: to protect its patrons from the trials put in front of its followers. You will go to Sunday school every Sunday. The Church will pay for your schooling, and I will be at your side to give you a life filled with love and friends and so much more. You grow healthy now, and know you have so much to look forward to."

Ariel tiptoed inside where her mother was asleep on the couch. The smell of alcohol surrounded her.

"I'm home!" Ariel said happily and as loudly as she could, the possibility that her mother would hear her remote. Ariel went to her room and wrote a note to leave on the coffee table next to the couch. She dated it three hours earlier. It informed her mother that she and Jose (the rat) were going out to dinner. Then she left once again. Andrea Lea. That would be her baby's name.

As dusk turned into night, Ariel continued to walk the streets until she arrived at Higgs Beach at dawn.

CHAPTER 55

PAULETTE STRUGGLED TO CONTAIN HERSELF as she pulled out her most casual California outfit from her still unpacked suitcases.

Next Monday would be her second week on the job, her third week in Key West. So much had transpired that she hadn't been shopping for a proper dresser. She was usually a very organized person: makeup in the bathroom, dirty clothes in the hamper, nutritious food in the refrigerator, and fairly good institutional food from the school cafeteria when in a pinch.

Enrico arrived in the latest model Corvette, the newest design cleverly amped up and riding low like the smooth, high-powered racing car it was. It was painted in the new apple red. The convertible top and interior were black. The top-off was the custom-made spin wheels.

How was she ever going to climb out of that seat?

They got coffee at Paulette's usual spot on Duval—could it be only three weeks ago? She ordered her usual coffee con leche.

"The cemetery is first on our agenda," Enrico said. "I made a loan the other day to one of the chiselers. He works there most Saturdays. Let's see if we can find him."

They parked at the back of the cemetery. "At one time a long, white picket fence with no gate was out front. Folks just walked in. When it rained, mud puddles were everywhere. Sort of eerie and much more fun than the new concrete entranceway. Actually, this isn't the original cemetery at all. Bodies were washed out, up, up, and away. When the bodies were recovered, they were given plots here in the center of Old Town."

"Because of a hurricane?"

"Yes, the one of 1846."

"Should we find a walking tour guide book? One of my new neighbors told me it was quite informative," Paulette suggested.

"We won't be that long. Eddy should be around here somewhere. He'll have much more direct information for us."

They walked through weedy, overgrown brush with makeshift walkways of sand and rock going in all directions. Many paths had large pieces of coral jutting out that, if dug up, would leave large holes in the ground. The look of neglect spread further as they walked along the uncared-for footpaths created by visitors trying to find their deceased relatives.

"If there weren't all these box houses surrounding us, wouldn't this place be kind of desolate? Even in broad daylight?" Paulette observed.

Enrico agreed. "I don't know the specifics, except with the reconstruction and finding owners and moving gravesites. Once upon a time, city planners had a vision about how this should all look by now. My guess is they either ran out of money or the citizens argued successfully that the charm and uniqueness would disappear."

At the back entrance, cars pulled through and stopped in front of gravesites and crypts. A few people stepped out of their cars, brought picnic baskets, and sat on concrete benches while eating their lunches inside the area marked off for family plots.

"To our right is the Spanish section, which was added to the informal one on the other side for original settlers. It's said there is gold in those tombs. Doing anything about it is tough. Locating the descendants has been the real issue. Tomb robbers have cleaned out most of them. Today they'd go to jail for it—if they got caught. Then there are the real ghosters out on the full moon." As Paulette looked around quickly, he explained. "No, no. They come out at night, usually around midnight. They stay behind the trees to wait for ..."

"Ghosts?"

"Yes. The ghosters bring sounds from South Africa and magic sticks from South America. If they're very lucky, they can brag about their getups. The most prized are the hand-me-downs from other longtime Ghosters. Deceased, of course."

"How do you know all this?"

"Stay around long enough, buy a few authentic souvenir books, and before long you'll sound like a native. You may notice the burial sites are on solid coral rock and all the crypts are above ground. They contain the names of early settlers and families who arrived from Spain, Europe, and the northeastern section of America. Many descendants are prominent residents. And don't forget about the Cubans who ran the tobacco industry for fifty years. The famous Curry Guesthouse? There was an original Curry family that had a large import/export business. Mallory Square got its name in honor of Ellen Mallory's son who was secretary of the confederate navy.

"Captain James Johnson: That's the man who interests me," Enrico said.

"Are you a history buff?"

"Of sorts. When I return to Miami, I'm going to do some research." They stood at the plot marked off by a small fence. "Captain James Johnson, died May 8, 1829. This is the oldest gravesite. Must have been one of those who floated out after the storm and was brought here. May he rest in peace. So much history all around." Enrico made a wide swath as he spoke.

"Eddy!" Enrico walked briskly toward a man holding a small chisel in one hand and a hammer in the other. As he chipped away, his face was close to the corner of a concrete slab.

"Been like this for decades," he said after shaking hands with Enrico and nodding to Paulette.

"How long have you been working on this one?" Enrico asked.

"'Bout a year. Every Saturday, like I told you at the bank. The committee located a distant relative who sent in funds to dig this one out of the tree. They hope to give the deceased a proper burial site.

"Look over here." He pointed to a pathway barely visible. "This one isn't too bad. Been working on that one on and off for three months. Relatives said the jewelry she wore when she was buried was no longer there. Only the dress and hat. We used to leave boards over the gravesites we were working on. No troubles then. Come back a week later, the grave would be the same. Nothin' stolen. Nothin' moved. Years ago we had one open for so long the book buried with the gentleman fell apart from exposure to the weather. No more.

"Too many ghosters around here. Kids playing on top of gravesites on the weekends, inquisitive tourists. We fixed the entryway, added a few new sections, added black metal fences around the exterior, closed the back entrance except for the hours of operation. Done no good. Now we bolt down open gravesites. Takes two of us to open one of 'em up these days."

"I am fascinated with the history." Paulette's voice was filled with a sense of awe.

"We have an even darker history elsewhere in this town. Besides buried pirates, criminals, and conquistadors who brought gold to the new land, there's Manuel Cabeza, in jail for killin' a Ku Klux Klan member. The entire Klan came out. They tarred and feathered his mixed-race wife, so he shot and killed one of 'em right on the sidewalk of Duval Street on Christmas Eve."

"You're kidding!" Paulette said, not in disbelief, but that such revenge could become a true fable.

"No kiddin' about it. The next day, Christmas, a posse—called that in those days—dragged him out of jail and hung him high. To be sure he was dead, they also shot him. Lots of books out. There's a lady in the main library who knows it all. Contact her when you get a chance."

"We saw a grave for Sloppy Joe Russell. Is that Sloppy Joe's owner?" Paulette asked.

"Yep. He was Ernest Hemingway's fishing guide and a Key West bartender at one of the smaller dives downtown until he opened his own place."

Paulette wanted to hear the rest of the stories, but it was time to move on and let the man return to his task.

Enrico and Paulette drove along White Street and turned south onto Flagler Drive where several mansions stood out along the way to the Casa Marina. Enrico said, "I'll take you there one night for drinks. Give you the history if you like. They recently finished redoing the exterior, saving the outside bar. Good spot for meeting other out-of-towners."

"Sounds like fun."

"Let's park here and 'walk Duval' as they say. Have some lunch. Later we can enjoy a few drinks and watch the view. I'll also show you the nightly action on Mallory Square, where trinkets and souvenirs are sold while the real artists and magicians work for tips."

There would be no hurrying around on Duval on a Saturday for this pair. Lunch was served inside a former mansion, a clear contrast to the available stands across the street with native coloring where pizzas, beers, lemonades, and onion baskets were sold.

White linen covered their table. The chairs rested on real hardwood floors. The original windows from the thirties had been scraped free of generations of paint and restored. Old-fashioned lights hung above the fireplaces in each individual serving room, decorated with a generous supply of real plants and antiques.

After a light lunch of salads with fresh pineapple, avocado, and pine nuts and a sweet white wine, they strolled along Carolina Street where an old lady dressed in a costume from the 1920s, complete with hat, umbrella, and feathers, was walking a tiny, wobbly baby stroller from the very olden days. Inside were two Chihuahuas dressed in pink baby dresses with matching hats covering their heads, their ears sticking out.

Enrico went up to her. "Where might you be going, Mrs. Johnson?"

"Why, of course, to the annual dog show at Mallory Square. We must finish in a few hours before the night shift comes in to claim their spots, don't you agree? Come and watch if you like."

"We'd love to, but we're on our way to the Pier House for a few drinks as the sun sets."

"Oh, there," she sniveled. "So crowded. Why not go to the open bar at the Casa?"

"Perhaps another time. Come by the bank and tell me that you won," he said as he took the crook of Paulette's elbow and they walked away, amused.

"That old lady owns half of Carolina Street. She's part of the original Johnsons who arrived here in the late 1800s to buy some property that became Carolina Street. Word is she has plenty of upkeep money from an inheritance. Her husband owned the first McDonald's in Maine. First she had the cash, then the property. Now she has a youthful, good-looking companion, and well she should!"

CHAPTER 56

ON THE WALK FROM CAROLINA Street to Mallory Square, there was about a half an hour before sunset. The entire area was filled with tourists: couples alone, couples with their families, families of several generations, and a few locals with visiting friends. When crowds were smaller, the event was less organized. First come, first served worked, and several stars had automatic spots on the concrete decking above the water.

"Cookies! Cookies! Two dollars a cookie." The voice behind the sales pitch was a dark-haired woman, too thin and in her fifties, her skin wrinkled from days in the harsh sunlight. She was riding an old bike with loose wheels, and a broken basket on the handlebars carried her home-baked goods.

She stopped pedaling and stepped onto the brick pavement when she saw Enrico reach into his pocket. "Oh my, what a handsome couple you make," she said, staring at him. "Thank you, kind sir," she added as he paid for two cookies with a five dollar bill, telling her to keep the money and the cookies.

Mounting her bike once again, she pedaled away, singing: "Cookies! Cookies! Mallory Square is alive with homemade cookies! Cookies! Cookies!"

They walked in between the people gathered around the magician. Soon the group dissipated as his female partner came closer to the crowd with a black hat in her hand. As Enrico and Paulette moved to the back to wait for the next show, the sun went over the horizon. There would be time for one more performance.

Enrico had another story. "For years there was a high-wire act right there." He pointed to the cement abutment in front of the water. If you check out some of the postcards, the guy's picture is still on it. He's gone, and so is the contortionist. The high-wire act I don't know enough about, except they say he went to Naples for the season because the tips were better."

"And the contortionist?"

"I knew you'd ask me that," Enrico said with a smile, showing a deep dimple on each cheek. "The story goes that when Mallory Square was updated, he moved from a free space to an assigned spot on the concrete platform."

"So?" Paulette said, wondering why that was important.

"Performing on the ledge next to the water brings in a lot more money than being in the center of the square. A *lot* more money," Enrico said with emphasis. "It turns out he and his wife made a deal that once she collected his final take on this one particular night, instead of coming out of the bag free of the chains, on the last turn, he would fall into the water still tied up while inside the zipped canvas bag. He would swim past the audience as usual, but when he was out of sight, instead of coming up, he would unzip his outfit and swim a short distance away, out somewhere along the shoreline. His wife would meet him there and they would take off.

"When they did that, a big scene followed with the fire and police departments arriving for the rescue. At great expense, they dredged the channel but never found the guy. A year later, exactly on the night of his disappearance, here he comes, his wife and daughter in tow. The three of them dined at the Turtle Bay Café, a little out-of-the way place popular with the locals. The manager called the police, who IDed the couple. That very night they ran them out of town. The city also filed a lawsuit for all the expenses that were never recovered."

"Where did they go? How did they have the nerve?"

"Who knows? Nerve? It doesn't take nerve to laugh at the city where you worked and made a good living for years. It only requires low class and stupidity."

After the sun set and the streetlights came on, the crowds on Mallory Square all but disappeared as jewelry sellers, carvers and painters, popcorn and clothes sellers, and finally the cookie lady went home.

When they reached the car and before letting Paulette in, he admitted, "I'd like to invite you to my apartment …"

"I'm not ready. This has been delightful. Thanks, I really appreciate it. Such a perfect day and evening."

"A kiss on the cheek then won't hurt either one of us," Enrico said as he wrapped his arms loosely around Paulette and pulled her closer. Gently lifting her chin as she turned her head slightly away, he pecked her cheek.

Paulette was definitely aroused, but the urge to retreat was when the hairs on her arms stood on end. This was her signal that something was not right. The urge to retreat was stronger than the urge to sleep with the handsome, sexy banker. Furthermore, even though it was the twenty-first century, Chris was the only one Paulette had ever kissed in that way, which at this moment, standing here like this with another man, felt like a betrayal. The real reason for her withdrawal, she had no idea. Emotions took over reason. She was not a schoolgirl, but she sure felt like one. Ridiculous. She wanted to explain further, but to say anything more, she would only ramble on and make the situation even more embarrassing.

❖

Jose caught Ariel in the hall. "I've called dozens of times. Why won't you let me apologize? I acted … I don't know. I wanted to tell you how I felt, but I screwed up."

"I'm not speaking to you."

"All I wanted to say is I'm sorry, and I am still your friend no matter what. And the only one who knows?" he stated with a question mark in his tone.

"Yep. The only one."

"What will you do?"

"Why is that any of your business?"

"At least talk to Ms. Marshall. She seems like a nice person. I like her. She's smart and she's funny."

"Just what I need: a therapist with a sense of humor."

"Will you come with me to the final dance like you promised? We had such a great time at the prom. Nothing more. Only for the last dance."

Ariel paused for a long minute and a half. "All right, all right," she said.

❖

The ringing of her front door startled Paulette. Hardly anyone knew where she lived.

"Who is it?" she asked.

"Ariel and Jose. Can we talk to you? Privately?" Ariel asked.

"I still have some furniture to buy," Paulette made light of the scarcity of accommodations as she led them to the two-seater couch and sat in the chair facing them.

"I ... we have a problem and I thought ... Jose thought I should come and talk to you. I was on part of that trip where Captain Maxy died—oh, not when he died—in the beginning," Ariel blurted out.

Paulette listened intently to every word Ariel uttered: How she left the captain and his two passengers. How she called Jose to pick her up. Even about the trip to South Beach, returning home only to hear her most trusted friend had died, and how guilty she felt. "There might have been something I could have done."

"First of all, there was nothing you were responsible for. So many decisions so young. It's a tragedy all the way around."

They did not tell Ms. Marshall about the baby, which would have only made everything so much more complicated. Nor did Ariel discuss the money taken from the safe, nor how she had exchanged the wills and kept the ring.

"If I were you, and you want some peace of mind," Paulette said, "I would make an appointment with Detective McKenna and tell him the truth. All of it," she said emphatically. "Only then will you be free of any guilt."

"I could go to jail!" Ariel gasped, looking over at Jose.

"I doubt it if you weren't on the boat for the return trip and you came home by other means."

"I ... he promised ... he said ... Max ... I stole money from him."

Paulette waited for the rest of the truth to come out.

"He paid me to go with him 'cause he knew I needed money. I took it again after first giving it back."

"What do you plan to do about that?"

"Return what's left. Jose and I ... I went to South Beach and spent some of it. I didn't ... I mean it was fun and all, but now I know it was stupid."

"About the money, a stupid mistake, yes. But if you are returning most of it, and you confess what you know, I'm not an officer of the law, but with a first offense, the department may decide not to bring charges."

"I guess so, but ..."

"The police know more of the pieces than you do. You might be of great help to solving this mystery. It's up to you to decide to do the right thing no matter what the consequences."

"You won't tell anyone if I don't go there, will you?"

"I'm concerned about you and your burden about this. If you don't talk to McKenna, this information will be too much to carry alone. From a legal standpoint, if you try to hide what you do know, you may look guilty to them somewhere down the road. If you confess too far after the fact, the department may bring charges, and the judge may not be as lenient, even to first offenders."

"You're right. You're both right," Ariel said as she looked from one to the other.

"Such a burden on a capable person's shoulders—yours—does not give the both of you a very good start for two teenagers caught in the middle of adult problems with no experience. I'm truly sorry about that," Paulette said. "Life will bring you many problems, but the day will come when you can use what you have learned, especially if you start out on the right foot."

"Yeah. Like don't do adult things with adults you trust."

Paulette looked at Ariel and contemplated what her offhand remark meant. She decided not to address it, but to add, "You are much luckier than so many others. You love each other and you have a bright future together.

"You have book learning, but so little knowledge and experience about how the world operates. Here you are, caught up in a web of despair, some of it your own doing. Let Captain McKenna decide your involvement. If there's a penalty to pay, pay it to the fullest and move on."

"Believe me, I have learned a big lesson. Lots of them." Ariel grabbed Jose's hand. "Jose is still on probation."

"Jose did not have anything to do with your involvement—unless you're holding back an important piece of the story. All he did was abide by your wishes and show up when you called."

"Did you know all of this?" Paulette asked Jose.

Jose, who had not said much of anything, shook his head.

"All right, then. Keep me posted."

CHAPTER 57

Jose drove Ariel to the police station. "You're on your own here, babe." He touched her shoulder then pulled her over for a kiss. She pushed him away. He said, "I know zero about all of this. You're the one who ..."

"I know, I know. Get ready, set, go. Okay?"

Ariel had been wrenching her hands, and they were sweating. She wanted to blame the heat, as everyone does, but honestly? It was the fear of going to jail for robbery. Even worse, maybe she really did contribute to Max's death.

Alan McKenna and a twelfth grader were sitting across from each other in his office in downtown Key West at local police headquarters. It was a not-very-large room with dark paneling on the walls. Luckily, there were no glass see-through windows, so officers rushing up and down the hall could not see in. The smell of mildew hung low except in the detective's office where an Air Wick was on top of one of the three-drawer file cabinets to the side of his desk.

After checking the books on his shelves, looking at family pictures, studying his messy desk and then looking at him, Ariel settled in. Finally she said, "I want to tell the truth, the whole truth, Detective."

McKenna waited for her to begin.

"I went with Max to get away from home. I often do, you know. Max has always been good to all of us, and ..."

"What time did you leave Garrison Bight?"

"Around six in the morning. The two Cuban guys were already aboard, and just as we were taking off, some big dude came aboard with two fifty-five-gallon drums. He handed Max two thousand dollars and stayed to himself the entire trip, like he was guarding his drums until we got to Islamorada. I steered us out of the channel! Actually, I am quite good at it."

"And?"

"I came here to tell you the rest," she said, taking a deep breath, convinced she was ready for the consequences. "I slept on the boat that night. I got up and caught the bus back to town. Have you ever been on one of those buses? Culture shock for sure. Before that ..." she hesitated, then began again. "Before that, I opened the safe and took out one of the envelopes that had a lot of money in it." A tremor took over in her voice as she continued. "I ... I spent some of the money on a weekend getaway to Miami. I'd been there once with my mother. What a miserable trip. This time I went for my own fun."

"That's where you caught the bus?"

"No, sir. That's a lie. I did not catch the bus. I called my friend, Jose Rodriguez, to come get me. We went together to South Beach. I had this envelope full of money, and I spent some of it."

"You had access to the safe?"

"I knew where he hid the combination: On the captain's desk under some maps. But I remembered it from when he told it to me when I was much littler."

"How many envelopes were in the safe at the time you opened it?"

"Maybe ten. Maybe more. I always heard about his numbering system and his famous brown book. It was just stacked in there. All that money."

"And you took how much?"

"The one envelope Max promised me."

"Why do you think he wanted to give you so much money?"

"For graduation ... and all."

"Do you have the money in your possession now?"

"Yes, sir."

McKenna waited as she unzipped her backpack and went to the bottom and took out a Kotex wrapper.

"I threw the envelope away," she admitted.

Inside the bag was a roll of hundred-dollar bills.

As she handed the money to the officer, she wished she had folded up the new will, taken it with her, and left the empty envelope that contained the new will where it was—under the sink aboard the Ramblin' Rose. Now she had a really big worry. When all the evidence was gathered, a lot of questions would point right at her.

"Do you have any idea how much this is?" he asked.

"Twenty-eight thousand dollars. More than I know how to keep. Its fool's gold as my daddy taught me. Witch's gold if I kept it. He thinks people shouldn't have that much money out of the bank no matter who they are. Can I give it to you—the rest, that is? As soon as I have a job, I'll replace the rest."

She watched as the captain thumbed through the bills, mentally counting them. She decided not to tell him about the five thousand she had tucked under her mattress at the back wall where her mother could not reach it.

"Then you and the captain were very close," he stated.

"Not more than he was with the other kids. He was good to all of us."

The look they shared told McKenna there was no way he was getting any further.

The report for the autopsy was in McKenna's possession, but he was not going to release it until roll call, which was following this meeting. The girl was not on site; therefore, she did not contribute in any way to the drowning. To go any further would be an intrusion into her privacy. No doubt she would have allowed him to probe further, but as an officer of the court, his duty was to also protect the innocent. To him, this also included the unaware and the very young.

"Will I go to jail?" Ariel asked.

"Over less than four thousand dollars and under the circumstances? I don't think so. At this point I can make no guarantees."

Tears streamed down Ariel's face.

After handing her a Kleenex, McKenna asked, "Were the two boys walking around with two open shopping bags filled with money? Did you see them bring anything like that when they came aboard?"

"No sir, I did not. They might have been in the drums, but I don't think so."

"What do you think might have been in the drums?"

"From the weight of them, when they were loaded onto the back of the truck, I would say drugs."

"Would you be willing to repeat what you just said in front of a court reporter? Go officially on record."

"Why?"

"It's a good idea for any future problems."

Oh, why did she even go to see Ms. Paulette? She made sense, but to admit wrong behavior and—well, Ariel was lost as to what to do next. She went to her apartment not for advice but for understanding. Certainly not to end up sitting in front of a cop. Not this at all. Now to put it on the record only made her feel trapped while the truth floated away like a rowboat without its oars and out of control. What she knew was no longer her own private secret.

McKenna called for a court reporter. After the swearing in, everyone settled down, ready to begin. "The sequence once more, please," he said, nodding to Ariel.

"I went with Captain Maxy—we all called him that—to Islamorada. Then I called a friend to come pick me up so I could go home. The reason I wanted to go home is I thought by the time the captain turned around, we wouldn't be back before my mother came in from Miami."

"What time did your friend pick you up?"

"Around 3 a.m."

"Where did you sleep?"

"In one of the beds on board. Downstairs. I told you that. I was more comfortable there. When I was a kid and my mom was fighting with me or drunk, that's where I would go."

"It wouldn't feel strange then to be there all alone late at night?"

"No sir, it wouldn't."

"Do you have a cell phone?"

"Not the kind that picks up messages from my house phone if that's what you're asking," she replied.

"Where were you during the financial transactions between the parties for the trip?"

"Me? I was down in the cabins. I stayed there most of the time, wishing I hadn't come. I had things to do. Homework. Chores around the house, food shopping. Not like when we were younger and had no responsibilities."

"We believe your fingerprints are all over the boat."

"Duh. Probably. We ... I go there sometimes with my friends. Sometimes I stop by to say hi by myself. The captain is ... was a really neat guy. A father to us kids."

"Do you know the combination to the safe?"

"Nope."

McKenna interrupted her. "Either you lied previously about how you knew the combination and opened the safe or you didn't.

CHAPTER 58

ARIEL STARED AT THE DETECTIVE for a long time before she continued. "I had the combination. I opened the safe. I took out one envelope," she said emphatically, "the one Max wanted to give me."

"Does his daughter, Susanna, also have the combination to the safe?"

"How would I know?"

"Just to keep you informed, the captain's daughter has opened the safe, and, to her knowledge, nothing was missing."

"Told ya." Ariel stopped. She stared straight across the desk and looked beyond the detective, slid down in her chair, and shut down.

"Word is everyone around him knew he kept a large amount of cash on his boat."

"True. I never saw any of it until that one time." Anger was growing inside Ariel.

"Damn it!" McKenna slammed his yellow pad on the desk. "The truth."

"I am telling the truth, Detective." The noise shocked her back to reality.

McKenna continued. "What did the two boys aboard look like?"

"How do you older people say it? They looked like typical teenagers. One was a few years older than his younger brother—if they were brothers. The older one was about six feet tall, thin, long legs and arms. Brown curly hair, dark brown eyes. A tattoo on his forearm that said something under a peace sign.

"The younger one was shorter. An inch taller than me. Cute. Baby face. Curly hair also. Thin, very thin. Oh, and he smoked."

"For someone who stayed below, you seem to know a lot. Maybe more than you're telling me," McKenna said.

"I don't want to be a cop if that's what you mean. In my neighborhood you have to keep track of every detail. It's not like the white side of town where floodlights light big houses. Half the time we don't have electricity. We're crammed into 850 to a thousand square feet. Most of us have to live with our parents. Either that or head for Miami for a proper job."

The witness's eyes were beginning to wander and disconnect from McKenna. Even so, before he stopped, he asked, so he could push her a bit further, "Did either of them see the captain put money in the safe?"

"I have no idea."

"Try to remember."

"Now how can I remember when I don't know what else may have been in the safe than what I told you earlier?"

"You knew the captain well enough. Do you think there was a prior arrangement between the parties, or was the exchange made on the spot?"

"Sorry, sir. I just told you everything I know, straight out. He seemed surprised when the drums arrived, but he took the money."

"Who was the friend who picked you up from the motel at 3 a.m.?"

"Why do you want to know?" Ariel asked, looking over at the court reporter.

"It would be helpful. He or she might know something more. Observed something you did not see," McKenna explained.

"Not if my possible fingerprints—and those of the two suspects—are all you found."

Smart ass, McKenna wanted to say. Instead, he continued. "If I supplied you with a series of photos, could you identify the last man who came aboard the boat just before you left the docks?"

"I guess so. Can I go now?"

The detective did not make a gesture or agree. He only kept looking over his notes written on a yellow legal pad. "The boys? Did they use their names? Say anything at all?"

"No, sir. The older brother called the younger one 'little bro'. That was all. The newspapers say they spoke no English. Not true. We call it Spanglish."

"Back to the boys. Could you pick them out in a lineup?"

"You think they killed Maxy? Captain Hernandez?"

McKenna looked over at the pictures on the side of his desk, glad he had sons. This girl was not only street smart, she was intelligent. She knew exactly how to handle him, and she was doing a good job of it. "Once again, you left Captain Maxy and his passengers behind because?"

"I told you. I wanted to get home before my mother. She was expected that night, but when I got home, there was a message that said she wouldn't be back until late Monday and that I should get myself off to school. Does any of this have to go on my record?" She glanced once again over at the court reporter typing into a small machine.

McKenna motioned for the court reporter to step out and take a short break. Once she shut the door and was out of sight, Ariel admitted, "One of the boys, the younger one with the curly hair? He made a serious pass at me. I was very uncomfortable."

"Did you tell the captain?"

"He had enough on his mind."

"Like what?"

"I really don't know, but I would guess it was about his wife, Rosetta. She's been after him to retire. She thinks he couldn't keep up, and he didn't have much judgment left about who he hired out to. Can I have something to drink? A Coke maybe?"

"Sure." He buzzed reception and soon an ice-chilled bottle appeared.

Ariel wiped the sweat off the bottle and took a sip. Putting the bottle in between them on the captain's desk, she said, "If I tell you more, ID your suspects, and I give you my fingerprints, will you keep the person who drove me home, a person who is in no other way involved—will you keep him out of the picture?" She held the bottle tightly and waited for an answer.

"Perhaps. For a time at least. Until we have a clearer picture of the entire situation."

They exchanged direct eye contact, and she handed him the bottle.

Uncomfortable as he was at being trumped by a teenager, McKenna's agreement and compromise was the end of the questioning. If the witness's story held up, neither one of them would end up with an arrest record anyway.

McKenna stood up and ended the interview with these words: "If anything else comes up, I'll call you. Wait in the lobby. Your mother is coming to pick you up. In the meantime, if we have anything else, I know where you'll be."

"Please do not catch me at school. Leave a message on my phone. Okay?"

CHAPTER 59

~~∽∽∾∾∞∞∽∽~~

IT WAS TWO MONTHS LATER. Attorney Frank Alberto (for business, Franco Alberto for family and friends), practiced in Islamorada. He had called the Hernandez family together for the reading of the terms of sea captain Maxwell Horatio Hernandez's last will and testament dated January 15, 2011.

As he looked around the room, he remarked, "Everyone looks well." Thirteen people were seated at the conference table or behind it in folding chairs. "I'm sorry for your loss. Maxwell Hernandez was a good man, a good father. Is everyone comfortable? Good. There's coffee and orange juice on the table to your left."

"No thank you," Susanna said for the group.

"Mrs. Hernandez, it has been too long," Franco said.

Rosetta did not reply. Her stare was a blank one as she looked around the room with little to no understanding, having previously discussed with Susanna and Michael that they would interpret all the legalese for her. If they agreed, then they were to handle Max's estate.

Beforehand she told them: "Your father knew the finances, and was of sound mind when he updated his will.

"Each of you has been given a full copy of the will executed on the date stated above," Franco began. "Forget the boilerplate. In essence, the items broken down on the sheet I have provided should cover all your questions. I would like to go through each of those sections first. Then if there are any questions, we can discuss them at the end. To begin:"

My wife, Rosetta Martinez Hernandez, is to stay in our home free and clear of any debts until her death. All expenses, including taxes and upkeep, are to be taken out of a special trust to be set up from the funds at South Shore Bank where such funds will be taken from safe-deposit box #201. Added to this new trust will be any monies remaining in my two checking accounts.

The attorney interjected, "Such sum amounts to $87,501.12 at close of business yesterday. I also took the liberty of checking with the corporation that issued the bearer bonds which we will discuss in a moment. Going on:"

Until such trust fund has been established, Mrs. Susanna Hernandez Ruiz, my youngest daughter, is to use the money, as outlined above, to cover all monthly bills. She is to send out a monthly report to all concerned parties as well. The new trust is also for my wife's care. Our daughter, Susanna, Mrs. Ruiz, is to be the only signer on the account. Included in this list is my wife's food, electricity, a clothing allowance, and a new car with good gas mileage. Son Michael Hernandez is to propose a list of automobiles, and Rosetta Hernandez is to choose whichever car she wishes from that list.

Alberto paused when his secretary knocked lightly on the door. The woman who entered had an unassuming manner about her. She was dressed in a plain beige dress, her auburn hair tied back in a ponytail. She was clutching a small, inexpensive, out-of-style handbag. Motioned to a seat, she sat to the side of the family.

"Continuing:"

The funds in box #201 at South Shore Bank are listed in a little brown book that is kept on board The Ramblin' Rose. There is $372,000 in cash and forty thousand in bearer bonds currently in the safe on the boat.

"From the information reported to me by Mrs. Ruiz, it seems the listing of those particular funds was halted several years ago. However, two current entries are not clear to her. Also, certain envelopes have been shifted around, and the total number is fewer than stated in this will. However, she does not see this as a problem since her father dealt in cash with everyone. Continuing to read:"

On my wife's demise, such monies remaining are to be put in a trust with equal rights divided among all five of my children.

Regarding the four houses, three of them are presently rented out. They bring in a total of $3580 a month. This is obviously very low against the index for Key West. However, these three houses are rented to close friends and/or their parents. Take special note that the rental rate is not to change unless and until each party decides to voluntarily leave the premises.

The fourth house is to be held in trust for Ariel Costas. The house must be repaired and updated. She is to live there rent free until she completes her education if she decides to pursue a nursing career. She formed this idea at age fourteen, and could change her mind. If she does, she has this estate's permission to stay in the premises for one dollar per month while she completes her education. At that time, she is responsible to pay all taxes and upkeep on the property. Further note that whatever career she chooses, her tuition is to be paid in full out of the family trust. Whenever she marries or has a child, the house is to be deeded over to her, free and clear.

"Now remember," Alberto cautioned, "this will was written four years ago. Continuing on:"

In case any member of my family questions this decision and sues my estate, he or she will receive one dollar with a reminder of how much each of my children has already been given such as educations, weddings, homes, and businesses. Therefore, no one will receive an immediate lump sum of money unless otherwise stated herein.

Of note is another safe-deposit box at South Shore Bank that I began over thirty years ago when the bank first opened. In my way of record keeping, there should be sixteen envelopes with $30 thousand in each envelope inside safe-deposit box #117. Note that all of this has been recorded in my brown notebook kept under the sink on the Ramblin' Rose. Susanna Hernandez Ruiz will also be in charge of the distribution of such funds.

"Remember again, these funds may be up or down for the reason Susanna states," Alberto said. "Going on:"

There is eighty thousand in numbered envelopes in the safe aboard the Ramblin' Rose. All are reminded this was my "slush fund." I have used these funds as needed for cars, down payments on houses, braces, private school for my grandchildren, buying restaurants, and home repairs on the four rental properties and the homes of four of my five children. Whatever is left on board the Ramblin' Rose is to be equally divided. Once again, Susanna Ruiz will be in charge of the distribution.

To Jose Rodriguez I leave all my tools and all the contents in the shed at the side of my house on Petronia. This should amount to thirty to forty thousand dollars worth of tools, boat parts, and supplies. Once he has reorganized and cleaned the place I have neglected these past years, he may sell or put to good use anything he salvages in any manner he sees fit. He is also to be given my old red truck "as is."

To Tom Jamison I leave the Ramblin' Rose with the hope that he will become a fisherman and take over my customers. In the event he chooses to further his education and become a lawyer (God forbid), his education is to be fully paid for out of the main trust.

To each of my grandchildren born before Rosetta passes, I leave one thousand dollars. A savings account is to be opened in their name. The funds are to be taken out of the newly established family trust. It is the obligation of my family to teach them to save as I have.

Lastly, for my former secretary, Julie Jackson, who worked so very hard during the years of a full operation where she booked four fishing vessels every single day and kept us all on schedule, for all her efforts, I leave her all the bearer bonds aboard the Ramblin' Rose and in the safe-deposit box #117 at South Shore Bank.

"That's about it," Alberto said.

Satisfied all their questions were answered, and Susanna had agreed to follow through wherever necessary, the family walked out together, leaving the outsiders, Jose, Ariel, and Julie behind.

CHAPTER 60

JOSE AND ARIEL SAT DUMBFOUNDED until the attorney folded up the file in preparation to exit the conference room.

Tom came over to them and said, "Can we talk outside?"

Settled on a bench in the open air, Tom began, "I was with Max a couple of nights before he died, trying to fish. He talked ... well ... he talked in a way I couldn't sort through. Not with an ending like this one." Tom released a deep breath and shook his head. "He told me I could have the boat and that the tools in the shed were for Jose. When I told him I was interested in setting up my own machine shop, we agreed to a switch. There are enough parts stored up in there to keep me occupied for a long while.

"He told me to have you take the boat, fix it up, and then to take over whatever was left of his seasonal business."

"I really don't know. I sort of promised my dad I'd work with him."

"Can't you do both? You once told me it only took a coupla days a week. Think about it and let me know. I would really love to dive into the mess in his garage and not the mess on that boat. Let me know what you want to do. We might have to wait a while for clearance on the exchange from the attorney."

"We will," Ariel piped in. "My idea is Jose should take the boat. He loves the water. Right now we're all too sad about Max to think clearly." She took Jose's hand, knowing in the way he wavered that it would not take much to convince him that the boat was his true desire.

When Tom separated from them, Ariel and Jose agreed they would dry-dock the boat for repairs. "We'll go to the police station with proof of ownership. Pick up the envelope that came from the safe that is rightly ours."

"How do you know all this?"

"Tom told me a while back that the envelope was put into evidence and would be released to the owners of the Ramblin' Rose. We're the rightful owners."

"I suppose. I hope down the road you'll take care of the finances."

Once they were in possession of the boat, Ariel would give the gold coins and bearer bonds to Susanna along with several personal letters. Then she would wait a few days to see what repercussions might occur. If there were none, she would take the funds sitting at the police station and open a bank account in Miami for her baby.

If for any reason there was a setback, at least Ariel had a house of her own.

Susanna and Rosetta were in the parking lot. "Ma, you cannot let what just happened in there stand. You have to fight," Susanna said.

"What for?" Rosetta answered. "It is what it is. I told you my wishes before we all came up here. We have plenty of money, all of us. The rest we pay taxes on anyway. I'm at the stage of wanting to divest."

"Divest? Where to?"

"By divesting I will have simplicity and the respect I deserve. And my own life. For the first time since I was eighteen. *Eighteen*," she mused. "My, my, such a long time ago."

Susanna did not mention the money on the boat to her mother. She was certain she could get the envelopes out of the evidence cage at the station with Tom's help. He would tell her the day the boat was to be released to Jose and take her to the police station before the release date.

In the meantime, she had access to two separate safe-deposit boxes and two blank, unsigned checks at her disposal. *Now who has the money?* she thought with a smirk. And now Susanna's ex-husband would be coming around. She was equal to him financially, and now she just might change her mind about still being crazy in love with him.

The lady who stayed behind to talk to the attorney, Julie Jackson, was someone none of the family recognized.

She said to Rosetta while the rest of her family was milling around: "Hello. I am Julie Jackson. I am sorry for your loss. He was a very kind man. I will see Susanna soon. When it is convenient, I will pick up the bonds. We live in Miami—my son and I. Mark graduates from high school this year. He has a partial scholarship to Yale in engineering. I had no idea about the bonds. This money is a miracle, and we thank you."

Rosetta said with a warm smile, "Don't thank me. Max was the saver. I was always the spender, but I don't have much to show for it."

"We're not sure what will be released when or if we have to go into probate," Susanna said, jumping in. She was surprised by her mother's change in attitude. This was not the mother she knew who whined and played victim all these years. Her mother was actually conversing with this woman in such a kind manner. She took her mother's reaction like it was a guarantee this woman Julie would get the bearer bonds without a hassle.

All of this seemed so unreal to Susanna—her mother being taken care of like this.

What Susanna got she got by hiding important information from her family. She felt rotten about it, but if that's what it took, then she would have to keep her secrets forever. For example, what about the fact that almost $300,000 aboard the Ramblin' Rose was booked into evidence? The envelope simply marked "To the owner of the Ramblin' Rose"? When Max was alive, everyone knew who that was. Now it was Tom himself, and while he was a nice guy who cared about her family, in no way would she believe he'd hand over that kind of money to anyone else. Rather, he would claim it for himself if he knew it was enough to quit his job and start fishing.

Susanna had lied to Tom when they visited the boat. She took a too-quick look and reported there were about ten envelopes. When it was time to go to the evidence room to sign out the bearer bonds to this Miss Jackson, Susanna would take all but two or three of the envelopes for her own keeping and no one else would be the wiser.

Susanna's present worry was for her son, Xavier. By the time he was in college, her mother would be gone and all five properties divided up. In today's market the houses could bring in as much as a million apiece. Divided equally by five, she would have the same million each of her brothers and sisters would receive. And very soon she would have the evidence packet from the police and access to two very full safe-deposit boxes.

On the way home in Michael's van, Rosetta whipped out a new iPhone and called a friend. She was smiling, making plans for a future trip, talking about how to decorate her house, and the new clothes she would buy. She ended with, "I am ready for the new adventures ahead!"

CHAPTER 61

IT WAS TWO WEEKS SINCE Max's death, and Ariel was dressed for the prom. She had on a loose-fitting white top over an eyelet blouse and black leggings like the other girls. But not *really* like the other girls. They were not pregnant. Unless they weren't talking about it. She had also been to the doctor and found a gynecologist to deliver her baby with in-between visits for proper prenatal care.

"Ready, Freddy?" Jose laughed nervously as he used one of his father's clichés. "You look absolutely gorgeous. Here,"—he thrust a bouquet at her and grabbed her hand—"this goes on the wrist, like the old days."

"How sweet," she said and smiled, wanting to be in his arms, but knowing at home, in her mother's presence, was the last place to show affection. "I'll thank you later," she whispered, looking downward in embarrassment and hoping her mother wasn't listening.

The way Jose looked at her lately, and especially at this moment, she knew tonight was the night.

Jose's head was spinning. Too much was happening too quickly, and he was not sure how to deal with any of it. One day you're a kid thinking and doing kid things, the next day you're determined to reach "home" in this game of hopscotch called life. Suddenly you step into the adult world prepared to make adult decisions, but you haven't any idea how to do it.

In the car Ariel said: "What about the boat? Are you really going to try and do something with it?"

"My dad wants me to take over his business. Says now that I'm almost graduated he'll be going on the road again. Last week he took his first drink since he came home two years ago."

"What a surprise," Ariel replied sarcastically. "You gonna do it?"

"What do you want me to do?"

"Your choice. It's your life."

"I wanted to talk to you about that."

Ariel was suddenly nervous. Her face went flush as she realized she was not ready for this next step. It was not at all like she thought it would be—how she would feel. "Right here? Right now? We'll be late. We're already late."

"Do you care?" asked Jose.

"Oh, sure. Miss Popularity here will be missed. They are definitely going to stop the dance because I ... *we* are not there."

Jose took Ariel's arm, the one that had the flowers he helped the florist put together for the corsage now on her wrist. "I've been thinking a lot about you since Miami."

"What?"

"Shh! It's my turn for once."

She leaned back and smiled.

"Since Miami, I haven't stopped thinking about you. I can't stop now. I want to share my life with you. If you'll have me. I ... We should get married."

"And the baby?"

"I want to take care of him."

"What if its a girl?"

"His name will be Max for a boy or Maxine for a girl."

"Yuck. It better be a boy."

"When ... that's not what I am trying ... what I am saying. You have a house now, and we graduate high school next week. I know you want to travel to parts unknown, go to Miami for a nursing program. Who's going to take care of our baby? Me?"

"What about you and your baseball career?"

"That was always a pipe dream. More Max's than mine. I know I'm good but not that good. Us. I want us to get married," he blurted out, his breathing shallow, his edgy voice waiting for the laugh and the no he expected.

"Do you love me? And the baby?"

"You know I do, already."

"Already what?" Ariel couldn't resist teasing him, or at least hold on until she had to give it up and act mature. It was part of her very nature when she was with those she cared about to think maybe they would understand and she would never have to grow up. Wouldn't that be fun? Besides, she was all excited inside. Thanks be to God, she was getting a second chance.

Seriously—very seriously—she was going to say yes. Even so, she needed him to suffer a little bit more.

Ariel also knew from somewhere deep inside that Jose knew who the father of her baby was, but he would never ask her. That just wasn't his way, and she loved him for it.

"Just answer me, damn it! Will you marry me!"

"Yes, Jose, we will marry you."

CHAPTER 62

TOM MCKENNA WAS READY TO wrap this case up and move on. The important witnesses had been interviewed, and high school student Ariel Costas had come forward. He believed her to be innocent. Just a kid caught in a dangerous situation who got out of it before the real trouble began.

Forensics had already been into his office with the results of the autopsy. Vernon had confirmed: "Accidental, boss."

"What about the bruises?"

"Normal bruises of a fisherman. The gash on his side might mean the boys tossed him overboard, but he was dead before he hit the water. Massive heart attack. He had digitalis in his system, so the symptoms were with him for quite some time."

"Can you be more specific?"

"We might be able to pin down the time of death within a few hours of the heart attack that killed him, but isn't accidental or intentional what we were after? His family are the only ones who could tell you about specific symptoms and when the onset began. They're not professionals, and they might not know. My tests say he was a goner before he hit the water."

"Anything else?"

"No fingerprints were found on the shoe floating further away. My guess is the victim lost it during the several hours in the water before the rescue."

"Can you determine whether he jumped on his own accord or was pushed?"

"If jumping or being pushed is an issue, your suspects may have more information. But you know they are going to give you answers that benefit them and not the case."

"Today's meeting is about good news and bad news, winners and losers," McKenna began at the daily roll call. "On the Hernandez case, results of the autopsy prove accidental death. The captain had a myocardial infarction, more commonly known as a heart attack, before he hit the water. So far as the authorities know, nothing in the safe was touched, so the case is closed. The money from the boat is to be released to its rightful owner, and the two Cuban boys will be cleared of all charges."

"But sir," Scooter interrupted. "Those illegals. Do they just get released out onto the street?"

"No, Scooter. They will be turned over to a different department and given a boat ride back to Cuba, and that's that. If we had more evidence or if the outcome was different, we might be able to bring the two suspects up on minor charges. The safe was inspected by a member of the family, and no monies or other valuables were missing. Case closed. We have some real criminals to catch. On the Hernandez case, where was the intent? Hard to prove with a death the result of health issues."

"Perpetrated by illegals," Scooter pointed out.

"Oh, now you're a lawyer."

The group laughed and McKenna continued. "My feeling is they were into mischief and then they were in the wrong place at the wrong time. A crime? Perhaps. They may have thrown the key overboard out of fear but to what aim we cannot ascertain. Apparently they've lost two bags of someone else's money along the way. The guess is about ten thousand dollars. Since it doesn't appear it was the captain's, we have no follow-through there either. Questions? ... Dismissed. Officer Jamison. Can I see you in my office in about ten minutes?"

McKenna and Tom arrived at McKenna's office at the same time. "Will you follow through on the paperwork?" he asked Tom. "By the way, how did you get that name, Tall Tom? It seems to have stuck. With a new crew here, would you like it dropped or are you okay with it?"

"Either way, sir. When Captain Hauser was in charge, there were two other Toms on staff. One was a small guy but a real fighter. After that, a medium-size guy came aboard. Then there was me," he said with a smile. "The rest of the guys are gone now and the name sorta stuck."

The captain chuckled. "Well, you decide. My purpose is to thank you for all your help. Without all the background information you supplied and how well you handled the delicate job of questioning people you have close relationships to, the force's budget would have been stretched, and the case would not have moved along as quickly. I know a few times you were put in a tough spot. I want you to know that as far as the department is concerned, at all times you handled yourself in a professional manner. To that end, I am putting a letter to that effect in your file."

"Thank you, sir."

Tom turned to leave and was called back.

"You're a hometown boy, aren't you, Tom? I envy you. On this case I saw the way everyone who has lived around here so long came through for each other. I've moved around too much to receive any of that. No real roots. No connections. You have them, and they will keep building. Are you going out on your own now that you have the possibility of owning a real machine shop in these parts?"

"Ariel told you?"

"She called, yes. Told me about the trade."

"No, sir. I plan to stay with the force. Max's shop is my part-time job—on the side, during vacations and time off. Next thing I need is a wife. After that, can we talk again?"

"You and me both. About needing a wife, that is—a good one. In the meantime, great job, and thank you."

The men shook hands, and Tom was dismissed.

Standing at the back of Garrison Bight Marina in uniform on the first weekend after learning the true fate of the Ramblin' Rose, Drew said to Scooter: "Those damned kids own that piece of junk. We can't bomb the piece of shit while it's dry-docked at Garrison. My cousin works there."

Scooter had a bright idea. "Let's go to Goodwill, pick up some fisherman's pants, a coupla plaid shirts, and a fishing pole and see what happens. Or we could wait 'til it goes back in the water."

"The money is booked into evidence. Remember? The widow or the smart-ass daughter who lives with her will sign the evidence envelope out more likely than the kids will. It's been a week since the reading of the will."

"I saw the chart. No one has shown up," Scooter said.

"We have to make our move before that daughter comes to collect the money. We can't just sit around and wait," Drew yelled. "What if someone else tries to get into the evidence room before we get there? So the evidence room is our best bet."

"I'm glad you finally see the mess we're in," Scooter replied. "Let's check the boat first."

Drew stepped into the boat. "Now that we're here, this is not a very good idea. Why do this? We should be in uniform, go into the evidence room on a slow day, and just take the damned envelope. Keep the bag and put it in our shirt on the way out. Who's ever going to find it in the mess back there?"

CHAPTER 63

~~∞∞∞~~

IT WAS JUNE, THE MONTH for graduations and weddings.

The invitation to Ariel and Jose's wedding was in Paulette's box at school. The ceremony was to be held at St. Mark's church the first Saturday following graduation.

How lovely, she thought. She may not have a natural son who appreciates her yet, what with his anger at the divorce and then having his mother leave for Key West at the same time he went off to college. However, here and in San Fernando there were still students near his age who considered her important in their lives, even if temporarily.

"Oh well, that's the breaks," she responded to the unspoken litany that remained in her head as she wondered if she had underplayed Billie's need for attention and overplayed her role with others as their caregiver.

"You know what?" she said out loud. "This invitation makes up for all the second guessing, even for the mistakes I made with my heart wide open while trying my best."

A few teachers were dashing around, no one listening to her self-talk. That was just fine with Paulette. She was being sentimental because she was tying up all the loose ends and preparing to go home to LA at the summer's end. She loved Paradise. It had taught her by example how to wind down and reassess her ambitions against those she had while married and living in LA.

As Paulette saw it, each generation alters the world, changes its music, believes they are the reason the earth rotates. All of this a result of newly infused genius from the Information Age via computers, tablets, and cell phones. This is their way to ignore the human condition each of us must face up to as we all make our way through the quagmires of life just as a captain steers his boat through the obstacles of the waterways until there is a clear pathway ahead.

As sad as Paulette was to leave, as much as everyone had been so wonderful, so kind, and so accepting, the time had come to make a choice: to immerse herself into the Key West lifestyle or move on. Her classroom was ready for the next person, and Paulette hoped that one would be as eager to counsel the at-risk students for the next school year as she was. Paulette had met the Girl Scout creed of leaving a place in better shape than she found it.

Paulette's Key West experience meant everything to her changes. She came as a woman who did not know her way around, dependent on another person for her decisions, her entertainment, her all. No one can fit that bill, at least not in today's world. And not since the first rumblings of women's lib one hundred years ago, fully activated during her mother's time.

Paulette and her mother would talk about that one of these days: the switch in the female point of view, what the shift meant to women raised in the fifties, and what her mother thinks of the new experiences since then?

In Key West, Paulette had developed into her own person. She was no longer just someone's daughter, mother, or wife while becoming involved in what she, like so many tourists, outsiders, and temporary visitors initially think—that Key West is only a land of play. It is so much more and then some. It embodies soul and freedom personified, a way of life envied by those who wish they knew how to let everything go and misunderstood by those who would never dare to try.

Visits made, relatives thanked, the wedding and end of the school year party attended, Paulette turned in her keys. It was finally time to hit the road. The high school was on her right, and Key West International Airport on her left, as she drove along Flagler Drive.

Circling onto US 1 and heading north, Paulette was sobbing, thinking of the chance she had been given to continue as a citizen of Key West for as long as she wished to stay and how she was not going to take advantage of it.

Billie would spend part of the summer with her in LA, or so he said. When would he understand how much she loved him? What could she do to make things right? She must tell him how sorry she was that he was an only child and sorry she did not adopt so all the scrutiny did not land on his misdeeds instead of his better qualities.

On her way home, she would stop in Wellington to visit her parents. She longed for an afternoon of shopping with her mother and some time with her father to watch him carve wood in his garage. Next, she would head for Palm Beach and a dinner with Iris Darby, her parents, her sister Sharon, and her husband Timothy J. Buckner, now head of his father-in-law's banking firm.

Iris told Paulette in confidence how she (Iris) was finally going to unload her secret that would blast the family apart after all these years, and she wanted her family and their third "sister" Paulette present for support.

"What I have to say will change the entire dynamics of the Darby family forever," Iris had said on her last phone call.

Knowing she was not ready to return to LA on any kind of permanent basis, Paulette was beginning to listen to the call from the Carolinas.

Billie was settled back in the Casa del Marcella and never home.

Home to help him unpack, she went to the San Fernando campus. The pull was not there either, so she went down to the District and put in for a year's leave of absence, which was approved. There were plenty of new, young hopefuls, new college graduates, ready to become do-gooders.

What Paulette wanted was to sit at her window in the Carolinas as fall arrived and watch the trees as their leaves change colors and then drop them in honor of the upcoming season.

Preview of
Palm Beach Interlude

The Paulette Marshall Series
by Lois Richman

Dreams do come true. One might have to wait a while, but they do. They do.

Paulette Marshall is so settled, her feet on solid ground for the first time in a long while, and she is content. She had always dreamed about coming home, but Palm Beach just wasn't the same, or was too much of the same. At this point, she had no opinion. She had only been a visitor, well-informed and with a long past history, coming from when she built her life in Los Angeles, California.

The West Coast, LA specifically, is where her castle in the sky, Casa del Marcella, held prestige and provided a spectacular view. Her ex-husband, still panting and hoping and with his checkbook wide open, still wanted to know: "How much do you want?" hoping she would change her mind and sell her half of the Casa so he and his new wife, her two kids, and their new baby could move in.

No way. Paulette had been holding onto the Marshall family home as payback for all the pain.

Son Billie was at UCLA, a mere seven miles and forty-five minutes away, but he has lived on campus, enjoying what all students his age want: to be in Westwood and let loose.

Paulette had been thinking about one of those condos where the HOA takes care of everything. She would have underground parking and security.

She is still attracted by the hills where trees grow naturally and tall, where woods are filled with all aspects of nature otherwise stripped from them by humans and their buildings.

Up on her two and half acres in the Carolinas, she has a small cabin now. It sits near the river that runs below her property. She and a helper have built pathways—passable but uninviting. She has a pen for horses she has not been brave enough to ride. She has also planted corn for next season, and her tomatoes are so sweet she would like to ship them to her friends, but by the time they would get there, they would taste like the store-bought vine variety.

The "why" of being up in the hills was obvious to her. She is living another dream, having found peace, quiet, and purpose after the settlement of a year of internal turmoil in Key West. The peace and quiet were obvious. But the purpose? It is to live the richness of life without earthly-made sounds of cars vibrating to the beat of their stereo systems and mama trucks with short dudes racing to outdo the even shorter ones.

Maybe she could find a purpose in just swaying with the trees and sitting by the fire during the winter, logs under the porch. For right now, that was quite enough.

The obvious truth to everyone else? Her Key West journey of self-discovery is behind her now, but she has not come back to a reality where there are loose ends that only she can settle and then let go of. Staying three thousand miles away has been helpful, but the day will come where she will have to confront it. For now, she hears the birds in the morning, sees a deer now and then, and the wonderful breezes between the leaves of untrimmed, shapeless trees that feed her soul. Her quiet time is all that matters for now … until the day of the call about Timothy J. Buckner.

It was Tim's daughter on the phone. "Oh, Miss Paulette, you have to come to Palm Beach! They have arrested my dad for the murder of his new wife."

"Honey, you need a lawyer, not me. I'm a counselor in semi-retirement for the moment."

"No. It's that he won't talk to anyone else. We've all been to see him. We put up his bail, but he won't leave until you come and talk to him."

"You're kidding. No, of course you're not. That's your father. I just don't know that I can."

She returns to Palm Beach, and thus begins the investigation of the death of Tim's second wife, Barbara-with-the-Four-Names as his kids call her. Why? Tim is her fourth husband.

This is Palm Beach. Money has changed hands, but old money still prevails in bank deposits, respect, and that certain silent, side-view envy expressed in so many subtle ways, even among their equals.

Beatrice Welch Darby said, "Palm Beach is not for your ordinary modern family. Heaven forbid!"

Neither was their family life supposed to go like this. "After all, we are still a well-known, well-respected Palm Beach family."

Beatrice lives by her good name and her showy mansion and appearances at parties and fund raisers. She and her sister, Claire, came from a poor family who lived in Green Acres, which in their day was where the wild ones were—plenty of trailers and dirt roads. They were thrust into better schools because of new rules about equal education and busing. She was never going back there, nor would she admit this was her beginning.

"We have a middle-size mansion next to the gigantic ones whose owners have raided and razed our homes only to return to their foreign countries and spend as little time in their mansions as many stateside American multimillionaires do each year," Beatrice would explain.

The Darby residence sits on more than two acres across the street from the Atlantic Ocean on Ocean Boulevard between the 100 and the 300 blocks. Mrs. Darby has said to her immediate family: "Our children went to the best schools and are considered to have established themselves among their fellow graduates from Harvard and Yale. We have been a generous family. We have educated our children and even helped our granddaughter's husband become a famous artist, tattoos and all. We knew of an executive who worked for MCA Records and worked out of the Tower in Hollywood—North Hollywood, to be precise. He produced the first record and got this newest member to the family his first "gig"—whatever that is.

"We have only one wayward daughter, Iris, but then who does not have a child that either runs away, marries out of her class, or rebels in dozens of less obvious ways?

"I suppose the eightieth birthday party for my husband is the best place to start. As usual, Iris was late, and everyone except my son-in-law, Timothy J. Buckner, a short-tempered, spoiled brat with no class, were continuing their exchange of stories as the buffet remained in care of the help who were already overworked from the large dinner party the night before."

Such a small thing to worry about—the pattern of my wayward daughter, Beatrice thought now. Small indeed, as it would be a short time before her favorite daughter—the one who looked after the family, really—was dead. Hit by a truck filled with sand, the driver swearing she stepped off the curb after he began turning right and thus was unable to stop.

Mrs. Darby said, "My son-in-law married again: an old, a very moneyed dowager, even by Palm Beach standards, labeled Barbara-with-the-Four-Names, a name spoken only behind her back.

"When Barbara was stabbed to death a year after their marriage, in what the police called a hate crime, Beatrice was beginning to think about the death of her daughter Sharon. If he had anything to do with either one of them—even though Beatrice did not know Miss Barbara as she liked to be called—Beatrice would personally destroy whatever was left of his dignity. If cleared of his charges and if he inherited Barbara's millions, Beatrice and her team of experts would start out taking those holdings apart. Her husband did not run a bank and teach her the art of the deal for nothing."

It is Madison, Sharon and Timothy J. Buckner's daughter, who is screaming into the phone. She is in California, eight and a half months pregnant. Her rapper husband is out of town, and she has to take care of her two and half year old daughter, so she cannot possibly help her father.

So at eight and half months pregnant, Paulette could not exactly say, "You do it! It's not my life, my drama." *Oh, well,* Paulette thinks. *Here we go again.*

Back in the day and periodically from then on, Paulette had been very close to his wife, Sharon. They were not only schoolgirl friends, they were best friends. They made a vow to look out for each other. In the early days of her marriage to Timothy, Sharon was vague with her answers to direct questions about his behavior. But if Paulette heard about any harm, which had been the talk for years, she would have immediately been on a plane for home to look into it. He was a cheater, a liar, a fool-around who married Sharon for her name and the position her father could offer. Sharon knew it, and that fact was the elephant at the table all these years.

Why should Paulette assist in Timothy's rescue, anyway? She never really trusted him nor liked him all that much, apart from Sharon's stories. Remaining right where he was would suit Paulette just fine.

Once Paulette left Key West (after a visit back to LA to check on her still-empty mansion), she went to the Carolinas where she bought a farm. There to enjoy the trees, the breezes, the change of seasons, and all the wildlife that surrounded her property, the last task she wanted to take on was to return to Palm Beach where the scenery was close to her heart but did not at all hold any emotional content to how her life was today.

What if Timothy was innocent?

Returning to two years ago, it is the eightieth birthday party for Iris and Sharon's father, to be held at the Darby Estate on South Ocean Drive in Palm Beach, Florida.

In attendance are Mr. and Mrs. Darby; daughter Sharon Darby Buckner; Sharon's husband Timothy J. Buckner; Sharon and Timothy's daughter, Madison; her rapper artist husband; a new, young girlfriend of Madison's who flew in from Hollywood for the occasion; Paulette; and her mother, Erin Marshall. And then there was Iris. As usual, she was late.

This time the excuse was she got lost; "So much repair work down here at South Beach, and now on I-95. I kept going west, thinking I was going north. You know my sense of direction," she said to her mother over the phone.

"Yes, dear. Get here as soon as you can. We will be serving in a few minutes."

The excuse was the usual weak one, and both mother and daughter knew that for Iris to come to the Darby residence and their portion of the beach always reminded Iris of being "that other daughter," the one who had never fallen in line with family expectations and traditions from the very beginning. She became an accountant and worked her heart out for her father, but when it came time for a promotion, she was the last one considered. She was not only a family member, she was a female—her father's words. Because of that, Sharon, who lived in the second Darby mansion several blocks inland, had been the favored sister.

The family might make it to dessert with pleasantries, but then the side comments would begin, sometimes carried to shouting matches, with Iris leaving early, her once powerful father now in a wheelchair and near death.

Iris would have made it on time except for the unexpected appearance of her young lover at the front door of her penthouse apartment in South Beach, Florida, as she was on her way out the door.